Turn of the Tides

WHITECAP

AN ENEMIES-TO-LOVERS SMALL TOWN ROMANCE

JESSICA PRINCE

To all the girls who had a crush on the popular guy in high school and thought you didn't stand a chance because he was out of your league.
He would have been damn lucky to have you.

Let's Connect

By signing up for my newsletter, you're guaranteeing you'll stay up to date on all new releases, cover reveals, giveaways, sales, and all the other exciting book news I have coming!

I pinky promise to use my emails for good only, not to spam you, and make sure each one is enjoyable for everybody.

Sign up on my website at www.authorjessicaprince.com

Discover Other Books by Jessica

WHITECAP SERIES
Crossing the Line
My Perfect Enemy
Turn of the Tides

WHISKEY DOLLS SERIES
Bombshell
Knockout
Stunner
Seductress
Temptress
Vamp

HOPE VALLEY SERIES:
Out of My League

Come Back Home Again
The Best of Me
Wrong Side of the Tracks
Stay With Me
Out of the Darkness
The Second Time Around
Waiting for Forever
Love to Hate You
Playing for Keeps
When You Least Expect It
Never for Him

REDEMPTION SERIES

Bad Alibi
Crazy Beautiful
Bittersweet
Guilty Pleasure
Wallflower
Blurred Line
Slow Burn
Favorite Mistake
Sweet Spot

THE CLOVERLEAF SERIES:

Picking up the Pieces
Rising from the Ashes

Pushing the Boundaries
Worth the Wait

THE COLORS NOVELS:
Scattered Colors
Shrinking Violet
Love Hate Relationship
Wildflower

THE LOCKLAINE BOYS (a LOVE HATE RELATIONSHIP spinoff):
Fire & Ice
Opposites Attract
Almost Perfect

THE PEMBROOKE SERIES (a WILDFLOWER spinoff):
Sweet Sunshine
Coming Full Circle
A Broken Soul

CIVIL CORRUPTION SERIES
Corrupt
Defile
Consume
Ravage

One

BEAU

My voice echoed through the living room, bouncing off the bare walls and the shiny tile floor like it was taunting me. I'd been torturing myself like this for hours, unable to turn the television off as I watched the recap of my earlier interview on every channel that aired it and my career highlights that inevitably followed. At that moment, I was tuned in to ESPN.

The ice rattled around inside my glass as I lifted it to my lips and drank deep, the burn of the whiskey the only thing providing the slightest bit of warmth at that given moment. I felt cold everywhere. Numb.

"It's been an honor and a privilege to be a part of such an incredible team all these years. These guys are more than just my teammates, they're my family, and I count myself

lucky that I've been able to spend my career side by side with them. But the time's come for me to take a step back—"

I'd finally reached my limit. I snatched the remote off the arm of my recliner and jabbed the power button with a lot more force than necessary, bathing the room in darkness. The only light was the silvery glow from the moon coming through the plate glass windows of my penthouse apartment.

I was a fucking cliché, sitting alone in the dark, drinking and having a pity party because shit in my life hadn't gone how I'd planned. But even though I knew I looked like a pathetic little bitch to anyone who could have seen me just then, I couldn't help myself. This wasn't how things were supposed to go. I was only thirty-four, for Christ's sake. I should've had a few more years left in me, at least. But my career, my dream, had officially ended earlier today. I was done. Who I was and how I defined myself—as a football player—for most of my life had gone up in a puff of smoke. I didn't know who the fuck I was supposed to be without football, what I was supposed to do.

My phone rang, filling the quiet space. My father's name on the screen made the whiskey I'd been drinking for the past hour turn sour in my gut. I pressed the button to silence the call, letting him go to voicemail. I already knew what he was going to say, and the last thing I was in the mood to hear was all the ways I had fucked things up or how he would have done everything different and that I should have listened to him. It was the same shit he'd been spewing all my life, from peewee to high school, even in college.

The best day of my life had been when I was drafted to Arizona because it meant I was finally able to get the fuck away from him. I'd listened to his shit, suffered his abuse on every fucking level my entire life. He was a bitter, cold bastard living a miserable life and making everyone around him just as miserable. He didn't have what it took to go pro. Hell, he hadn't even been able to make the team in college, so he'd spent my entire existence living vicariously through me. I was pretty sure that was the only reason he'd agreed to have a kid in the first place. Only, it seemed like he envied the talent I was born with that he lacked. So even though he pushed me harder than a parent should, he was also a raging asshole because he knew he'd peaked and I still had a long way to go.

It was always a catch twenty-two with him. I was damned if I did, damned if I didn't. So eventually I just stopped trying.

I scrubbed at my face with my free hand then brought the glass to my lips and tossed the rest of the smoky amber liquid back before pushing out of the chair and heading toward the kitchen where I kept the booze. I poured more whiskey over the ball of ice in the bottom of my glass—because that was the kind of guy I was now, a douchebag with a million different shapes of ice—flavors too—thanks to my housekeeper. Christ, I had cucumber and melon infused ice, ice with lemon slices, rosemary, ice made out of coffee—that one I actually liked—you name it. Fancy fucking ice. Most of which sat in the freezer untouched unless I had a woman over. They loved that shit.

It was amazing the kind of shit you started doing when you had more money than you knew what the hell to do with.

My phone started up again just as I brought the refilled glass back to my lips and drank. I let out a growl and snatched the phone from my pocket, ready to tell my old man to fuck off before I hung up on him. But it wasn't him. It was actually someone I'd be happy to hear from. A welcomed voice in the shit show that was my life at the moment.

I answered quickly and brought the phone to my ear. "Sam. How's it going, man?"

"It's going good. You know me, got no complaints. I'd ask how it's going with you, but I already know."

He would. If there was anyone who understood what I was dealing with just then, it was Sam Killborne. The man was a Pro Football Hall of Famer, and someone I looked up to and respected beyond measure. He'd been my mentor when I was younger, knowing I not only wanted to go pro, but I needed it if I had any hopes of getting the hell away from my old man. It was a toss-up who hated Hank Wade more, me or Sam.

Sam was always pushing me to be a better player and a better man. He was the antithesis of my dad in every way. He'd always been patient and calm, taking the time to teach me, never getting frustrated or angry if I didn't get it right the first time. I was one of the best QBs in the league because of Sam, or I had been. Until today. Or more accurately, until a sack fucked my shoulder to hell and back and it never healed properly. I'd had surgeries, physical therapy, anything to try to get my throwing arm back to 100%, but it hadn't been in the cards. The injury was just too bad. Doctors did what they could, but my mobility was never the same. And the league didn't have room for an aging quarterback who couldn't throw anymore. So I'd been given a choice—if you could call it that. Announce my retirement myself, keeping my dignity intact, or be dropped once my contract was up. Simple as that.

After what the last scans of my shoulder showed, I knew it was well and truly over. My agent confirmed what I already knew. No other team was going to take a chance on me, not in this lifetime. The only choice was to bow out gracefully, like it was my idea.

"Figured today was a hard hit. Wanted to call and

make sure you weren't currently sitting at the bottom of a bottle."

Ah, and another thing. Sam was never one to mince words.

I looked at the whiskey bottle sitting on the counter. "Not the bottom. Think I'm floating in the middle somewhere."

"If I tell you to put a lid on it for the rest of the night, you gonna listen, kid?"

I would have liked to say no, that I fully intended to drown my sorrows for the rest of the night, and maybe even into some of the morning. But I had too much respect for the man on the other end of the line. He'd earned that from me in more ways than I could list.

On a sigh, I moved over to the sink and dumped my glass containing at least fifty bucks worth of whiskey and that stupid fucking ice ball down the drain.

"Nah, I'll call it," I replied as I recapped the bottle and shoved it back into my liquor cabinet. "Probably for the best anyway. Spare me an even worse hangover in the morning."

"Smart." There was approval in Sam's tone. "Appreciate that. Besides, I've got something else to talk to you about."

I moved to the fridge and pulled out a bottle of water, then dumped a few painkillers into my hand. If I wasn't drinking anymore, might as well do what I could to combat the hangover coming in the morning. "Hey, if it's not about football, I'm all ears."

He chuckled deep. "I didn't say it wasn't about football. But it's not about your retirement if that helps."

I let out a snort. "Well, it sure as hell can't make anything worse. What have you got?"

"A job, actually. That is, if you want it. Not trying to pressure you into anything."

I brought the bottle of water to my lips and drank. "What do you mean? What kind of job?"

"A buddy of mine happens to be the new head of the athletic department at Oregon University, your alma mater. The head coach over there retired at the end of last season, and they've been on the hunt for his replacement ever since with no luck. I mentioned I might have someone to fit that bill. When I said your name, he just about lost his mind. I think it'd be nice for you to get back to where it all started for you."

It felt like a ton of information to take in all at once. Too much for me to try and wrap my head around while I was on my feet at least. I'd had enough booze to knock most people on their asses. I collapsed onto a stool tucked beneath the island and rubbed at the tick that had developed in my left eye right around the time my publicist shoved that bullshit hearts and flowers speech at me to read in front of the cameras. "Wait. You want me to coach college football? What the hell do I know about coaching?"

"Probably nothing. At least not yet. But you can learn, and you have all the skills you need to teach those boys to be good men and good goddamn football players. I believe in you."

Well, that made one of us. "Why haven't you taken this job, Sam? Between you and me, you're the one most qualified."

He scoffed through the line. "You know it's not for me. Besides, I'm happy right where I am."

Sam coached, sure, but he coached high school football, had been since he retired from the pros and moved to my hometown of Whitecap, a small coastal town in Oregon. He said he preferred to teach them before they were old enough to form shitty habits and attitudes. He liked to claim that helping me made him realize his second calling. He said he lived out his first calling as a professional NFL player, and when he couldn't do that anymore, he was lucky enough to discover a second one coaching kids who dreamed of going down that same road. Or, hell, who just wanted to have a good time on that field with their buddies.

I'd been one of those kids once.

"I get that you need to think about it, son. I'm sure

your agent's throwing shit your way left, right, and center."

He wasn't wrong about that. He'd been throwing around words like guest commentator and broadcaster. The truth was, I had zero interest in being in front of the camera like that. I loved football for the *game* not the celebrity. Just thinking about going down that path created an anxious knot in my gut.

Out of all the options I'd been given, the easiest one to stomach was coaching. There was just one key thing stopping me from pulling the trigger.

"Man, I don't know. I'd have to go back, and I just don't know if I'm ready for that. You know how badly I wanted to get the hell out of there."

"I do. But that was a long time ago, Beau. You aren't a kid anymore. Don't let your bastard of a father dictate your life. You're stronger than he is, and I don't just mean physically, and you know it."

Logically, I did. But the thought of living in the same place as that man again threatened to give me a skull-splitting headache.

"I'm not asking for an answer now, son, only that you consider it. You have options, Beau, but if it's any consolation, I really think you could be good for those kids. Make a difference, you know? Besides, it would be nice to see you back in that Wolverine blue and white," he continued as I sucked back the last of my water. I tossed the empty bottle across the kitchen toward the recycling bin and winced at the fire that shot through my shoulder, reminding me why I was where I was in the first goddamn place.

"I'll think about it," I promised him. It was the least I could do for him, after all.

"Appreciate it." And in the next breath, he shifted gears. "If you take it, maybe that means you'll be home in time for the reunion. Something to think about."

The reunion.

At the reminder of my upcoming fifteen-year high school reunion, I looked at the invitation that had come in the mail a few weeks ago. I hadn't given it much thought at the time. To be honest, I'd intended to throw the thing away but hadn't gotten around to it before my house-keeper had stuck it up on my refrigerator. It had stayed there simply because I didn't cook, so I wasn't in my kitchen all that often. Out of sight, out of mind and all that.

On that reminder of the reunion, my mind traveled back to the past. Or more to the point, to one specific person.

"Yeah," I said, speaking my thoughts out loud as I pulled the image of her up in my mind. "Definitely something to think about."

Two

PRESLEY

Late mornings were my favorite time at Dropped Anchor, Whitecap's local watering hole. My last few calm moments before the kitchen came to life as my waitstaff finished preparing for the lunch rush to start.

I had an office in the back where I did most of the administrative tasks that came with managing a bar, but at this time of day I preferred to do what I could at the bar, sitting in the middle of the place that had come to feel like a second home to me. I started working here when I was just eighteen and desperately in need of money to help pay my way through college. If it wasn't for this place, I would have had to drop out before earning my degree.

I'd started waiting tables, then worked my way back behind the bar where tips were even better, and now, all these years later, I was the manager. The current owner,

Diane, had started talking recently about selling the old place so she and her wife could tour the country in their RV before they got too old to enjoy it. I couldn't imagine someone else coming in and taking this place over. With new ownership came changes—not always good ones. The last thing I wanted was for this place to lose all its charm and history by being turned into something trendy. Whitecap was a tourist town, and that meant there was no shortage of city folks coming in and trying to change shit up that had worked perfectly well for years.

I couldn't let that happen here, so I was determined to be the one who bought it from Diane when the time finally came. The problem was, I didn't have the money on hand to do it, and banks didn't consider a college degree in business and a can-do attitude as proof enough that a person was worthy of a loan.

Assholes.

But I wasn't giving up. This place and the people who worked here meant something to me. I was determined to get that loan. I just wasn't sure how. At least not yet.

Before I could travel down the road of how the hell I was going to manage to secure my future and the future of all my employees and friends, the door to the bar burst open and my best friend came flying through like a tornado.

Colbie's gaze darted around the bar frantically. "Presley? *Presley!*" she practically shouted.

I dropped the pencil I'd been using to work on the staff schedule and raised my hand in the air. "I'm right here, crazy."

"Oh, thank god you're here. I was going to try calling or texting, but I lost my phone again." That had to have been the third time this month. I loved my best friend dearly. We'd been thick as thieves since I moved to town back in middle school and she'd been more than a little scatterbrained the whole time.

"Uh . . ." I held my hands up at my sides. "I'm always here at this time. Where else would I be?"

She gave me a start when she grabbed me by the shoulders and yanked me into her, hugging me so tight my ribs groaned and my lungs nearly popped like overinflated balloons.

"Colbie—" I croaked, but she cut me off.

"Shh," she cooed in my ear as she petted the back of my hair. "Shh, it's okay. It's all going to be just fine, I promise."

"Jeez, Colbs, loosen up, would you?" I managed to squirm out of her hold and sucked in a deep breath. "Good lord, woman. What's gotten into you? You're acting even crazier than usual. Shouldn't you be at work right now?"

"I just came from there. I'm on my break right now."

I raised my brows and teased, "And you didn't bring me a coffee? Rude." Colbie worked as a barista at the local coffee shop, Drip. The girl might have been a tad flighty, but she could make one hell of a cup of coffee, and the owner, Monica Killborne, liked to claim that she couldn't run the place without her.

She looked at me with wide, bewildered eyes. "Wait. You haven't heard?"

I shook my head, my brows dipping in confusion. "Heard what?"

"Shit," she hissed before clamping her mouth shut and rolling her lips between her teeth.

"Colbie," I said, warning in my tone. "What's going on?"

She began shifting from foot to foot anxiously, "Um . . . well . . ."

I swiveled around on my stool, pinning her with a look. "Start talking."

She let out an exasperated puff of air. "All right. Well, I *was* working at the coffee shop earlier, and Monica told me something." She paused again like she was building up the courage to finish. "Then a bunch of customers came in and were all talking about it. I didn't believe it at first, but then Luna showed me an article on her phone." She rolled her eyes. "I could have looked it up myself if could find my freaking phone—"

I held up my hand to stop her from saying any more. "Colbie, babe, you're rambling. And your phone probably fell under the driver seat of your car again."

She smacked her forehead. "Gah! I didn't even think to look there. I should go check now."

I grabbed her by the elbow before she could take off. "Colbie, focus."

Her attention returned to me. "Right."

"What did you see in some article that had you rushing over here to check on me?"

Her face pulled into a wince. "It was about Beau Wade."

Tension poured into my body, coating every muscle and joint until I felt as stiff and brittle as a stale pretzel stick. It took serious effort to keep my expression neutral, to not give away that my blood was suddenly cold and my heart was racing, but I managed. I'd gotten really good at it. I didn't have much of a choice, after all. Not in Whitecap.

Beau Wade was this town's golden child, the good ol' small-town boy who went on to make it to the bigtime. The famous football player everyone could brag about and be so damn proud of.

It was as if going pro was reason enough for everyone to forget all about the spoiled, entitled little shithead who got off on relentlessly tormenting those he felt were beneath him. For some reason, I had been his favorite punching bag back then. All through middle school, high school, and into college, that prick had taken special exception with me, going out of his way to make my life a living nightmare.

For all the love he got from everyone in this freaking town, that was how much I hated the bastard. The best day of my life was when he'd been drafted into the NFL, all the way to Arizona. I didn't even care that he was getting to live his dream by going pro like he'd always wanted, because it meant he was leaving. I mean, sure, it might have been nice if just *once* the asshole got what was coming to him instead of everything he freaking wanted, but finally, I'd get some peace from the never-ending ridicule and teasing. I didn't have to worry about the one-upmanship and competition—the childish games he always forced me into, time after time, whether I wanted to play or not.

I hummed, trying my best to come off like I didn't care as I looked back down at the schedule I'd been working on before Colbie burst in like a psychotic hurricane. But if there was one person who could see right through me, it was Colbie. She'd been there every time Beau made me cry or rage or any of the other unpleasant things he made me feel.

"What about Beau Wade?"

"Well, uh . . . he—he's coming back."

I didn't realize how tightly my entire body had locked up until the pencil in my hand snapped right in two. I cleared my throat, dropping the pieces, and hopped off the stool, rounding the bar and grabbing a bottle of vodka off the shelf. I poured myself two fingers and tossed them back, hissing at the burn it caused as it made its way down my throat.

"Uh, Presley? Babe, are you okay?"

I opened my mouth, breathing like a dragon as I blew out the fire caused by the liquor. "Of course I am. Why do you ask?"

"You mean besides the fact it's ten-thirty in the morning, you're on the clock, and just downed two shots worth of booze?"

I probably would have poured myself another if she hadn't pointed it out. Morning drinking on the job was the last thing a person who wanted to own a bar should be doing.

"Okay. Point taken." I twisted the cap back onto the vodka bottle and returned it to the shelf. I braced my hands on the bar and pulled in a calming breath, willing my heart to slow down. I wasn't going to let that man cause me to backslide.

"Now, when you say *back*, what exactly do you mean?"

"Apparently he retired recently, and the reports are saying he's taken a job coaching at OU. It was just announced yesterday. It's all anyone who came into Drip this morning could talk about."

A small spark of hope flared to life inside of me. "Hey, that could just mean he's coming back to Oregon, not necessarily Whitecap. Just because he's taken a coaching job doesn't mean he has to come back *here*. Maybe he's choosing to stay closer to campus?"

The pitying look on her face told me all I needed to know. She shook her head. "Monica told me herself he was moving back home. Got that straight from her hubs, and you know how close Sam and Beau always were."

I let out a defeated sigh and dropped my head. If that came from Sam it might as well be taken as gospel. I never understood that relationship. Sam and Monica Killborne were two of the best people I'd ever met. Monica had the biggest heart and Sam was usually so good at reading people and spotting bullshit a mile away. I never understood his relationship with Beau. It didn't make sense that he wasn't able to see through him the way I did.

I pulled in a fortifying breath, steeling my spine and

straightening my shoulders. I could do this. I was an adult, for God's sake. I could handle some stupid guy.

"You know what? It's fine. This is fine. Totally fine." Maybe if I said it enough I could will it into becoming the truth.

Colbie looked like she believed me just as much as I did. "Are you sure? I know how you feel about the guy."

I lifted a brow. "You mean how I hate him?"

The corners of her mouth wobbled with suppressed laughter. "Exactly."

"It'll be fi—" I bit down on my tongue to stop myself from saying *fine* again when her brows lifted high on her forehead. "All right, it sucks. I'll admit that, but I can handle it. This isn't high school anymore. I can't speak for him, but I'm a hell of a lot more mature than I was back then."

She lifted a hand and tilted it from side to side. "Well..."

I threw a clean hand towel at her face. "Shut up, assface. I am!"

She laughed, holding her hands up in surrender. "You are. I believe you."

She didn't. But that was okay. I didn't believe me either, so it would be a double bonus when I proved us both wrong.

God, I hoped I could prove us both wrong.

I decided to move on from that and said, "Besides, Whitecap might be a small town, but it's not microscopic. I'm sure it'll be easy enough to avoid him if I work extra hard at it."

She held up both of her hands, crossing her fingers tightly. "I'm rooting for you, babe."

I appreciated her support, but I had this. I could do it. I'd worked too damn hard to build my life into what I wanted. Into something I could be proud of, and I'd be damned if I'd let a man come in and mess things up. Beau Wade meant nothing to me. Actually, *less* than nothing. He wasn't even a blip on my radar. And I'd make damn sure to keep it that way.

Colbie shook her hands in front of her like she was trying to clear the negativity from the air. "Enough about that flaming dog turd." She smiled big and waggled her brows. "Let's talk about something else . . . like our high school reunion coming up next weekend," she spit out quickly, making sure to get all the words out before I could cut her off.

I let out a pained groan and dropped my head back dramatically. "Colbie, *no*," I stressed. This was only the thousandth time she'd mentioned that stupid reunion since the invitations were delivered. "I told you, I'm not going to that thing. High school wasn't exactly a time in my life I'd like to reminisce about."

She blew out a dramatic raspberry. "Please. High school reunions aren't about reminiscing. They're about seeing people you haven't seen if fifteen years and being able to show them how much better you're doing than they are."

I gave her a bland look. "I see two flaws in your logic already. First," I lifted my index finger in the air, "half our graduating class still lives here, just like us, and I see most of them on a regular basis when they come into my bar."

"Ah, yes. But that's only half."

My middle finger joined the first one. "And therein lies the second issue." I lifted my arms out at my sides. "I'm the manager of the same bar I've worked at since I was eighteen, living in the same town. I'm happy with my life, sure, but I don't think those assholes we went to school with will consider that something to brag about."

Her face turned fierce. "Screw the haters," she declared with ferocity.

"I love you like crazy. But no. Just no," I told her for the millionth time. "I'd rather lick the floor of the men's bathroom than set foot in that reunion."

She gave me her big puppy dog eyes, clasping her hands in front of her chest. "Please, Presley? Pretty please? For me?"

I let out a snort. "Not a chance in hell. And stop using that face on me. It won't work."

Three

PRESLEY

DAMN COLBIE and that stupid pouty face. It had totally worked.

I blamed her for why I was currently wearing a dress that I never would have thought to buy for myself and ridiculous heels that pinched the living shit out of my toes as I made my way toward the Whitecap High School gymnasium.

"This is my nightmare. How the hell did I let you talk me into this?" I grumbled as I tugged at the inappropriately short hem of my dress, trying to cover more skin.

Colbie smacked my hands away. "Will you stop fidgeting?"

I had to admit, the dress somehow managed to make me feel classy and sexy at the same time, a combo I hadn't even known existed until Colbie snatched it off the rack last weekend and insisted I try it on. The sweetheart neckline of the corseted bodice and ultra-thin spaghetti straps exposed everything from my neck down to the subtle hint of cleavage. The bubble skirt might have been nice and flowy, but it barely reached mid-thigh.

Colbie had squirted some kind of bronzing crap on my chest, shoulders, and legs that gave me a sun-kissed look and created a pretty shimmer, like my skin was covered in crushed pearls or something, as I rubbed it in.

I had to fist my hands to keep from tugging at the hem again. "I feel like I'm seconds away from flashing my cooch to everyone. I'm not used to showing this much skin."

"Well, you look like a freaking sex kitten. And I told you, that red totally works on you."

I felt like I stood out like a sore thumb, especially in such a bold color. But I appreciated her attempts at making me feel better. "You look amazing too," I told her, speaking the god's honest truth. Her dress was equally as short as mine, but completely strapless, fitted, and in a pale lavender that looked great against her pale skin. "Absolutely stunning, sweetie."

She fluffed her thick hair, preening theatrically, feeling a hell of a lot more comfortable all dolled up than I did. "Well, thank you, darling," she said in a dramatically accented voice, replacing the "L" in darling with a "W". "I do try." We closed in on the gym entrance, and I felt

Colbie's entire demeanor change as her body went from loose and breezy to stiff as a board.

Her throat worked on a swallow, her eyes pinned to the door. "Hey," I said quietly. "You okay?"

I didn't understand the lightning-quick change until I heard a deep voice speak. "Ladies." I whipped my head back around and spotted none other than ruggedly sexy Sheriff Kincade Michaels.

Well, that explained that. I curled my lips between my teeth to keep from smiling like a lunatic, because the only thing that would fluster my best friend beyond compare was her ultimate crush. The man she'd been pining after since she'd been a teenager and he'd been a freshly minted deputy who could wear the hell out of a uniform.

"Sheriff Michaels," I greeted, taking the reins since I knew my girl wouldn't be able to form a coherent sentence. He stood at the entrance to the high school gym dressed in that khaki uniform shirt, jeans, and his gun belt. "Since when does the big man have to do such menial tasks as security detail?"

He grinned and chuckled, and I swore I heard a muffled choking sound coming from Colbie's direction. She was either having a heart attack or an orgasm. Honestly, I wasn't sure which one I'd have preferred.

"Since the deputy scheduled to do it got a nice little

case of food poisoning and there was no time to find anyone else."

"Ah, so you pulled the short straw," I teased. "Pulling babysitting duty on a bunch of grownups to make sure they don't get too rowdy."

He shrugged, his smirk probably threatening to give my bestie heart palpitations—if the organ in her chest was even still working. "Someone's gotta do it. You ladies have yourselves a good time in there. And be safe, yeah?"

I threw him a jaunty salute. "Sir, yes sir."

He shook his head good-naturedly as I looped my arm through Colbie's stiff one and guided her into the gym with me. She moved woodenly until we cleared the door, then her whole body slumped.

"Oh god." She sucked in a ragged breath. "How bad was that just now? Did I totally embarrass myself?"

"In order to embarrass yourself you would have actually had to speak. You just stood there like you were a marble statue of a woman in shock."

She slapped her hands over her face and made a noise that sounded an awful lot like a dying animal. "What the hell is wrong with me? Why do I always go stupid around that man?"

I tugged her arm, giving her a little jostle. "Hey, I personally think it's cute. You've been crushing on the dude nearly half your life. I'm just waiting for the day when something actually happens. It'll be like watching a real-life Hallmark movie."

She snorted loudly. "Please. Like he even knows I'm alive."

"He knows you're alive, sweetheart," I assured her.

"Only as the weird girl who freezes up and goes silent every time he looks in her direction. He probably thinks I'm hiding something with how ridiculous I act. Like a meth lab in my basement or a trucker's head in my freezer."

"Forget about him. Tonight's not about meth labs or trucker's heads, remember? It's about fun and showing off these awesome dresses," I told her as we reached the sign-in table.

She looked over at me with a tiny smile. "They are pretty awesome, aren't they?"

"Oh my God, Presley Fields, is that you?"

I looked over to the woman manning the registration table who was handing out nametags and forced the smile to stay on my face. "Hey, Anna. How are you?"

Anna Waters was one who'd stayed in town like me after graduation and one I'd have been happy with leaving. I hadn't been that lucky.

She'd been a pain in high school, and had only grown to be an even bigger pain in the fifteen years since we'd graduated. She was one of those women who felt if

27

you weren't a wife and a mother who spent their days in the kitchen with a child strapped to their hip, you weren't doing your job as a woman, and she loved to throw that opinion around like confetti. I was even lower than the other non-mothers because I also worked at a bar, which to her was an insult of biblical proportions or something.

"Oh, I'm just wonderful, as always." Of course she was, because to hear her tell it, everything in her life was utterly *amazing*. It was as though she'd deluded herself into forgetting we lived in a small town where everyone liked to talk. Those picture-perfect children of hers were anything but perfect. It was spread far and wide that her youngest had been kicked out of daycare after breaking the skin of the fifth kid he'd bit, and her fourteen-year-old daughter—the one she'd gotten pregnant with just before graduation—had been picked up with an older group of kids who had tried robbing a liquor store in the middle of the freaking day, no masks and only blocks from the sheriff's station.

Definitely not the brightest crayons in the box.

And her husband . . . Well, I *did* work at a bar, after all. A bar Garth Waters was a fan of frequenting, drinking too much, and picking fights he didn't have a chance in hell of winning. More than once my staff had to call the cops to get him out when he got too unruly and started breaking shit. He'd spent his fair share of nights in the drunk tank. But according to her, they were all misunderstandings.

I might have felt bad for her if she wasn't such a sanctimonious bitch all the damn time.

She looked me up and down with obvious judgment. "Wow. Look at you. Who knew the local bartender could clean up so well?" Her smile was anything but kind, and I had to bite my tongue to keep from saying something nasty. "Looks like someone's come tonight to find herself a husband."

My smile was brittle, my eyes flat as I replied, "Oh, no, Anna. No husband for me, at least not at the moment." I lifted my shoulder in an easy shrug. "I'm still having fun. No quite ready settle for the same old boring dick night after night after night for *years* just yet. Know what I mean?" I hit her with a sugary smile. "Speaking of husbands. Where's Garth? He stay home to sleep off last night's bender?"

So much for not saying anything nasty. But sometimes it couldn't be helped. That woman just pushed my damn buttons.

Colbie coughed beside me and proceeded to choke while I scanned the table for our nametags. I didn't bother waiting for Anna to lift her jaw off the floor and answer. I simply snatched them up and handed Colbie hers. "You have yourself a lovely night," I told her with over-the-top sweetness in my voice. "Maybe I'll see you in there later." I gave her a little finger wave, enjoying the way her face burned beet red way too much. Then I grabbed Colbie's arm and yanked her along with me into the party.

"The same old boring dick night after night after night?" she asked from the corner of her mouth, her voice trembling with suppressed laughter.

"She deserved it," I defended. "She pushed until I had no choice but to push back."

"Oh absolutely," she agreed cheerfully. "That woman's always been one of Satan's minions. That was fun to watch."

"Yeah, well, the night is young," I said, hoping like hell that coming here wasn't a huge mistake. "Let's hope that's not the only excitement we have tonight."

Colbie looked at me and waggled her eyebrows. "Drinks?"

"God, yes," I exclaimed. Getting through this night was going to require booze.

The gym had been decked out for the reunion, the committee members clearly sparing no expense. I had to admit, I was pleasantly surprised. I'd been expecting balloons and crepe paper streamers, but they'd done a lot better than that. It didn't look cheesy or gaudy. It was actually nice. Round eight-seater tables were gathered along the sides of a large area left open for dancing, covered in white table clothes and chair covers sporting our school's colors. A DJ was set up at the front of the dance floor and there were at least four small bar stations strategically placed throughout the gym.

A large screen hung from the ceiling behind the DJ booth, projecting images that had been pulled from the yearbook as well as some personal photographs sprinkled throughout. The centerpieces were also in the school colors but somehow managed not to look gaudy. The place reminded me more of a wedding setup than a high school reunion.

"Wow, this place doesn't look half bad," I murmured as we headed to the closest bar station. There was a gaggle of women in front of us, waiting for the bartender to finish whipping up their fussy pink drinks.

I recognized a few of them as they huddled together, heads close, voices hushed but excited. The others I struggled to place, but they weren't a group who had stayed in town.

Colbie and I stopped a couple feet back to wait when one of the women lifted her head, her eyes rounding as soon as she spotted me and my bestie. "Presley Fields and Colbie Hart?"

I was at a loss for who the chick was. Fortunately, Colbie didn't have the same issue. "Pam Culver?"

The name jogged my memory and I remembered that

Pam Culver was on student council and drill team. We shared a few classes together and she'd always been nice enough, but we didn't really run in the same circles.

"Yeah, that's me! Well, Pam Davis now, but yeah! It's so good to see you guys." She surprised me by pulling us both into tight hugs.

"It's good to see you too," I returned, letting out a breath of relief when the bartender finished with the pink concoctions and passed them around. Colbie and I moved up to the bar and I quickly ordered a vodka soda.

I smiled at the bartender, tucking extra bills into the tip jar as she passed me my vodka soda and Colbie's white wine. Just as I lifted the glass to take my first fortifying drink a commotion started near the entrance. People flocked, blocking my view, but it was clear something big was happening.

I pointed in that direction with my glass. "What's going on? Why does it seem like everyone is freaking out?"

"You didn't hear?" Pam asked, her eyes dancing with excitement.

Colbie shrugged and shook her head in confusion when I looked her way for an answer. "Hear what?" I asked.

She made an *eek* face before dropping her bomb. "Beau Wade is coming to the reunion."

I choked on the sip I'd just taken, my eyes going wide

with panic as I struggled to cough the vodka out of my lung. "*What*?" I squeaked as I felt the color drain from my face.

"Yeah, apparently it was a really last-minute deal. Isn't that awesome?" She did a little hop in place and clamped her hands together. "And it looks like he just showed up."

Oh shit.

This couldn't be happening.

Four

PRESLEY

My stomach pitched before falling to the ground at my feet. Despite what Pam and everyone else thought, this was *not* good. I looked in Colbie's direction and found she was already staring at me, her eyes as wide as mine were.

"So good to see you again, Pam. Will you excuse us? Thanks," she sputtered quickly, barely finishing her sentence before hooking her arm through mine and pulling me away. "I had no idea," she hissed quietly before I could get a word out. "Swear to God. I never would have guilted you into coming with me if I thought there was even a chance he'd be here tonight."

I pulled in a calming breath as we stopped in a quiet corner near the DJ booth, far away from the hubbub taking place near the entrance. It was easy enough to avoid curious stares given how nearly the entire graduating class was flocking around Beau like he was something special. The asshole threw a ball for a living, for Christ's sake. It wasn't like he invented the cure for cancer.

"I know," I said, giving her a small smile as I took her hand and gave it a reassuring squeeze. "I know you'd never do something like that."

Her gaze moved to the entrance where the crowd still gathered before shooting back to me. "We can leave. We don't have to stay if it makes you uncomfortable."

My nostrils flared on a deep inhale. "No." My voice was firm, determined. And maybe slightly petulant. "No, I'm not leaving. This is *my* high school reunion too, damn it, and I have every right to be here."

Colbie nodded enthusiastically, ever the supportive cheerleader. "Yeah. *Yeah*. You're totally right. Screw that guy."

The pep talk was actually working, and I could feel myself getting pumped up. The only thing missing was "Good Vibrations" blaring in the background to really set the mood. "Exactly. Screw him! So what if I didn't want to come here in the first place. I was still here first. I'm not going to let that self-righteous ass run me out."

Colbie looked like she was getting as jazzed as I was. "No way. Nu-uh. If anyone should leave it's him."

"Yeah. This is *my* town," I declared with a tiny stomp

of my high-heeled foot, "and if he has a problem with sharing the same space, he can be the one to leave."

The crowd parted then, and I felt my righteous indignation falter when I got my first in-person glimpse at Beau Wade in years. It was impossible to avoid the man completely, especially when working at a bar, and even more especially when that bar's clientele came in most Sundays to watch his team specifically. I knew far more about his career and stats than I wished I did. But somehow, seeing him on those screens every week didn't do him justice.

Damn it. The asshole was like a fine scotch, only getting better with age. It wasn't fair.

He'd always been good-looking, a fact that annoyed me to no end. It wasn't right that a guy that awful was able to turn the head of every single female he walked past. It was a major flaw in society that a person's shitty behavior was overlooked simply because they were hot. And as much as I would have liked to deny it, I couldn't. Beau Wade *was hot*, and I would have been lying if I claimed not to see the appeal as I stared at him from across the gymnasium.

He looked even taller than the last time I'd seen him in person, standing a good few inches above most of the people gathered around him, all broad-shouldered, strong-chested, and narrow-waisted. He wore dove gray slacks and a matching blazer, tailor-made to fit his long, cut physique.

He'd skipped a tie, leaving the pale blue button-down open at the collar, showcasing his thick neck.

A prominent brow rested over his blue eyes that I knew from experience were like pure ice, cold enough to freeze you in place when he looked at you. The rest of his features were just as strong, from his sharp cheekbones, regal nose, and square jaw to his sandy-colored hair. It bordered right on the edge of blond, nearly tipping over into light brown, the sides buzzed short with the longer strands on top styled to perfection.

God, he looked good. *Too* good.

Lifting my cocktail to my lips, I took a long drink, the icy liquid coating my tongue and sliding down my throat.

"Damn," Colbie breathed from beside me. "Is it just me or has he gotten even hotter?"

My attention darted back to her as she curled her lips between her teeth before shrugging. "Hey, glare at me all you want, but you know I'm right."

I let out a heavy sigh. "Damn it, you're right. He's gotten even better looking. He must have made a deal with Satan or something."

"Well, Mr. Devil Man is certainly living up to his end of the bargain then."

That he was, I thought as I chewed on the skinny plastic cocktail straw in my glass, unable to look away.

"You sure you're good?" Colbie asked, pulling me from my ogling.

"Yeah, I'm good," I said with a slight pout.

I felt a tingle start at the base of my neck and work its way down my spine. The sensation caused goosebumps to spread across my skin. I let out a shiver as I turned, looking back over my shoulder to find Beau already staring in my direction.

His gaze bore into me like it always had when we were kids, stealing my breath. My cheeks flushed and my heart sputtered and turned over in my chest like an old car engine. I could practically feel his eyes trailing over my bare skin, causing heat to build inside of me.

It suddenly felt like the walls were closing in on me. Even with an entire gym between us, there still wasn't enough space, and I started to worry that maybe Whitecap *wasn't* big enough for both of us.

It almost looked like there was a smile tilting the corners of his lips upward as he took a step away from his adoring fans, as though he was starting in my direction. Panic streaked through me at the thought of a confrontation just then. I wasn't properly prepared or nearly liquored up enough for that.

Fortunately, I was yanked from that worry by a tap on my shoulder. I started, ripping my gaze from the last man on the planet I should have been giving any of my attention to.

"Presley Fields. It's been a while."

I took in the man standing in front of me and recognition flickered in my mind like a lightbulb turning on. "Oh my god, Mike? Mike Perry?"

"Yeah," he said with a laugh. "Hi. I wasn't sure you'd remember me."

"Of course I remember you." Fond memories flooded, overcoming all the bad that came with the sudden appearance of Beau. Mike Perry had been my high school crush. The cute, shy, slightly nerdy boy I'd been lab partners with in biology. I'd spent most of my senior year hoping he would notice me in time to ask me to prom, but it never happened. Instead, he took Cinda Carter and I spent my prom night curled up on my couch, feeling sorry for myself with a pile of junk food and romantic chick movies guaranteed to make me weepy. He went out of state for college, and this was the first time I'd seen him since graduation.

I remembered thinking he had a very pretty smile and kind eyes back then, and looking at him now, he still did. I returned the quick hug he gave me and pulled back to take him in.

From the corner of my eye, I saw Colbie's head bouncing side to side between us, intrigue written all over her face. She knew all too well how much I'd liked Mike back then. I glanced her way and bugged my eyes out in silent communication.

Being the best friend she was, she understood and started to back away. "I'll go grab a couple refills, let you guys catch up." She added ridiculous finger guns before realizing she looked like a goober and turning away with a roll of her eyes at herself.

"I see you're still friends with Colbie."

"Yeah, I am." I bit down on my bottom lip nervously while lifting my shoulder in a shrug. "She's my bestie for life."

He gave me that polite smile. "I like that."

"Yeah, me too. Wow." I shook my head in disbelief that Mike was really there, standing in front of me. "It's really good to see you. You look great." And he did, that was for sure. Mike had always been cute in that clean-cut, sweet-boy-next-door kind of way, and that had always worked for me.

"Look who's talking," he returned, taking hold of my upper arms and holding me out at arm's length. "My god, you're even more beautiful than you were back in high school. Didn't think that was possible." A tinge of pink rose up on the apples of his cheeks as he admitted, "You know, I had the biggest crush on you back then."

My cheeks pinched as my smile widened. "Aw, you

did? I had no clue." I lowered my eyes, feeling my own cheeks flush with heat. "I crushed on you back then too."

His whole face lit up. "I'm actually moving back next month. If you're not seeing anyone, I'd love to take you to dinner. You know, if you're interested?"

"I'm single," I said quickly and with a little too much enthusiasm. I cleared my throat, trying to regain my cool. "And I'd love to go to dinner."

"Great. I'm really looking forward to it."

I could still feel that tingle along my spine, but I refused to look and see if Beau was still watching. "Yeah. Me too."

I tucked my hair behind my ear, feeling downright giddy. I'd gone from dreading this whole thing to coming out of it with a date with a guy I used to be so into.

We went about exchanging numbers, excitement and nerves making me fumble a few times as I tried to key his in. Finally, it was done.

"Well, I guess I should"—he threw his thumb over his shoulder—"probably mingle a bit more. But I'll see you later?"

"Yeah. Of course."

"Great," he repeated as he backed up, slightly awkward and all kinds of adorable. "Then I'll see you around."

He started away, looking back at me over his shoulder

every few seconds until he almost slammed right into another person.

Colbie reappeared just then, passing me a fresh vodka soda. "That looked like it went well."

I did a little hop in place, bringing the black plastic straw to my lips and taking a sip. "It really did. Turns 0ut he's moving back soon and asked me to dinner."

She did a little dance for me, letting out a squeak of excitement on my behalf. "Oh, yay! You had such a crush on him back in school."

I bit down on the straw and grinned goofily. "I know. And get this. He said he had a crush on me back then too."

Her smile fell just a touch, taking her enthusiasm with it. "He did? Then why didn't he ever ask you out?"

I lifted my shoulder in a shrug. "I don't know. I guess he was just too shy?"

Her brows pulled together as she let out a low, "Hmm."

I arched a brow and cocked my hip, feeling defensive all of a sudden. "*Hmm*? What's *hmm* supposed to mean?"

"Nothing!" she insisted before quickly amending, "Well, okay, not *nothing*. Doesn't that seem a little flaky to you? I mean, you never really struck me as the kind of woman who'd go for a dude who didn't have the balls to make a move."

I clamped my lips shut on the argument I was going to

issue, because there really was no point. She was totally right, and if I said otherwise she would have seen right through me.

I rolled my eyes as I took another drink, the excitement I'd felt moments ago petering out like a tire slowly leaking air. "Okay, you're right. But that was fifteen years ago," I asserted. "I mean, maybe he's changed. It only took a few minutes for him to ask me out this time."

She didn't look convinced. "I don't know. Maybe."

I narrowed my eyes. "Well, I'm going out with him anyway, and I bet I have a really great time."

She opened her mouth, but before she could get a word out her eyes rounded on something over my shoulder. "Oh shit, this isn't good," she muttered to herself.

"What isn't—?"

"Well look at you, Bubbles. All grown up."

Ah hell.

Five

BEAU

I'D BEEN on the fence about whether or not going to the reunion was a good idea, but the moment I stepped into that gym I knew I'd fucked up. I hadn't RSVPed or told anyone I planned on attending, yet somehow the word had gotten out.

It was easy to forget how small towns operated after being in the city for so long. It had totally slipped my mind how everyone seemed to know your personal business whether you shared it with them or not. Or how gossip spread faster than the clap through an Old West era brothel. Ironic, really, given those were two of the main reasons I'd wanted to get the hell out of Whitecap so damn bad when I was younger.

And now I was back.

It had only been a couple weeks since I'd made the

move, and it still didn't feel quite real yet. I wasn't even fully settled in my new place. The whole move had been a whirlwind. In the span of two weeks, I'd interviewed for a new job, uprooted my entire life to move back to a town I swore I'd never set foot in again, and started my new role as head coach for my alma mater. On one hand, stepping back onto that field all these years later felt kind of like coming home again. However, on the other, doing it as a coach instead of a player was foreign territory. The start of the school year and the football season was right around the corner, and practice was officially underway. I'd been coaching my guys now for a week, and I still didn't have a goddamn clue what I was doing. I had two Super Bowl rings, for fuck's sake, yet I still felt like a fraud every time I brought that whistle to my lips and blew, demanding everyone's attention.

I was convinced the only reason I hadn't made an ass out of myself yet was thanks to the rest of the coaching staff. They'd been a godsend.

Honestly, my time would have been put to better use if I'd just stayed home to unpack a handful of the million boxes that cluttered my four-thousand square foot beach-front home, but one look around the cardboard castle I'd been living in lately had overwhelmed me to the point I'd had to get the hell out of there.

I was sure the house would be nice once I was doing

more than squatting in it—at least the pictures my assistant had shown me online before I told her to pull the trigger indicated it would be—but I hadn't had the time to breathe lately, let alone unpack. I woke up each morning before dawn for a five-mile run on the beach, then headed home with just enough time to shower and suck back a cup of coffee before I had to be at the school. On top of coaching, there was a shitload more paperwork than I'd been expecting, and I was still trying to get my footing with the rest of the OU athletic staff.

After practice I hit up the weight room with the kids to make sure I didn't start slipping. By the time I got home, I was usually wiped. I had just enough wherewithal to order something for dinner, pour myself a drink, and sit down to go over the stats on all my players so I could make sure we were ready for the start of the season. Then I usually forced myself to unpack two boxes each night before allowing myself to fall into bed and crash, only to wake up and start all over again.

Sam and Monica had invited me over to their place for dinner twice now, but I didn't have the time. A high school reunion was the very last place I had any business being when there was still so much on my plate, but the thought that I might get to see *her* pushed me to be something I hadn't allowed myself to be in a very long time: Reckless.

It had been ten years since I set eyes on Presley Fields and the draw to see her again after so long was too great to ignore.

"Oh my god! Beau Wade, it's so good to see you!" The woman sitting behind a long table filled with name tags shot to her feet and jogged around the best she could in her heels. I was caught off guard when she latched onto my shoulders with her long acrylic nails and lifted up to place a kiss on my cheek, awfully close to my lips and way too familiar for my liking.

I yanked my head back, out of the line of fire and gave her the same smile I reserved for dickhead reporters who liked to ask backhanded questions after a loss just to rub that shit in my face.

"Uh, yeah. You too . . ." I trailed off, at a loss for who this chick was supposed to be.

"Anna?" she said like that wasn't one of the most commonly used names in the English language. "It's Anna Waters now, but you probably remember me as Anna Clark."

The name rang a bell, but it took me a moment to put it together with the woman standing in front of me. Then it hit me. "Ah, right," I said with a snap of my fingers. "Anna Clark. I remember now."

She used to run in the same clique as my on-again-off-again girlfriend during senior year, Larissa Johnston. If high school was a cliché, they'd have been the group of mean girls who ran around making everyone else feel like shit. Most of them had been cheerleaders and *all* of them were spoiled brats.

If I were being honest, I hadn't liked Larissa all that much, even when I was dating her, but I'd been a horny little asshole and she let me have sex with her.

"Good to see you."

She smiled like she'd just won the lottery and clung to my arm as a group began gathering around me. I stood there, gritting my teeth to keep from telling everyone to back the fuck up as I received back slaps and high fives from my graduating class like they were my best friends instead of people I hadn't spoken a word to in a decade and a half. My heart rate had picked up. I was starting to feel claustrophobic as the group got even bigger, the walls closing in on me, and even though I was doing my best to keep from snapping at everyone, it was getting harder by the second.

I was about to lose it when a gap formed in front of me and a flash of vibrant red caught my attention. I looked past the mass of people vying for my attention, and the moment I realized who I was looking at, my heart started beating faster for a whole other reason.

She was the one person from back then that I would recognize anywhere, no matter how much time had passed.

Presley Fields stood across the gym looking like a goddamn vision in crimson. Her long wheat-blonde hair hung down her back in fat loose curls that shined like spun gold beneath the overhead lights.

I hadn't known whether or not she'd be here tonight, it was just my luck that she was and it took no time at all for me to find her. I'd been prepared to search her out, but finding her so easily in a sea of people like this felt like it was destined, like fate had stepped in to make it happen.

That sinfully sexy dress revealed a mile of smooth, tanned legs and ended in a pair of heels that made me imagine what they might feel like digging into my back as I buried my face in her pussy. That flirty little skirt was just begging to be flipped up as I bent her over the nearest flat surface and pounded my cock inside her.

As if she felt me staring, she glanced in my direction and those eyes I remembered being the sweetest shade of honey and cinnamon locked on mine. The blood rushed from my head, traveling straight to my dick with that one look. All these years later and it was still the same effect she'd had on me when I was a hormone-riddled shithead who couldn't control his boners.

She made me hard without even trying, but when we battled, when we went head to head and I pushed those buttons of hers that lit fire behind her eyes and made her cheeks flush, well, I hadn't found a single thing that could compare to that feeling.

She'd always been so damn good, so polite and bubbly. Always in a sunny mood. The goody two shoes who bent over backward for everyone else. Everyone but me. There was something exhilarating about being the only one who could rile her up, who could dirty up that good girl exterior she worked so hard to keep polished to a shine.

What Presley made me feel back then bordered on unhealthy. I was well and truly fixated on her. And as we stared at each other across the expanse of glossy maple flooring, I felt that same pull to her that had plagued me from middle school all the way through college.

I felt myself start in her direction, that invisible string between us tugging at me, and I would have been lying if I said the way her eyes flared with a hint of panic just before she ripped her gaze away didn't make my heart beat even harder, pounding against my sternum like it was a drum. It only solidified my decision to make my move. But before I got more than a few feet, I saw another guy come up from behind and tap her on her shoulder.

The way her whole face lit up at the sight of that dickhead Mike Perry made my blood run hot, and a haze of red coated my vision when she threw herself into his arms for a hug. I stood frozen in place, unable to tear my focus from the two of them as they talked. My hands clenched into tight fists as Presley's smile turned even brighter, and I nearly lost my shit when she ducked her head and looked up through the thick fan of long lashes in that bashful way I'd seen her do a million times growing up. I'd met more than my fair share of women over the years, and even the most practiced at seduction couldn't pull off that look, no matter how hard they tried. And the real kicker was, she wasn't even trying to be seductive when she looked at you like that. It was just her, that hint of shyness mixed with her bubbly personality. It was the most intoxicating combination.

I fucking hated when she gave other men that look because I knew exactly what it made them think. It made them want her. I knew because that was what it did to me every goddamn time, even when that look wasn't pointed in my direction.

It took every ounce of my carefully honed self-control to keep from going over there and driving my fist into that fucker's face. He might have come off as the shy, unassuming good guy back in high school, but I knew the truth. I'd warned him off Presley once before, and from the looks of it, I was going to have to remind him that she was well and truly off limits.

The voices around me sounded like they were coming from deep within a tunnel, muffled and barely recognizable as the woman in red across the room stole my attention completely. All those irrational feelings she'd stirred in me years ago came rushing right back to the surface, causing me to feel like I'd shot back in time to the kid I used to be.

"Beau, remember when we played peewee together? Think you could put in a good word for me with your agent?"

"Could I get your autograph, man? I bet I could sell it for a buttload on the internet."

"How about a selfie?"

"What's it like being famous?"

"Did you really bang that pop star?"

"Now that you're back, maybe we could get together for dinner, or . . . you know."

The intrusive and highly inappropriate questions came from all sides. You would have thought I was sitting in the middle of an interview, for Christ's sake, not my high school reunion. I didn't bother responding to any of them, only looking down at Anna, who'd clearly just propositioned me, and giving the gold band on her ring finger a pointed look before arching my brow.

Jesus, is this what these people were like back in school?

I shook my head and heaved out a weary sigh, something I'd been doing a whole lot of lately. I was contemplating turning around and heading back the way I came when that bag of dicks, Mike Perry, finally walked away from Presley, giving me my opening.

"Excuse me," I mumbled to no one in particular as I wormed my way out of the throng of former classmates. My feet carried me across the gym, the heels of my dress shoes clicking against the glazed floor as I closed the distance between us.

I recognized the pretty woman who'd rejoined her as her best friend from childhood, but I couldn't remember her name. Presley used to run around with her all the time back when we were kids, the two of them practically attached at the hip.

Presley's back was to me, so her friend was the first to see me coming, and I couldn't stop the smile from spreading across my face at her deer-in-the-headlights expression. A soft chuckle of anticipation rumbled through my chest as I stopped a foot away. If her friend's reaction was anything to go by, Presley wasn't going to be very happy to see me. Not that I could really blame her. I tended be a bit of a . . . well, prick back then. But pushing her buttons was a compulsion. The only time I got a break from being Beau Wade, football player or Hank Wade's son was when I was battling her, and as much as she might have hated the little games we played, they were the only light I had back then. When she refused to fawn over me like everyone else, that made me feel more normal than anyone or anything, and I hadn't been able to give that up.

"Well look at you, Bubbles. All grown up." And *damn*, but she had grown up well.

She turned around slowly, and as soon as I got an up-close look at her face, at that fire spitting and sparking in her cinnamon eyes, my dick went hard as stone. Christ, she was even more beautiful than I remembered.

Even with rage billowing from every pore on her pretty face, she was enough to take a man's breath away. Sleek, perfectly arched brows rose over intriguing eyes that couldn't be classified simply as brown. The color could change with her mood or what she wore. If she was in her usually pleasant, sunny mood they could radiate a golden glow that had the power to feel like the sun warming your skin, but if she was gearing up for a fight—like she usually was with me—that fire tended to peek through, giving the brown more heat that reminded me of those delicious warm spices on cold winter days. And sometimes the gold and spice blended together in the most beautiful shade of amber.

I was getting all that spice at the moment, and I wasn't mad about it.

Her pert little nose was scrunched up angrily, the tip just slightly upturned. Her round cheeks prevented her from having that model sharpness that so many of my exes paid a fortune to obtain, but I much preferred the real deal that was all Presley over the surgically enhanced women I'd dated over the span of my career for no other reason than we looked good next to each other in photos and in magazines.

Her normally full, pouty rose-petal lips were pursed in disdain, but even with the daggers she was throwing my way, she was the most beautiful woman I'd ever laid eyes on.

"Don't call me that," she ground out, her voice low and throaty, almost feral.

Game on, I thought as my grin tugged wider.

Fuck. Something was seriously wrong with me that I got off on screwing with her in such a big way, but I couldn't help myself. Presley Fields made me feel alive. Even when she was hating me.

As it stood at that very moment, it was taking every ounce of strength I had not to tangle my fist in her hair and yank her against me so I could taste that luscious little mouth of hers. To see if it was as delectable as I remembered, or if my memory had somehow faded over time.

"Saw you talking to that asshole, Perry. You still have a thing for losers and Momma's boys?"

That comment deepened the pink on the apples of her cheeks. "He's not an asshole or a loser."

I held a finger in the air. "Ah, but you didn't deny he's a Momma's boy."

Her friend's nervous gaze bounced between us like a ping-pong ball. "Uh, you know what? I think I see someone I'd like to catch up with over . . . far away. I'll meet up with you later, Pres."

"Colbie, don't you dare—" she started, but her friend booked it in another direction.

"Good to see you, Colbie," I called over my shoulder, and I could have sworn it looked like she stumbled over her shoes before righting herself but didn't stop.

Presley stared after her and huffed out an exhale. Her pinched lips moved, and I was watching them so damn closely I could see her silently mouthing a count to ten, like she was desperately struggling to stay calm.

When she finally looked back at me she'd schooled her features. "I don't know why you're here, but I'm really not in the mood for whatever this is."

One corner of my mouth kicked up in a smirk. "Pretty sure I'm here because it's my reunion too."

Her nostrils did that little flare that always happened when she was trying really hard not to lose her shit. She let out a low, angry growl that made my dick twitch behind my fly. "That's not what I'm talking about and you know it. Why did you have to come back *here*? To Whitecap. Everything was going so—" She stopped herself and

57

slammed her eyes closed, her lips moving as she counted to ten again.

I lifted a brow and stuffed my hands onto the pockets of my slacks to keep from reaching out to touch her. "You know, you almost make it sound like you haven't missed me."

"You know what? I'm not doing this with you. I'm not going to play whatever twisted little game your mind is set on. Welcome home, I guess. Hope to not see you around."

With that, she spun on her sexy-as-fuck heel and stormed off, leaving me to the ravenous vultures flocking over once I was alone. And how pathetic was it that once she stormed off, it only took moments for me to miss her, to want to hunt her down and throw her over my shoulder. To maybe, just maybe finally *keep* her?

I'd give her that play, at least this time. Because she'd be seeing me around whether she liked it or not. She'd be seeing a *lot* of me. I'd make damn certain of it.

Six

PRESLEY

Sundays were spent at my parents' house. It had started as a weekly dinner shortly after I returned from college and had become a tradition, but as the years went on and my parents got older, I started coming over earlier and earlier. First it was in order to help my mom cook so she didn't have to stay on her feet in the kitchen for so long. Then I started to notice things around the house that needed fixing, like the siding on the house needed to be power washed or pickets in the fence that needed replacing. Bulbs that needed to be change or water stains on the ceiling that needed to be painted.

My father was a proud, hardworking man who'd spent his entire adult life busting his ass for other people. He made his living as a handyman of sorts, painting houses, fixing garage doors, mowing lawns, and cleaning pools.

You name it, he did it. A quintessential jack of all trades. But he gave so much of himself to his clients—primarily the Whitecap elite, those with more disposable income than my family ever had—that he didn't have the time or energy to fix things in his own home.

He still gave too much of himself to people who didn't appreciate how hard he worked for them. Now he did it with arthritis that would have crippled most other people, but he was too strong to let it keep him down.

Where he made home repairs, my mother cleaned and cooked for the families who owned those homes, both of them working too damn hard this late in their lives. They deserved more and were both working their way toward retirement with dreams of gardening and fishing, lazy days on the beach with a stack of books waist-high. So I spent my Sundays helping them with their own home so they could have a bit of a break.

As I pulled up to their house, I noticed the white picket fence around the postage stamp-sized front yard was looking a little dingy and put a fresh coat of paint on my list of things to do, along with weeding the front flowerbeds.

I turned off my car and grabbed the grocery bags from the back seat before heading to the door. "Guys?" I called out as I finagled the door open with my arms loaded down. "I'm here."

My mom appeared in the entryway, wiping her hands on a dish towel. "Oh, honey. You didn't have to carry these in all by yourself." She draped the towel over her shoulder and moved to me. She pressed a quick kiss to my cheek before taking one of the bags from me so I could close the door.

I followed her into the kitchen, taking in the sink full of soapy water and dishes as I placed my bag on the counter beside hers.

"What's with the sink?" I asked as I began unloading everything I bought to make her famous roast chicken with broccoli and cheddar casserole.

"Oh, that? That's nothing." She blew the sudsy dishes off like it was no big thing. "The dishwasher's on the fritz again is all. I'm just washing by hand until your father's finished fixing it."

That was the third time in the last six months that the ancient dishwasher had gone "on the fritz." It didn't need to be fixed, it needed to be replaced all together.

"That's it," I grumbled as I turned and slammed my hands down on my hips. "I'm buying you a new dishwasher. I don't care how much you argue."

Before she could do just that, my father entered the kitchen from the door that led to the backyard. His features—drawn tight with the constant pain he lived with—smoothed out at the sight of me.

"Hey there, puddin' pop." He dropped his toolbox on the old, scarred-from-use butcherblock counter and came over to wrap me in one of his classic bear hugs. Arthritis or not, Alan Fields didn't skimp on hugs, and the ones he gave me were as strong and warm as always. "Good to see you."

"Hey, Daddy," I said softly, snuggling deeper into him for a few more seconds. It had to be said, my mother's home cooking could cure any sickness, but my dad's hugs could cure pains of the heart.

He placed his hands on my shoulders and pulled back, holding me at arm's length so he could take me in with a tender smile like he did every time he saw me. "My beautiful girl," he said affectionately. "How's tricks?"

"Tricks are good, same as always. And I was just telling Mom I'm going to buy you guys a new dishwasher, so no need trying to fix this one."

He blew a raspberry past his lips and waved his hand at me. "Not necessary. I got this. It'll be fixed in a jiff."

"Dad, that thing is a piece of junk," I said in exasperation. "How many times have you had to fix it? Just let me do this for you."

My mom spoke up then as my father started rummaging through his toolbox. "Honey, we can't let you do that. Aren't you still trying to buy that bar of yours?

You need to save every penny, not blow it on a silly dishwasher."

She wasn't too far off the mark. But buying them something that would make their lives easier wasn't "blowing money" in my opinion.

I was trying my hardest to buy the Dropped Anchor, but it turned out a bar manager with little more than a single credit card with an embarrassingly low limit and a buttload of student debt wasn't a very appealing candidate for a loan.

I needed to show the bank that I could come up with at least ten percent before they'd even consider giving me the money I needed to make my dream come true. But a new dishwasher for my folks was the very least I could do. And I did mean the *very* least.

"Everything on the bar front is fine," I lied. "Just let me do this for you, okay? You guys have done so much for me. I want to return the favor."

She reached out to give my cheek a gentle pat. "You're such a good daughter. Now, how about we get started on dinner? That chicken isn't going to roast itself."

I didn't miss the way she tried to navigate past the current topic, but I'd let it slide. For now, at least.

"You remember my friend Marjorie from book club," she started, and I had a feeling I was going to like this new topic of conversation even less. "Well she was just telling us about her son's recent divorce. He's about your age, and we got to thinking, wouldn't it be nice if the two of you went out on a date?"

Yep, I was right. I'd have rather talked about my serious lack of money than have my mom try to set me up on *another* blind date.

"God, Mom. Not this again."

"Oh, Shirley, let the girl be," my father said in my defense. "You're always trying to fix her up, and it never works out."

I bit down on the inside of my cheek to keep from laughing.

Mom slapped a hand on her hip and kicked out a foot. "Well excuse me for wanting my daughter to be happy. It's not like she's putting herself out there. Someone's gotta do it or the only grandkids we'll end up with is a whole mess of cats."

"Hey," I cried in offense. I didn't even like cats.

She gave me a look like she didn't want to hear it. "Oh please, all you do is work, work, work. If you can't find a man yourself, I'll have to do it for you."

Sure, because that would make for an incredibly healthy relationship.

I crossed my arms over my chest, my bottom lip sticking out in a pout. "That's not true at all. As a matter of fact, I went to my high school reunion last night with Colbie. So there."

Her face instantly lit up. "Oh, that's great! How was it? Did you guys have fun?"

"It was, um . . . Well, it was good. I actually ran into the guy I had a crush on back then and he's moving back to town in a few weeks." I smiled as I remembered my unexpected and pleasant run-in with Mike the night before. Before the whole thing went sour, thanks to that asshole Beau. But I wasn't going to give that guy another moment of my time. "We have a date planned when he gets back, so I don't need you to set me up with your friend's divorced son." I lifted my chin in the air. "I'm perfectly capable of finding a man on my own."

My father spoke then, turning the conversation toward an even worse topic. "You know, speaking of the reunion, I heard that little punk made an appearance."

So much for not giving him another moment of my time. It was almost laughable to hear my father refer to Beau Wade as a *little punk*. My old man was no slouch, but Beau still managed to beat him out in height and brawn. Even before arthritis put a hunch in his strong, capable frame. But he'd been a *little punk* in my father's eyes when we were kids, and clearly nothing had changed.

"He didn't give you a hard time, did he?" Dad continued, his voice almost threatening, like he would have given anything to hunt Beau down and deliver one hell of an ass whooping. "Because so help me, I'll—"

"It's fine, Dad," I said quickly, cutting him off before he could get good and riled. To say my parents weren't fans of the boy who'd made my school days a misery was putting it lightly. "All that stuff happened years ago. We're adults now. There's nothing to worry about."

But as I thought back to how his sudden appearance the night before had initially left me flustered, and how off-kilter I felt after our little run-in, I wasn't so sure about that. But my parents had enough on their plates as it was. They didn't need to worry about the petty little squabbles their daughter had with her high school bully.

It would be fine. It had to be.

"Honestly, I doubt I'll see much of him around town. I'm sure he's got a lot going on with his new job, and it's not like we run in the same circles."

"I never understood why he seemed to target you the way he did," my mom said with a shake of her head. "I swear, he was like a little boy on the playground pulling the pigtails of the girl he had a crush on."

A startled burst of laughter fell past my lips as I turned to give her a bewildered look. "Believe me, Beau Wade never had a crush on me. Not for a single, solitary moment. The only feelings between us were hostility and contempt."

I was leaving out some key details from my and Beau's extremely tumultuous, confusing past, but they didn't need all the gritty details. It was better for the sake of my sanity if I just pretended like it never happened. I'd spent the past ten years doing exactly that. There was no reason that had to change just because he had unexpectedly popped back up in my life.

Mom lifted her shoulder in a shrug as she turned and went back to the few remaining dishes in the sink. She picked up a glass and began to dry it. "If you say so."

I jumped at the loud clang my father caused when he dropped his wrench back into his toolbox with far too much force. "Of course she says so, Shirley." He snorted indignantly. "My girl's smarter than that. She'd never get involved with that boy." He shook his head as he rummaged through the tools again, snatching at things in agitation. "Always said that boy was from bad stock. I highly doubt the apple fell far from the tree."

My head whipped in my father's direction, my brows pulling together, the skin between puckering as I tried to make sense of that last statement. As far as I'd always known, Beau's parents, Hank and Catherine, were as much Whitecap royalty as their son. A wealthy family who lived on the right side of our little town. A doting stay-at-home mother, and a business-savvy father who ran not one, but *two* local car dealerships. My dad's comment about bad stock was the first I'd heard to the contrary. Then again, I'd always gone out of my way to avoid the Wades. The few run-ins I'd had with Beau's father always skeeved me out a little. I wasn't sure why, but the guy just gave me the creeps.

I felt my mom's attention on me and quickly smoothed my expression out, giving her a tight smile as I resumed unloading the grocery bags. The last thing I needed was for her to start suspecting I cared about anything related to Beau Wade.

Seven

PAST

Colbie came skipping up to the table, dropping her tray down with a clang that jolted me back into reality and pulled me out of the book I'd been reading as she slid into the chair across from me.

"Whatcha reading?"

I flipped the cover of my book closed so she could see the front. She let out a short whistle and waggled her brows at the image of the half-naked Duke clutching the nanny with the heaving bosom to him on the cover. "Another one you stole off your mom's shelf?" she teased, knowing I was a sucker for my mom's old-school bodice-ripper romances.

For the nerdy girl who didn't get much attention from the boys in school, it was nice to read about the lengths a man would go to win over the woman he loved. If I couldn't have a real relationship, at least I had these books. They were a much-needed escape from reality a lot of the time.

Colbie gave me a look as she peeled the rind off the orange on her tray. "You keep your face buried in those books, you're going to miss out on everything happening around you."

The doors to the cafeteria opened just then, almost as if her words had some sort of magical power, and my mood immediately plummeted to the floor. "You say that like it's a bad thing," I grumbled as I watched Beau Wade and Larissa Johnston walk into our school's cafeteria, hand in hand, like they were the king and queen of the freaking senior class or something.

As far as the rest of the kids we went to school with were concerned, they might as well have been. He was the quarterback of the football team and she was the captain of the cheer squad. They were the clichéd popular high school couple who treated everyone they thought was beneath them like crap, and it just so happened I was a favorite target for both of them. Individually and together.

I quickly slammed my book shut and stuffed it into my

backpack, knowing if either of them saw what I was reading, there would be no end to the crap they'd give me.

Colbie looked over in the direction I'd been staring and let out a scoff. "God, they're the worst," she mumbled as Beau took a seat at the head of the popular table and pulled Larissa into his lap. She let out an over-the-top giggle like the two of them didn't push the limits of the school's policy on PDA on a regular basis. If she wasn't climbing him like a tree in the hallway for everyone to see, they were sucking face against the lockers or grinding all over each other in the parking lot. They had no shame. Anyone else would have gotten into serious trouble, but it was like everyone looked the other way for them, teachers and students alike. Like they were special.

I looked away with a roll of my eyes and picked up my plastic fork to move the food around on my tray without taking a bite. My appetite had disappeared the moment those two had shown up.

"I really can't wait for graduation," I mumbled. "Hopefully I'll never have to see them again."

Colbie lifted her hands in the air and crossed her fingers with a huge smile on her face. "Here's hoping they go off to college somewhere far, far away and never come back."

My head fell back on a deep, genuine laugh. "God,

wouldn't that be amazing?" I asked with no small amount of glee in my voice.

Just then an intense prickling sensation began to crawl up the back of my neck. In a room filled with kids my age who hardly ever noticed me, I suddenly felt like I was being watched. I twisted in my seat, trying to be as discreet as possible as I attempted to find out the cause of that sensation. As soon as I did, my gaze locked on with Beau's chilly blue eyes.

I needed to look away. I knew that. But there was something about the way he was staring at me that caused a shiver to work its way down my spine. A shiver that should have been my body's reaction to fear or revulsion, but instead it was a shiver that made me feel things I'd never felt before. Things I couldn't explain but left me out of sorts.

"Uh, Pres?"

I ripped my eyes off of Beau's before Larissa could notice. The last thing I needed was to end up on her radar —*again*. I cleared my throat as heat spread upward from my chest over my neck and pooled in my cheeks. "Yeah?"

She was looking at the popular table with a furrowed brow, confusion painted across her face. "Why is Beau staring at you like that?"

I didn't have the first clue, but I had no intention of sticking around to find out. After all, having his attention never ended well for me. "Who knows," I said as I pushed back in my chair and hefted the strap of my backpack over my shoulder. "He's a weirdo creep." I grabbed up my tray, my lunch uneaten. "I need to get to the library. See you after school?"

She nodded, popping a slice of her orange into her mouth. "See you," she returned with puffed cheeks, and with one last wave in her direction, I booked it out of the cafeteria, refusing to look in that jerk's direction as I passed his table. Even though I felt him staring the entire way.

That feeling of being watched returned the moment I stepped into Spanish later that afternoon, and I knew without having to look that Beau was at his desk near the back of the class, watching me just like he had been in the cafeteria. Usually, I considered the day a win if I managed to get though all my classes without notice, but something about today was different, and I didn't understand why. I didn't know why he held such an interest in me today, but I knew the reason couldn't possibly be good, so I decided the best thing I could do was ignore him.

I refused to turn around, even though it left me feeling

like I was ignoring a persistent itch between my shoulder blades or fighting a sneeze. I did my best to focus on what our teacher was saying. Usually I thrived on being studious, but today was proving to be exceptionally hard. I was having trouble focusing as I frantically scribbled notes in my binder, more to give myself something to do than anything else, and when I read over what I'd written, it was clear I'd only picked up every fifth word or so that Ms. Garza said, because what I'd written didn't make any sense.

I glanced to the clock hanging over the whiteboard at the front of the classroom and let out a sigh of relief. Only five minutes left in class, then I didn't have to see Beau for the rest of the day, God willing.

I was almost scot-free. At least that was what I'd thought, until Ms. Garza spoke again. "All right class, now for your homework." Groans filtered through the room from my classmates, but I sat with my pen poised over a clean sheet of paper, ready to go. "Beneath each of your desks you'll find a card. It'll either have a picture or a Spanish word. What you're going to do is partner up with the person whose card has the word or image that corresponds with yours and together you're going to create a two-page conversation in Spanish that you'll read in front of the class. You'll have two days to complete the assignment, so I suggest you find your partners and work out a schedule. And remember," her voice rose as the kids in the room grew louder while hunting for their partners, "pronunciation counts."

Group projects were something I dreaded. I would have much rather done the work on my own. Well, except for my science lab, but that was only because I was partnered up with Mike Perry, and I was just *waiting* for the day to come when he'd finally ask me out.

My heart lodged in my throat and anxiety made my chest tighten as I twisted around in my desk, trying to find a card with the word that went with the drawing of a house on mine. As the seconds ticked by, more and more of my classmates partnered up for the assignment. Finally, I spotted a card with the word *casa* scrawled across it, and when I looked up to see who it belonged to my stomach bottomed out, plummeting to the floor at my feet.

Beau was kicked back in his seat, long legs stretched out in front of him. His eyes were on me, a smirk that could only be described as evil stretched across his face. *Man*, it really wasn't fair that he was so freaking good-looking. It was like a cruel joke that someone so ugly on the inside would be so cute on the outside.

The blood drained from my face and my mouth went dry as the sounds in the classroom dulled beneath the roar of blood rushing in my ears.

"Looks like it's you and me, Bubbles," Beau called with a cocky grin that had too many people focusing on us. My eyes narrowed and my hands balled into fists. *God*, I hated that stupid nickname. Like going out of your way to be nice instead of a raging jerk to everyone was a bad thing.

I wanted to scream. Or at least throw back a biting remark that would even the score between us, but I couldn't get my mind and mouth to work in sync. Instead, the bell rang and I quickly stuffed my things into my backpack, barely taking the time to zip it up before storming out of the classroom.

There was no way I'd be able to work with him. I'd do the project myself and let him get the credit for it if that got me out of having to partner with him. Even with all my other work piled on top, it was still better than being stuck in his presence for however long the stupid assignment took.

By the time the last class of the day ended I was feeling good about my plan. It was the perfect solution, really. I didn't like Beau and he sure as hell didn't like me, so I bet he'd be thrilled to find out I was willing to do all the work for him if it meant we didn't have to spend time together.

I headed for my locker to get everything I'd need to do the Spanish assignment on my own, stuffing my backpack so full that it was going to be a pain to carry, but I wasn't one of the lucky kids whose parents had the money to buy them a new car the moment they turned sixteen.

Colbie caught up with me just as I slammed my locker

shut and heaved my backpack on. "Jeez, you're going to give yourself scoliosis or something."

I snorted as I hefted the straps up higher, trying to get the bag settled in just the right place that it wouldn't be impossible to carry on my walk home. "Comes with the territory, I guess."

She blew a raspberry past her lips as she fell in step beside me. "Maybe if you're a certified genius taking a bazillion AP classes. But not when you're a normal, middle of the line student like the rest of us."

I laughed and shook my head. She wasn't wrong about my class load, but I didn't take so many advanced classes and extracurricular activities because I was a genius. I took them because it was the only way I could hope to get a scholarship, and that was the only way I'd be able to attend college without incurring a ton of debt. As hard as my folks worked, they couldn't afford to put me through a university.

I'd been busting my butt for years to get as many grants and scholarships as I possibly could, but each one felt like a competition. I didn't realize it at first, but it eventually came out that a lot of the ones I'd lost out on were because Beau had gotten them, and I was convinced he'd done it on purpose, applying for the same grants as me as just another one of his sick little games.

It wasn't like he needed them. His parents had more

money than mine would ever know what to do with, and I was sure he was going to receive a football scholarship to any college he wanted. He basically had a first-class ticket to anywhere he wanted to go, so I didn't understand why he couldn't leave the academic stuff to those of us who needed it, the students less . . . athletically inclined. That was the nicest way I could think to describe my complete lack of coordination in pretty much every sport on the planet.

And that was just another bone of contention where Beau was concerned. I had to study my ass off to get straight As, but he didn't seem to have that problem at all. He'd been on the honor roll every year since the seventh grade. He was part of the National Honor Society, *and* summa cum laude. All of that, and I'd hardly ever seen him crack a book. It wasn't fair!

We pushed through the glass doors and stepped out into the crisp, breezy spring day. The muscles in my neck were already cramping, and I could feel knots forming between my shoulder blades, but I gritted my teeth and carried on. Fortunately, we didn't live too far from the school.

The parking lot was emptying quickly, but there were a few stragglers still lingering, students still visiting with their friends or the person they were dating. And of course, one of the kids still lingering had to be Beau.

My heart began to beat faster at the sight of him pressed up against a gleaming black Jeep Wrangler with Larissa latched onto his face.

Colbie spotted them just seconds after I did. "Eww." She scrunched her face up in disgust as the two of them practically dry-humped in the middle of the parking lot. "They don't have any shame, do they?"

I let out a huff and rolled my eyes as I discreetly picked up the pace. "Don't worry. I'm sure they'll break up for the millionth time soon enough."

She snorted out a laugh. "True. Talk about a toxic relationship. Those two fight and break up at least twice a week."

My chest sank on a breath of relief just as we passed by the Jeep. Unfortunately, that breath came too soon, because before I could make my escape, Beau's deep voice called out, "Yo, Bubbles." I froze in place, momentarily thrown before turning stiffly to face him. At some point, he'd pushed Larissa away, and I now had his full attention. He jerked his chin toward the Jeep and ordered, "Get in."

My jaw fell open, hanging in the wind at the same time Colbie and Larissa both squeaked, "*What*?"

Eight

BEAU

PAST

I sensed her before she'd even walked out of the school. It had been like that since she moved to our little po-dunk town back in middle school. I would have been lying if I said I hadn't been watching for her. Then again, the freaking girl had my attention every time she entered a room. Even if I didn't want to notice her.

We didn't hang with the same people, have the same friends, or have a damn thing in common, as a matter of fact. She was a goody two shoes all the way through. The girl never got in trouble because she wouldn't even bend a rule, let alone break it. She did extra credit work just for the hell of it and spent most of her time with her nose stuck in a book. She wore a smile almost constantly, polite to pretty much everyone to the point that I was surprised the sun didn't shine out of her butt.

She was the opposite of me in every way, but there was something about her that drew me to her from the moment she and her folks rolled into town. I could still remember the first time I saw her walking through town, smiling at everyone with that bright, rosy smile of hers. I was barely twelve, but I remembered thinking I wanted that smile for myself and feeling frustrated that I couldn't have it.

I started to call her Bubbles because of her bubbly personality, but the name stuck because, well, it just fit her perfectly. There was also the added fact that she couldn't stand it. I was sure it said something about me that I got off on screwing with her, but I didn't care. The fact she was so damn polite with everyone else, but wouldn't hesitate to go head-to-head with me made me almost feel special.

Man, I was really screwed up.

She and her friend Colbie were laughing as they hit the sidewalk in front of the school. My gaze dragged right along with her, like it was being pulled on a leash, watching closely enough that I didn't miss the way she kept tugging at the straps of her overflowing backpack.

The damn thing looked like it was packed with bricks and couldn't possibly be comfortable.

Annoyance clawed through me when I tried pulling away from the death grip Larissa had on me only to have her latch on tighter.

"Come on, Beau," she said in that whiny voice that always made me roll my eyes. "Why don't we go back to my place?" She bounced on the toes of her flip-flops as she batted her eyes. "My parents won't be home for *hours*."

I blew out a breath and pushed her back for the second time. She'd latched onto me the moment I got to my Jeep and held on with the strength of a freaking anaconda. "Told you already, I have shit to do."

She went from sweet to sour in the blink of an eye, slamming her hands on her hips and throwing daggers my way with her eyes. "What do you have to do that's so freaking important, huh? You seeing another girl?"

I didn't bother hiding my eye roll that time. I was so over this shit. Any time I had other plans or wasn't in the mood to hang, Larissa accused me of cheating on her. Because, god forbid, I didn't actually want to spend time with her when all we really ever did is fight. I was really getting sick of whatever this relationship was.

"I'm not having this conversation again, Riss. I told you, I have a project I gotta do for Spanish." Done with this conversation, I looked in Presley's direction and called out, "Yo, Bubbles." I had to bite the inside of my cheek to keep from smirking at the stiff, wooden way she turned to look at me, and I sure as hell didn't miss the way Larissa's eyes bounced back and forth between us, but I didn't give a shit. I jerked my chin toward the passenger door. "Get in."

All three girls looked at me like I'd just grown an arm out of my forehead or something, but while Presley stood there like her feet were glued to the concrete, her friend and Larissa both squeaked, "*What*?"

I didn't take my eyes off Bubbles as I looked at her like I was just daring her to argue. "We got that project for Spanish we have to work on. Or did you forget already?"

My dick twitched behind my fly when her eyes went from wide and frightened to narrow and vicious. "I didn't forget," she hissed, her apple cheeks taking on a pretty pink flush. The same pink as her rosy lips. "But I don't need your help. I can do it myself and you can just take the grade. Win-win."

I lifted a brow and leaned back against my car like I didn't have a care in the world. "And risk a shitty grade? Don't think so, Bubbles." Truth was, I'd spotted her card the moment she pulled it from beneath her desk. Mine had a picture of a fence on it so I'd made quick work of finding the kid whose card went with Presley's and basically scared him into trading with me. It was the same asshole who stared at her boobs and ass when he didn't think anyone was looking. Like hell I'd let that little perv partner up with her.

The fixation I'd felt toward Presley was only getting worse the closer we came to graduation. It was as if there were a clock in my head ticking down. My time was running out. I was borderline obsessed with the girl, and when Ms. Garza announced this project, I saw it was the perfect opportunity to make a move.

"Don't call me that," she growled, giving her foot a tiny stomp. "And it won't be a shitty grade. It'll be an A, just like everything I do." She lifted her chin proudly as she made that decree, and I liked that she had so much faith in herself. The girl was smart as hell. She deserved to own it.

I would have been more than happy to stand there all day and fight with her—while secretly wondering what it felt like to kiss her pretty mouth—but I knew if she stayed in Larissa's orbit for another second, things had a chance of getting ugly. I couldn't let that happen, so instead of throwing something back, I moved to her, reaching out and grabbing the handle at the very top of her bookbag, and pulling it off her shoulders. I let out a grunt at the weight of it, a wave of aggravation sliding over me at how heavy it was. Christ, she could hurt herself carrying something that freaking heavy.

"Hey!" she cried, taking off after me as I beeped the

locks on my Jeep and yanked open the back door. I tossed her backpack onto the backseat, and it dropped like a boulder hitting water. "What do you think you're doing?" she yelped as she scrambled for her bag, but I slammed the door shut before she could get to it. "That's stealing!" she shouted.

I shrugged, crossing my arms over my chest. "You want your bag, you gotta get in. I'm not letting you do this assignment yourself and risking my GPA." I leaned in closer to her, breathing in a fragrance that smelled fresh and citrusy with a hint of something floral underneath. Like honeysuckle and oranges. "Get. In."

I could see the panic swirling in her light brown eyes before she turned to look back at her friend. Colbie gave her a shrug like she didn't know what to do, and I didn't bother hiding my grin, knowing I'd won.

With an angry huff, Presley stomped her feet against the ground as she rounded the hood and snatched open the passenger door. I grabbed the handle of my own just as she slammed the door hard enough to shake the whole Jeep, but before I could get in, Larissa's hand shot out, her fingers wrapping around my arm. "If you leave with that loser, we're so over," she threatened. Like I gave a shit. The only thing in that whole sentence that could cause a reaction from me was her calling Presley a loser. But defending her would have put a bullseye in the middle of her back.

I shrugged and pulled my arm out of her grasp. "Works for me. See you around." With that, I climbed in behind the wheel and shut the door on a fuming Larissa and confused Colbie, sealing myself alone with the girl I'd been infatuated with for way too long.

From the corner of my eye, I caught her fidgeting in the seat, her hands clasped tightly in her lap. "Where are we going?" she asked as I twisted the key to start the engine.

I looked her way, something swelling in my chest at the sight of her in my car for the first time ever. Damn, she looked good sitting there. Too good.

"My place," I answered in a low, clipped voice. "My folks won't be there, so there won't be any interruptions." The thought of being alone with her was nearly enough to drive me crazy.

"Beau." She said my name on a breath that had my fingers gripping the steering wheel tighter as I backed out of the spot and shot out of the parking lot. She didn't say my name often, but when she did, it always sounded so damn good coming from her mouth. "I don't know if that's a good idea."

I smirked as I pressed harder on the gas pedal, wanting to get as far away from the school and her side of town so she didn't have any choice but to depend on me to get wherever she needed to go. Truth was, I just wanted to spend some time alone with her, and now that she was in my car, I wasn't sure I'd be able to let her go. "What's wrong, Bubbles? You nervous to be alone with me?" I glanced in her direction, shooting her a wink. "Worried you won't be able to control yourself?"

I glanced in her direction to find her glaring at me like she wanted to stab me, but I knew by the way her cheeks were burning red it was more than just rage.

"First, *stop calling me that*," she said on a growl that shouldn't have sounded as hot as it did. "Second, the only thing I wouldn't be able to control is the desire to strangle you."

Christ, she was cute as fuck. "If you say so."

From the corner of my eye I saw her cross her arms over her chest and push herself back in the seat with a pout. I much preferred her fire to the nervous, panicked energy she'd been giving off earlier. She was so much stronger than she thought, and I hated to see her cower. Not when she was better than all those assholes that caused her to do it.

Myself included.

Nine

PRESLEY

Past

I never thought I'd say it, but I was actually grateful for the fact Beau was annoying the ever-loving crap out of me because it helped distract me from the fact that I was in his car. With him. Heading straight into the lion's den or pit of hell or wherever it was he lived.

The scent of spice and something outdoorsy, almost woodsy, filled the cab of the Jeep. I would have loved to say it was a gross smell that only succeeded in giving me a headache, but that would have been a lie. Truth was, being stuck in that seat, surrounded by that intoxicating smell that was all Beau was . . . comforting. Don't ask me how that was possible, but it was the truth. It almost felt like being wrapped in a blanket. Sure, there was a narcissistic asshole trapped in there with me, but it was comforting all the same.

Which actually worried me, because I had to have been losing my mind to feel that way.

"You got quiet all of a sudden," Beau pointed out as the businesses and storefronts of downtown Whitecap gave way to pretty homes with well-maintained yards. I knew if I were to roll down the window, the sound of the waves crashing against the shore would steadily grow louder as we got closer. We were quickly leaving the quaint, quiet neighborhoods I was familiar with and getting closer to the ocean, closer to the luxurious houses that lined the coast. Closer to where the town's wealthiest residents lived. Because *they* could afford those beachfront homes.

Of course this would be where Beau lived. I don't know why I was surprised.

I stared out the window, refusing to look in his direction. "I don't have anything to say to you."

I heard him let out a snort and caught movement out of the corner of my eye. As discreetly as possible, I slid my gaze in his direction, taking in the way he drove with one arm lazily draped over the steering wheel, almost carelessly. His other hand rested on the console between us, his long fingers drumming out the beat of whatever song was playing quietly from the speakers. Looking at him, it was easy to think he was just a normal high school boy. The gorgeous, popular quarterback on the football team, not the spawn of Satan himself I knew him to be.

"Careful, Bubbles. You might end up bruising my ego."

It was my turn to scoff, my eyes rolling so hard it was a wonder they didn't get stuck facing the back of my skull. "Oh please," I cried indignantly. "Narcissists can't get bruised egos." I waved him off. "Besides, there's no way a *loser* like me could ever make you feel bad about yourself," I threw in, repeating the insult I'd heard his girlfriend use only a handful of minutes earlier.

"Don't say shit like that," he barked, his voice hard and bordering on violent. So much so that my head whipped around in his direction, my eyes bulging in their sockets.

I might have actually been frightened of the sudden change in his demeanor if the thought of him defending his spoiled brat of a girlfriend didn't piss me off to no end. "Excuse me?"

But then he said something that struck me speechless, something I never in a million years would have expected him to say. "Don't call yourself a loser," he gritted out, his molars clamped together so tight the muscle in his jaw ticked like crazy. "You're not a loser, so don't say it."

My mouth fell open so wide my jaw was practically resting in my lap. "I—what?"

His face fell, his expression growing dark in a way I had never seen before. "You heard me," he grunted in response.

"I—I don't think I'm a loser, Beau."

He took his gaze off the road for a second to shoot me a frown. "Then why'd you just say that?"

"I was mimicking your girlfriend," I replied snidely.

"She's not my girlfriend," he bit back. "And you shouldn't listen to anything she has to say. She can be a real bitch when she wants to be. Which is most of the time."

"Yeah, tell me something I don't know," I grumbled, deciding to ignore his comment about her not being his girlfriend. It was only a matter of time—probably hours—before that changed again.

"Anyway, I know I'm not a loser. I don't care what other people think. I know exactly how awesome I am."

He shocked me again by smiling, the mood in the car changing drastically for the second time in less than five minutes, and muttering, "Good. Because you are."

Had something happened? Had I fallen on my way to get into his Jeep and given myself a concussion? Was I asleep and this was some kind of weird dream? Or maybe Beau had driven us right into an alternate dimension somehow where he *wasn't* a raging hemorrhoid.

Or maybe this was another one of his twisted games.

My eyelids dropped into slits as suspicion took hold of me in an iron grip. "What are you doing?" I asked, my tone accusing.

His brows pinched together, his eyes coming back to me for a split second, just long enough to see that the normally frigid blue was decidedly warmer than usual. "What are you talking about?"

"Why are you being nice to me? You're *never* nice. We hate each other."

"That's not true," he argued bewilderingly. "I don't hate you."

Okay, maybe I wasn't the one losing my mind. Maybe it was him. Either way, I wasn't playing whatever this game was, so I decided to ignore him and looked back out the passenger side window.

I'd learned over the years that the best way to handle Beau when I wasn't sure what he was up to was to ignore him. Easier said than done when I was stuck with him, but I'd do my best.

A few minutes later, Beau turned his Jeep into a circular drive, stopping in the middle of it right in front of one of the biggest houses I'd ever seen.

I knew my father had done some work on the Wade house a few times, but this was the first time I'd seen it, and it was just more proof that Beau and I came from two totally different worlds.

This house was *ridiculous*.

I was so busy staring up at the mcmansion outside my window that I hadn't realized Beau had turned off the car and gotten out until he appeared in front of me, pulling my door open.

"You gonna get out so we can get this project done, or sit here and gawk the whole time?"

"I—Beau, this was a mistake. I think you should just take me home." I didn't belong here. That much was evident.

He rolled his eyes like I was being ridiculous. "Will you stop being dramatic? We have to do this project, so let's go." Instead of waiting for me, he leaned across me and unbuckled my seatbelt before grabbing my hand and tugging me out, giving me no choice but to follow after him.

He didn't bother releasing my hand as he dragged me from the Jeep and up the steps of the impressive front porch to the heavy beveled-glass double doors.

If the outside was impressive, it was nothing compared to what the inside of the house looked like. I couldn't imagine what it would have been like to live in a place like this. It didn't feel cozy or comfortable like my home did, but that had nothing to do with the size. My house actually felt like a *home*. This place felt like . . . a museum.

I stared around in awe, oblivious to where Beau was

leading me until the toe of my shoe caught on the edge of a step.

I gave my hand a little tug, trying to get free or at least slow him down. Neither happened as he continued up the staircase at the same pace. "Where are you taking me?"

His answer had my stomach bottoming out. "My room."

I stumbled, nearly faceplanting on the stairs. "Beau, wait." I tugged harder on my hand. That finally got him to stop, but he still didn't release it. The heat from his palm seeped into mine and traveled up my arm and through my entire body, sparking like a live wire. "Maybe we shouldn't—"

The rest of my objection died on my tongue when he turned to look back at me. "What are you so afraid of, Bubbles?" he asked, something in his voice sending a shiver up my spine. "You scared of me?"

Was I?

It didn't really matter whether he scared me or not, because I'd never let him know. That would have only given him one more thing to hold over me, and I would be damned if I added to his arsenal.

"Please," I scoffed indignantly. "You don't scare me. You're just another spoiled, self-centered jock with too much money and not enough sense."

His brows inched higher on his forehead. "Then

what's the problem?" The way he phrased it made it feel more like a challenge than a question, and I'd be damned if I was going to be the one to back down.

Lifting my chin, I squared my shoulders and shook off any of the lingering doubts I'd had only moments ago. "Not a thing. Lead the way."

However, as I followed him the rest of the way up the stairs and down a long, plushly-carpeted hallway, I couldn't help but feel like I was being led by the devil himself.

"I'm telling you, we should go with what I suggested."

I rolled my eyes at the ceiling and threw my pen down on the textbook I had open on Beau's bed. I let out a huff and looked to where Beau sat in the rolling chair that he'd pulled over to the bed from his desk so he could kick his feet up on the mattress and relax.

"I'm not writing that down," I argued for the millionth time. We'd been working on our project for the past hour. And what a surprising hour it had been.

I wasn't sure what to expect when I'd been teamed up with Beau, but I could admit that some of the worst-case scenarios had filtered through my head. I was shocked when he'd taken the work seriously—well, with the exception of trying to get me to sprinkle a few sexual innuendos into the conversation we had to create. But other than that, we'd actually worked pretty well as a team.

I definitely hadn't seen that coming.

Another thing I never would have expected in a million years was that . . . I was actually having a good time. Color me surprised as hell, but it was the truth. When he wasn't going out of his way to piss me off or make me miserable, Beau Wade was actually pretty funny. I was seeing a side of him I'd never known existed. I could have actually seen us maybe being friends. Or at least friend*ly*.

I didn't even mind the nickname so much anymore.

"Come on, Bubbles. Bet she gives us extra points for creativity." He winked at me and I felt my cheeks flush with heat.

I balled up a discarded piece of paper and tossed it at his head with a laugh. "More like we'd get expelled." I picked up my pen and pointed it in his direction as he lifted the soda can to his lips and drank. "Don't push it. I'm kinda sorta starting to not hate you a ton. Let's not ruin that."

He placed his hand to his chest. "I think that's the nicest thing you've ever said to me," he joked playfully.

I looked down at my notebook, grinning as I wrote down the next sentence we agreed on. "Well, it's not like you've given me much to make nice comments about. What with you hating me and all."

I expected some smart reply or teasing insult, but he went silent. When I looked back up, he'd shifted in his chair, lowering his feet to the floor and leaning closer to me. His features had gone hard and the air charged. The atmosphere had gone from fun and playful to intense.

"Beau? What's—?"

"I don't hate you," he said, rendering me speechless. "I've never hated you." Something in his voice made it impossible for me to move, to look away. "Not for a single day."

It felt like there was static electricity in the air between us. I didn't realize I'd leaned closer to him as well until the textbook slid off the bed and clattered to the floor. I blinked back into reality and jerked away, clearing my throat. "Um . . ." I reached up with a trembling hand and tucked my hair behind my ear as my gaze bounced around Beau's room. It was so much bigger than mine, everything in it so much more expensive, yet, mine felt homier. "Well, you could have fooled me," I said with an awkward laugh, trying to infuse lightness back into the situation that suddenly felt extremely heavy. "You've been really good at pretending otherwise."

He moved closer still, and a thought suddenly blinked into my head. *Is he about to kiss me?*

That thought was followed by an even more insane one. *God, I want him to kiss me.*

I'd never been more confused in my life. This was a boy I hated, my high school bully, my nemesis, and I wanted him to kiss me like crazy. I wanted him to kiss me the way I'd seen him kiss Larissa all those times. Like he couldn't help himself.

"Presley." I was so used to him calling me Bubbles that the use of my name momentarily threw me off guard. "I've never hated you. Not for a single day."

It was going to happen. He was going to kiss me. And something told me it would probably be the best kiss of my entire life.

His eyes flew down to my mouth when my tongue darted out to wet my lips, that clear, pale blue growing darker than I'd ever seen it before. This was it. It was happening. He was going to kiss me. And that voice inside my head that should have been yelling at me to back away was nowhere to be found.

But then the door slammed downstairs, giving both of us a jolt, and just as fast as it had come on, the moment splintered before shattering into a million pieces.

"Beau," a loud, deep voice called from downstairs, causing me to shoot up straight, my spine going rigid.

"Is that your dad?" I asked in a whisper, my own eyes rounding as the fire in his died out.

"Yeah," he grumbled, the air in the room growing frigid.

"Should we be up here?" I continued to whisper for some inexplicable reason.

He returned his feet to the mattress, taking on a laid-back, casual position that didn't match his sudden mood change. "Don't worry about it. Just ignore him."

That was easier said than done, especially since I could hear the man's footsteps climbing up the stairs as he called for Beau again, his voice much closer this time.

A few seconds later, the door to his bedroom flew open, banging against the wall behind it hard enough to startle a gasp out of me.

"Boy, what did I tell you about answering me when I —" His rant cut off when he spotted me sitting cross-legged on his son's bed.

I lifted my hand in an awkward wave. "Uh, hi, Mr. Wade. I'm Pres—"

He looked to his son, dismissing me before I could even get my whole name out. "I need to talk to you. Outside," he ordered to Beau before turning on his heel and storming out.

The door closed behind him and I glanced back to Beau as he pushed out of his chair, his jaw clenched so tight it ticked, and tossed his notebook onto the mattress angrily. "Be right back," he grunted without sparing me a single look as he stomped out of the room, leaving me alone and feeling incredibly awkward.

Seconds ticked into minutes. The more time that passed, the antsier I got, like a million tiny bugs were crawling beneath my skin. At one point I could hear raised voices, but they'd moved far enough away that I couldn't make out what was being said.

Finally, the door flew open and Beau reappeared, face red and eyes that all-too familiar chilling ice blue.

"Come on," he clipped as he snatched his keys off the desk and stuffed them in his pocket.

"Uh, where are we going?" I sputtered as I made quick work of stuffing my things back into my backpack.

"I'm taking you home. Think we've done enough on that conversation for one day."

"Oh." My stomach sank as disappointment spread through my limbs. Despite everything I thought I knew about Beau, I'd actually had fun this afternoon and I was sad it was over.

The ride back to my place was made in silence. The fun-loving, funny boy I'd gotten to know was gone, but as he pulled up in front of my house and put his Jeep in park, that niggling of hope that we could stop being enemies for the first time in years was still alive in my chest, blooming into something.

"Thanks for the ride," I said quietly as I reached for the handle.

"Sure. No problem."

I tugged the handle and pushed the door open but something stopped me from climbing out. I wasn't sure what had happened between him and his father earlier, but I hated that, whatever it was, it had upset him enough that he'd gone from joking and playful to broody.

"Hey, Beau?" He turned his head to look at me but remained silent. It took a few calming breaths, but I eventually found the courage to say what I truly felt. After all, we'd crossed a hurdle today, and I didn't want to risk backsliding. I hadn't been able to stop thinking about that almost-kiss for a second, and I would have been lying if I said I didn't hope the opportunity arose again. "I had a lot of fun with you today," I admitted quietly.

He smiled for the first time since his dad barged into his room. "Me too, Bubbles."

I returned his smile. "And for what it's worth, you're not so bad. Who knew, right?" I threw a wink his way that made him laugh, and on that sound, I hopped out of his Jeep and shut the door, giving him a wave before he took off.

As I headed into school the next morning my footsteps were lighter than they'd been in a really long time. The smile on my face wasn't forced or stiff. I felt . . . good. Excited to get the day started, actually. I couldn't wait to see how things would change now that Beau and I had reached some sort of ceasefire.

I spotted him standing at his open locker and felt my smile get bigger as I started in his direction. I hadn't been able to stop thinking about the kiss that didn't happen to the point I'd hardly gotten any sleep the night before. I was seeing Beau Wade in a whole new light, and it was so much more flattering than the one that used to shine on him. I could see us as friends. And, hell, given the intensity I felt between us yesterday, maybe even something . . . more. But I wouldn't get ahead of myself.

"Hey," I started once I reached him. "So, when do you feel like getting together again to finish up our project?"

He turned slowly, his expression totally blank as he looked me up and down in a rather dispassionate way.

My smile turned into a frown as I reached out to place my hand on his forearm. "Hey, you okay?"

Just then, something—or should I say some*one*

slammed into my shoulder, knocking me off balance, and if I hadn't reached out to catch myself, I would have fallen on my butt right there in front of half the senior class.

"Excuse me, *loser*." I looked up just as Larissa snuggled up against Beau's side. Seeing her cling to him like that sent a sharp pain through me, but it was the way he so casually lifted his arm and hung it over her shoulders, pulling her into him like he actually wanted her there, that turned that stab of pain into a burn.

She sneered at me as she all but glued her front to his side, dragging her long, pointed nails down the cotton covering his chest and stomach. "What do you think you're doing touching *my* boyfriend?"

My gaze darted back and forth between the two of them. I kept waiting for Beau to put her in her place, to tell her to shut up or push her away. But instead, he just kept looking at me like I was nothing.

"I-I didn't—I'm not—"

"Da-da-da," she mocked before breaking into laughter. It was when I heard other kids behind me start to laugh that I realized we'd drawn a crowd. "Is your brain not working, freak? I asked why you were putting your gross, loser hands on my boyfriend."

My heart sank, landing with a dull thud on the ground at my feet.

"Beau?" I whispered, the pain in my heart reflecting in my voice.

"Oh my god," Larissa cackled. "Look at that! How pathetic. The loser's got a crush on the popular guy." More laughter rang out all around me, each one like a slice of a razor-thin blade. "Oh, that's so sad," she continued with a dramatic pout of her bottom lip. "What do you think, baby?" she asked, pressing her boobs even harder into Beau's side. "How's it feel to know this freak's got a crush on you?"

He looked down at Larissa with a smile, pulling her up for a forceful, deep kiss that squeezed the breath right out of my lungs before finally looking back at me with that blank expression. "Don't really think about her at all. Not like she's on my radar."

Larissa's head fell back on a cackle, like that was the most hilarious thing she'd ever heard. But I was done. Done being the butt of these jerks' jokes, of being ridiculed and mocked, of being tricked into thinking there was something deeper to Beau Wade than there really was. He was as shallow as a puddle, and I'd let him play me.

But never again.

Tilting my chin high, I schooled my expression, refusing to let these assholes see my pain as I spun on my heel and stomped away from them. From him. The bell for first period hadn't rung yet, so I made one quick stop before heading to class.

Ms. Garza's head came up when I knocked on the frame of her open door.

"Good morning, Presley. Can I help you with something?"

"Yes ma'am," I started, stepping into her classroom. "It's about our Spanish project. Sorry to be a pain, but I need a new partner."

Because I was done with Beau Wade for good.

So freaking done.

Ten

BEAU

MY SHOES BEAT against the packed wet sand near the edge of the shoreline where land met ocean, kicking up clumps behind me as I ran. Every inhale filled my lungs with the salty sea air and every crash of the waves sent up a refreshing mist of spray.

I'd forgotten what it was like to run on the beach. It was so different from that dry desert air I'd grown used to. Each breath was fresher, purer somehow. The wind whipping off the water was downright pleasant. That would change come winter, however. The icy spray would feel more like needles piercing my lungs, but I could deal. I'd done it before, in a past life.

I'd taken my earbuds out halfway through the run, enjoying the sounds of the waves crashing and the gulls crying over the hard beat of the music I usually ran to.

It had been a week since the reunion, and I hadn't seen Presley once in that time. And that wasn't for lack of looking. When I was out, I had my eyes peeled. I was starting to grow anxious. Sure, I had a new job I was focused on, one I wanted to do well, one that took up a hell of a lot more of my time than I'd initially expected, but it would have been a lie if I said she wasn't a large part of the reason I'd decided to set my roots back in Whitecap after having dug them up so many years ago. I could have found a place closer to the university, in one of the other small towns that bordered the one I'd grown up in. But *she* was here. And after so many years of wanting her but having to keep her at arm's length, I was finally at a point in my life where no one else could dictate what I did or who I was with.

I wanted her, goddamn it, and I was *finally* going to take my shot if it fucking killed me.

My mind filled with memories of Presley Fields as I pushed myself harder, ran faster. My running shoes sank into the sand with each pounding step and that twinge in my shoulder made itself known with each swing of my arms, but I'd grown used to the discomfort, accepting that it was just a part of my life now. My shoulder had healed. It might not have been good as new, but it was as good as it was going to get, so I'd have to deal because there was no way in hell I was having *another* surgery on the damn thing.

I pushed the twinge to the back of my mind and focused on thoughts of Presley and how she'd looked the night of the reunion. She'd changed so much, yet somehow stayed true to the girl I'd known, the one I fixated on for so many years.

I spent an embarrassing amount of time stroking my cock to the images of her in that red dress and heels over the past several days, each time coming harder than I had in a really long time. I fucked my fist to Presley Fields on the backs of my eyelids so much, it was a wonder my dick wasn't chafed.

But, God, she'd really taken my breath away that night. She'd always been beautiful. Most beautiful girl I'd ever laid eyes on, but seeing her all grown up for the first time . . . well, she was something else. All curves, long toned legs, and smooth, creamy skin. I wanted to mark that perfect skin, sink my teeth in and turn it pink so everyone could see who she belonged to. Then I wanted to strip her bare and mark the places only my eyes were allowed to see.

I pushed myself harder, faster, hoping to work off some of the sexual frustration coursing through my blood since that goddamn reunion. I felt like I was coming out of my skin, and it was taking everything I had not to track Presley down. That would probably freak her out, and I had enough working against me as it was. The last thing I needed was to scare her into getting a restraining order against me.

By the time I took the boardwalk from the beach back to my house, my legs were shaking so hard it was a wonder I could stay upright. I hadn't pushed myself like that in a long time, but the exhaustion in my muscles felt damn good.

I was looking forward to a hot shower to loosen up before I had to get ready for work. But when I rounded the curve to my driveway, I noticed a car I didn't recognize sitting in front of my house. The black luxury sedan didn't have a speck of dirt on it, the pristine paint job gleaming beneath the early morning sun.

I slowed to a jog, then finally a walk, never taking my eyes off the car. As I reached into the pocket of my hoodie and pulled out my keys, the driver side door opened and the tension I'd been carrying in my shoulders and neck melted away.

My mom beamed at me as she held her arms out wide. "There's my boy," she greeted, wrapping her arms around me and yanking me down into a bone-squeezing hug the moment I got close enough. "Oh, honey. It's so good to see you."

"You too, Mom," I said as I lifted back to my full height, grinning down at her.

"It's been too long." I chuckled and shook my head.

Leave it to her to lay on the mom guilt within seconds. "Way too long."

A twinge of guilt moved through me. I hadn't exactly been the best son when it came to my mother. I'd been so focused on getting the hell away from my old man, that once I made that my reality, I didn't look back. I'd offered more than once to fly her to Arizona for a visit, but only if she came alone, something she wasn't willing to do. Despite knowing exactly how big an asshole my father was, she never stopped pushing me to, in her words, mend fences. Something I had no intention of ever doing. It was probably the biggest thing we argued about. Even with me moving back, I'd shot down her countless invitations to come over for a visit, refusing to set foot in the same space as that man.

"I know. And I'm sorry. I'm trying to get settled here, but I planned on calling once I got all unpacked. Maybe have you over for dinner or something. But I still have boxes everywhere."

"Yes, well, I suppose it's the thought that counts," she said with an arched brow and a knowing look as she patted my cheek none too softly. "Boxes or not, I'd still like to see my son. You have time to invite your mom in for a cup of coffee?"

I didn't, but I'd make it anyway. "Of course I do," I told her, flinging an arm around her shoulders and leading her up my front porch. "Come on in. Don't mind the mess."

I led her inside and into the kitchen. To keep from going insane, I'd decided to unpack one room at a time, and the kitchen was the one I'd started with, so it was by far the cleanest. She took a seat on one of the high back barstools my assistant had purchased on my behalf. In fact, most of the new furniture in this place was chosen by her. I hadn't had the time to do it myself—or the desire, really. I didn't give a single shit about interior design. My philosophy was, as long as it was comfortable and not butt ugly, what did I care?

"Oh, Beau. This is such a lovely home," she said as she looked around while I went about starting the coffee maker. "But I don't understand why you don't just hire someone to come in and finish unpacking."

"Because I've had my fill of strangers traipsing through my place. What with the movers, the guys from the furniture company, and the people who set up the alarm system. It was too much. This is my space, it's basically the one place I have where I can kick back and relax, and I'm tired of having other people in it," I explained.

She drummed her fingers on the sleek porcelain countertop and let out a thoughtful hum. "Okay, then I'll do it. Problem solved." She held her hands up like she was a genius. "I'm hardly a stranger, after all."

That was true, but the thought of my mom being in my space day in and day out was, well, if I was being honest, a bit of a nightmare. Don't get me wrong, I loved my mother like crazy. There wasn't much I wouldn't do for her. But to say she was pushy would have been an understatement of laughable proportions. And it wasn't only the pushiness that made me hesitate. It was also that she'd have an opinion about *everything*, from what I owned to where I put it, and as far as she was concerned, her way wasn't just the best way, it was the *only* way. That was the very last thing I needed to deal with when shit in my life was still so damn chaotic from basically starting my life over.

"I appreciate the offer, Mom. Really. But I got this. Honestly, I don't mind the boxes so much. I barely see them anymore."

The coffee gurgled and sputtered, the stream thinning out as the pot filled. I pulled two mugs from the cabinet beside the fridge and set them on the counter.

"Sweetie, you really should have those in the cabinet right above the coffee maker, don't you think? It's much more convenient."

I took the moment when my back was to her to roll my eyes. Like I said . . . opinionated.

"Yeah, sure, Mom. You're probably right," I placated as I filled the mugs. "Milk and sugar?"

"Two splashes, please. No sugar."

"You got it." I made quick work of preparing her coffee how she liked it and slid it across the island to her.

"Thank you, darling," she said as she brought it to her lips and sipped it in that dainty way that was all her. For as long as I could remember, she always held her mugs like she was having tea with the Queen of England or something. Back rod-straight, pinkie out.

"So," I started after drinking from my own mug, my coffee straight black, "What brings you by?"

"Does a mother need a reason to visit her son?" She arched a brow, and the effect with that damn pinkie still out made me feel like I was being chastised by a goddamn royal or something.

"Of course not. I was just asking."

She hummed. "I missed you is all. You've been back in town a few weeks, and I haven't seen hide nor hair in all that time. I was beginning to think you were avoiding me."

I gave her a look to let her know she was laying it on a little thick. "You know damn well that's not true. Things have been crazy lately, what with packing up my entire life and moving it halfway across the country and starting this job. I've had a lot on my plate. I need to prove myself not only with the school, but with my team."

She blew out a raspberry and waved her hand like she

thought I was being ridiculous. "Oh *pfft*. They're lucky to have you."

"You think that because you're my mother, and you've always supported me, but that's not what this is about. I can't get by on my name and reputation with these boys. I need to earn their trust. I have to prove myself to them."

She smiled warmly. "And I don't have a single doubt you'll manage to do that. I don't want you to lose track of the other things that are equally as important. Such as making time for yourself. Having a personal life."

I had to admit, there wasn't much of a personal life happening lately, but I fully intended on fixing that. "I know. I'm working on it, I promise."

She stared down at her mug as she quietly tapped the side of the ceramic with her nail. "And family," she added in a hushed tone before finally looking up at me. "Beau, your father—"

I held my hand up to stop her. "I've told you a million times, Mom. I don't want to hear it. Whatever you have to say about that man, save it, because it's falling on deaf ears."

"Son, he's your *father*."

"That man is nothing to me," I barked loud enough to make her jump, nearly sloshing her coffee over the rim of her cup. I hadn't meant to be so cold with her, but my vision was starting to cloud red. "You know how I feel and why I feel that way. Christ." I lifted a hand and raked it through my sweat-slicked hair. "It's not like you didn't see it for yourself. I don't know why the hell you insist on pushing this. Why you constantly defend him."

"Because he's my husband."

The stabbing pain to my chest that comment created was nearly enough to knock the breath from my lungs and rock me back on my feet. It felt like she'd reached out and slapped me.

"And I'm your *son*," I said in a low, craggy voice. "Your fucking *son*, Mom. Jesus. Does that mean anything?"

She looked stricken, heartbroken, but at that very moment, I couldn't find it in me to feel bad for what I'd said. Too many years of taking second place to him, even though that son of a bitch didn't deserve a single second of anyone's loyalty, had jaded me too fucking much.

"Of course it does," she whispered in a pained voice. "You two are my family. I just want my family back. Is that too much to ask?"

"Yes," I answered with finality as I gave my head a disappointed shake. "Look, Mom, I love you, nothing will ever change that, and I'll always be here for you. But what you want, it's never going to happen. And he's the only one you have to blame for that."

I moved to the sink and dumped my barely-touched coffee down the drain before turning back to her. "But if

116

you keep pushing this, you're only going to succeed in pushing me away. So I'm asking you, please, just stop."

She brushed at the single tear that fell down her cheek as I rounded the island, the tension I'd managed to run off earlier now back two-fold.

I bent and brushed a kiss to her temple. "Feel free to finish your coffee, but I need to get ready for work. I'll see you later."

Then I walked out of the kitchen and down the hall to my room. Something told me that hot shower wasn't going to be nearly as enjoyable now.

Eleven

BEAU

THE SUN WAS high in the sky, the cloudless baby blue so brilliant it would have improved anyone's disposition. Well, anyone but me, apparently. After the shit with my mom earlier that morning, the beautiful day actually only succeeded in pissing me the hell off. And as shitty as it was, I'd been taking it out on my team. I couldn't help myself.

"Goddamn it, Johnson, you should've had that!" I barked at my starting wide receiver, a kid barely old enough to drink or grow facial hair, for fuck's sake. "Why the hell should I keep you on my team if you can't catch a simple pass like that, huh? The ball slipped right through your fucking fingers!"

"Sorry, Coach." The kid hung his head in shame as he moved back into position, and I immediately felt like shit for coming down on him so hard. It wasn't *that* good of a pass.

I was just in a shitty mood, and no matter how hard I tried not to take it out on my players, I couldn't stop snapping at them. No one had been spared from my wrath today.

I was being an asshole. Truthfully, I wasn't behaving much better than my father had back when I'd been in school. He never failed to berate me after a game, pointing out all the shit I did wrong and how I should have known to do better.

With that realization, I blew the whistle around my neck. "That's it for today," I called out. "Hit the weights then the showers. See you back here tomorrow."

They started jogging for the field house, not a single one of them meeting my gaze as they passed, doing their best to avoid me and my shitty-ass mood.

I gathered my stuff and looped the strap of my gym bag over my shoulder just as my assistant coach came over. "Hey. You good?"

Like the rest of the athletic staff at OU, Bradley Brentwood was solid. He had a good reputation and the patience of a goddamn saint, which made him a godsend for a college team. I hadn't gotten the chance to know him very well yet, but what I did know about the guy, I liked.

"Yeah. Yeah, I'm good."

He crossed his arms over his chest, his gold wedding band glinting in the sunlight. "You sure about that?"

I shook my head at myself. "Sorry, man. I've been in a piss-poor mood today and I've taken it out on everyone here."

He blew me off with a laugh. "You kidding? Come on, man. This is football. If someone's not yelling, we're doing something wrong."

I appreciated him trying to make me feel better, and while I knew yelling wasn't unusual, I still felt like a prick. It was different when it was deserved, but the boys hadn't deserved all the shit I'd thrown at them today, and I didn't want to be one of those coaches who thought the best results came by being a dick. I'd never responded well to coaches like that, and I didn't expect the guys on my team to either. I'd meant it when I said I needed to earn their trust, and that kind of coaching style didn't necessarily breed trust.

"Thanks. I appreciate it."

He hiked his thumb over his shoulder. "You heading to the weight room with the guys?"

I usually did, but I figured I'd spare them from my mood for the rest of the day. "I think I'll give them a break from me and head home for the day." A hard, grueling workout would have probably helped ease the tension coiled into a sack of knotted rope in my neck and shoulders, but I could use the equipment setup at my house to do that. If I felt like it. "I'm not very good company today anyway."

He clapped me on my shoulder and started walking backward, calling out, "All right. Tomorrow's a new day."

"That it is. See you tomorrow."

He threw me a two-finger salute. "See you tomorrow, Coach."

I headed out, making the drive back to Whitecap from the college. I could have gone straight home and used the extra free time to unpack more boxes, probably should have done that. But instead, I found myself detouring and going through the main drag of downtown to the local coffee house, Drip. Sam's wife, Monica, had opened the place years ago, and since then, it had been the favorite coffee house among Whitecappers. Even the tourists preferred it.

It took five minutes to go less than thirty feet from where I'd parked my SUV right in front of the small strip of businesses, to the entrance of Drip. Everyone who had been walking by wanted to stop and *catch up*, which basically meant they wanted to gossip.

The frustration I'd been dealing with all damn day had settled behind my eyeballs, stabbing at the backs of them, but I managed to keep my composure as I politely ended the conversations and finally made my way inside the coffee shop. Unfortunately, it didn't get any better from there.

"Well, if it isn't Beau Wade."

The sound of that voice was like nails on a chalkboard, causing my molars to clamp together and an unpleasant shiver to skitter down my spine.

I turned, pasting on a small, polite smile I certainly didn't feel like giving. "Hi, Larissa."

My old high school girlfriend stood from a small bistro table tucked beneath one of the large plate glass windows and moved toward me. There was an exaggerated sway to her hips that was completely unnecessary as she walked across the small space that separated us.

She hadn't changed all that much from when I'd last seen her. She still wore her makeup thick and her clothes tight. She still had that man-eater look in her eye as well, the one she always thought was sultry and seductive but came off as more of a warning to the guy she'd set her sights on. I knew that firsthand. She was more likely to chew you up and spit you out than seduce you.

She stopped in front of me and smiled a smile that would probably have worked on a man who didn't already know her, but I'd been there and done that, and I had absolutely no desire to go for a repeat. "Heard you were back in town." She brought a hand up and slowly dragged her long bubblegum pink nail down the center of my chest. "Was wondering when I'd see you."

I looked down at her hand, noticing the tan line from what could have only been a wedding ring wrapped around her ring finger. I didn't know if it was an old tan line or if she'd just removed the ring when she spotted me, but I honestly didn't care to find out. "Should have come to the reunion. It was a good time. We could have caught up then."

She rolled her eyes and scoffed. "Yeah, I don't think so," she said like she was above everything and everyone. "I had much better things to do with my time."

"Yeah? Like what?" I asked, calling her out, knowing she was most likely full of it. She'd done the same shit back in high school too, acting like she was so much better than everyone around her, even her friends. It was sad to see she hadn't grown out of it fifteen years later.

I didn't miss the way she blanched. "Anyway," she started, shifting the topic without answering my question. "Now that you're back, we should catch up." She pulled her bottom lip between her teeth and bit down as she stepped even closer, invading my personal space and practically dragging her tits across my chest. "We used to have a lot of fun together. Bet we still could."

A bubble of laughter burst past my lips. "Is that how you remember it, Riss? As fun?"

She blinked in confusion, falling back on her heels and putting the tiniest amount of space between us. "Huh?"

I couldn't recall our relationship being *fun* at all. That relationship—if you could even call it that—was straight up toxic. All we did was fight and break up. The only reason we kept getting back together was because we were young and stupid and driven by hormones. But, again, that wasn't something I felt like getting into just then.

"You know what? Never mind. It was good seeing you, Riss." I patted her on the shoulder and took a step back. "Enjoy the rest of your day." With that, I turned away from a bewildered Larissa and moved toward the counter.

My steps stuttered when I saw that it wasn't Monica working the shop today. It was Presley's best friend, Colbie, standing behind the counter, an apron in Drip colors with the Drip logo tied around her front. She was currently standing there with a deer-in-the-headlights expression on her face as she stared at me.

I couldn't help but smile, wondering if maybe my shitty day was finally taking a turn. I hadn't been able to track down the one woman I wanted to see most, so her best friend was definitely a close second. "Hey, Colbie. Good to see you."

She blinked owlishly wide eyes. "Uh . . . it is?"

"Of course." I gave her my most charming smile, hoping it would warm her toward me. It was the same smile I'd used in countless magazine article spreads—when they weren't wanting me to, in their words, *smolder*. Whatever the fuck that was. It was the smile I used during interviews and red-carpet events I'd been forced to, and hopefully it would disarm her enough to get her talking about her BFF.

I knew that wasn't going to be the case when she went from wide-eyed to suspicious in a single beat. Her eyelids narrowed into slits and her head canted to the side as she studied me. "What's happening right now? What are you up to?"

Well, that certainly hadn't been the reaction I'd expected, and I had to admit, it threw me off my game a little. "What are you talking about? Can't a guy be nice?"

I'd misjudged this woman, that was for damn sure. I thought she'd be easy to sway to my side so she could talk me up to her friend, but she had a hell of a lot more steel in her spine than I'd given her credit for. That was my mistake.

She slapped her hands down on her hips and hit me with a look that screamed *don't bullshit a bullshitter*.

"Forgive me, but I don't think you're all that nice."

Well ouch.

My head jerked back, my chin tucking into my neck. "You don't think I'm nice?"

"I don't," she said firmly. "Have you forgotten? I'm

friends with Presley Fields. Have been for years. And I know exactly the kind of jerk you can be because I saw how you treated her. You made high school hell for her."

I didn't miss the fact that she hadn't said anything about college, so I could only assume Presley never told her about what went down between us. I wasn't sure if her keeping a secret like that from her best friend was good or bad. I was under the impression that women told each other everything. Was she so ashamed she'd never told anyone what happened?

I pushed that thought to the back of my mind to deal with at another time and held my hands up in surrender. "I can't argue with that. But it's been fifteen years. I'd like to think I've changed since then. That I'm not the same little asshole I was when I was in high school."

I caught the flicker of understanding in her gaze before she covered it up. Her only response was to hum noncommittally.

"Look, how about we start over, yeah?" I extended my hand across the counter for a shake that she didn't take me up on.

She crossed her arms over her chest. "If you're serious about starting over, you should start with Presley, not me. You owe her about a million massive apologies from my count."

I arched a brow, one corner of my mouth pulling up

127

with it. "I don't suppose you'd be willing to tell me where I could find her?"

She grinned then, a wicked little grin that let me know there wasn't a chance in hell of that happening. "Ha! Fat chance."

"Okay, fine. But can I at least get a coffee to go?"

On that, she relented, thank Christ, because after dumping the cup earlier that morning after my mom's visit, I hadn't had a chance to make myself another, and the headache the lack of caffeine caused was worsening by the hour.

She moved behind the counter, banging away on the complicated-looking machine. Whatever she was doing looked complicated as hell, but she radiated confidence. Clearly, she knew what she was doing back there. Finally, a few minutes later, she handed me a tall paper cup with a lid on it.

I looked at her with the same level of suspicion she'd given me earlier. "You didn't poison this, did you?"

Her eyes rolled to the ceiling. "Please. If there's one thing you should know about me, it's that I'd never compromise the integrity of my coffee."

I started to laugh but when her expression didn't change, I realized she hadn't been kidding and quickly swallowed it down. I lifted the cup to my face, leaning in to sniff the

128

concoction she'd just made me through the tiny hole used for drinking. I was hit with the scent of cinnamon and something else that had that same sweet spiciness. "What is it?" I asked, my top lip curling up ever so slightly. "I usually take it black."

She gave me a put-out look. "It's perfection in a cup, that's what it is. And you can drink your boring black coffee when you're at home."

Well consider me properly scolded.

She arched her brow, arms crossed over her chest once again as she watched me, like she was waiting for me to take a sip so she could see my reaction live and in person. So much for chunking it in the trash the moment I walked out the door.

Here goes nothing, I thought to myself as I brought the cup to my lips and took a sip. I was fully prepared to fake that I liked it. Luckily, I didn't have to. My eyes widened with surprise. The coffee actually tasted like, well, *coffee*. She hadn't masked the flavors with a bunch of sugar, but instead, somehow enhanced it with the steamed milk and whatever she'd added.

"Wow. Colbie, this is good. Really good." I stopped to take another sip. "Excellent, actually."

"Of course it is," she replied, not bothering to act humble when she knew damn good and well she'd created something perfect. "I'm an artist, Beau. You may be a hotshot football player, but this is my house, and here, I'm the MVP."

My head fell back on a laugh. This chick was something else. I could see why she and Presley's friendship had remained so solid all these years. She was a trip.

I quickly paid, shoving the extra bills in the jar by the register for a generous tip, knowing damn good and well I'd be a frequent customer now that I'd tasted what this woman could do, and wanting to stay on her good side for it.

"You have a good one, Colbie. And thanks again for the coffee."

"You're welcome. Now go make things right, because the last thing this town can handle is the nuclear blast that is you and Presley if you don't squash this beef between you."

Oh, I fully intended on it.

I just had to figure out how.

Twelve

PRESLEY

IT WAS BARELY eight in the evening, and I was already dead on my feet.

I'd come into work early this morning to meet the beverage distributor and get some paperwork done. It was supposed to be an easy day, but then two of my servers called out sick during the lunch rush. The same happened later when one of the bartenders who was supposed to close called off as well. Apparently there was a nasty stomach flu going around the local daycare and the kids of Whitecap were taking their parents down.

I'd hoped that would mean a light evening, maybe even one where we could close earlier, but no such luck. The customers had come out in force, meaning the rest of the staff and I had been running our asses off all evening.

I carried a tray of empties to the large oval-shaped

bar that separated Dropped Anchor into two sections and glanced at my watch. There were still three hours until close, and it was going to take a hell of a lot more coffee to get me through this shift. Fortunately, tomorrow was my day off, and I planned on sleeping in. The thought of climbing into my bed and curling up, surrounded in my nest of pillows, made me whimper. I was that tired.

"Donovan," I called as I rounded the bar, tossing the empty beer bottles in the trash and getting to work on washing the glasses so we didn't run out, "Go ahead and take your fifteen."

He looked out at the crowd that didn't seem to be getting any thinner as the hours ticked down. "You sure, boss?"

That was one of the reasons I loved this place so much. The staff was more like a second family than just co-workers. Once I'd graduated from college and Diane had promoted me to manager, she'd taken a big step back, letting me run the bar how I saw fit. I'd been in charge of the hiring, the firing, and everything in between. I'd hired every one of the people here, and I was proud as hell to say they helped me run this place like a well-oiled machine. Even on crazy nights like this.

"Positive." I moved behind him, patting him on the shoulder and gently guiding him toward the opening at the back of the bar. "Take your break. You've more than earned it. I'll cover while you're gone."

"Thanks. I'll be right back."

I grabbed a bar rag, quickly wiping up a spill before turning my attention to the customers waiting for a drink. I wouldn't consider myself a pro when it came to bartending, but I'd gotten pretty decent at multitasking. I was able to pull a draft and handle a cocktail shaker at the same time, and with the other two bartenders working alongside me, we made quick work of the building crowd.

I smiled as I poured drinks, made change, swiped credit cards, and took keys away from those who'd tied on one too many, slowly working my way down the bar toward the end. I'd hit a rhythm that helped me forget how tired I was.

"Hey, Freddy," I greeted, smiling fondly at the old man who occupied this very stool night after night, no matter how packed or empty the place was. We had our share of regulars, but Freddy was more like an unofficial part of the Dropped Anchor family. He'd never gotten married or had kids, so instead of spending his evenings at home alone, he spent them here, with us. Some nights he'd tie one on, but most of the time he was content to simply hang out, eat a burger, and drink Cokes with cherries tossed into the glass.

Despite the fact the man was knocking on the door of eighty, he'd also designated himself as a kind of bar security, hanging around until closing most nights and walking the ladies on staff to their cars to make sure we got there safely. When the holidays rolled around and we closed the bar to the public for our staff Christmas party, Freddy was the only person not on our payroll who got an invite.

"You good, hon?" I pointed at his nearly empty glass. "Need a refill?"

"Much appreciated, sweetheart," he said in his signature raspy smoker's voice.

I grabbed the soda gun from behind the counter and pointed it at his glass, filling it with Coke before tossing in a few of the cherries he loved so much. "Anything else? You order dinner yet?"

He lifted the glass to his lips and sucked the fizzy liquid through his straw. "Nah. Figured I'd wait 'til things slowed down. Didn't want to get in your hair on such a busy night."

That was Freddy, kindhearted to his very core.

"Don't you even worry about that. You're part of the crew here. I'll take care of you."

"You're an angel, darlin'. This town's lucky to have you."

I hopped up, leaning across the bar to place a quick kiss to his grizzled, ruddy cheek before shooting him a wink and heading to the back to put his dinner order in with the kitchen.

Despite being so tired I was in a pretty good mood. Working both shifts in the front of house meant the tips were going to be pretty damn good. That money would make an even bigger dent in what I was trying to save so I could get that loan to buy the bar. Reminding myself of the end goal was enough to keep me going, no matter how exhausted I was.

I headed back for the bar, hoping to get back into that flow, but jerked to a stop when I spotted the person who'd just pulled up a stool two spaces down from Freddy.

"Evening, Bubbles."

Well shit.

After nearly three weeks of not seeing hide nor hair of Beau Wade, I'd actually started to think my luck was going to hold out and our paths wouldn't cross. I should have known better. I mean, sure, there were other bars in and around town, but Dropped Anchor was a favorite for most people. It was only a matter of time before he'd come walking through my door.

Damn it. Why does he have to look so good? a tiny voice in the back of my head lamented.

It really wasn't fair.

He was dressed like anyone else, in a plain tee and faded jeans, but the way his gray T-shirt molded to the muscles beneath was downright criminal. I was sure if he stood up, I'd get a front row seat to the ass of the century and strong, thick thighs. But at that moment, all I had to gawk at was the arm porn on full display. Wide, veined forearms that could make a woman orgasm all on their own rested on the bar top between us. The way his elbows bent made his impressive biceps strain, testing the limits of his sleeves.

If I thought he'd looked good in that suit at the reunion, it was debatable if he was better dressed down and casual, which only worked to irritate the hell out of me.

My eyes traveled back up to his, and I knew by the pleased smile that stretched across his face and showcased perfect white teeth that he'd caught me leering. *Son of a bitch.*

"Good to see you. I was starting to think we'd never run into each other."

"If only," I deadpanned. I would have loved nothing more than to kick him the hell out of my bar, but he *technically* hadn't done anything to warrant it, and the last thing I wanted to do was cause a scene. Scenes led to curiosity, curiosity led to gossip, and gossip eventually led to questions I had no desire to answer. So I kept the lid on my frustration, telling myself he was just another customer. I'd serve him and move along. It would be easy.

I hoped.

I placed my hands on the bar and cocked my hip to

take some of the weight off my feet. They were really starting to hurt from standing for too many hours. "What can I get you?"

He blinked, and if I didn't know better, I might have thought he was actually bothered by my lack of small talk.

"Deschutes, IPA if you have it on tap."

I nodded and moved back down the bar, grabbing a pint glass and filling it with a local beer. "You paying now or starting a tab?" I asked once I placed the glass in front of him. *Please pay now. Please pay now*, I chanted silently. Because starting a tab meant he intended on staying, and my night had been going so well.

He lifted the pint glass and took a sip of the rich golden liquid, studying me over the rim the entire time. It was almost enough to make me fidget, but I held myself steady. This was my turf. I wasn't going to let him make me uncomfortable on my turf.

"If I start a tab does that mean I'll get a little conversation?"

Not if I could help it.

With one arm braced on the bar, I waved the other wide, encompassing the entire bar. "I don't know if you've noticed, but it's a little busy in here. Not to mention, we're short staffed. I don't exactly have time to chit-chat. Sorry."

Why the hell did he want to talk to me anyway? It wasn't like we were friends. We'd tried that once. Or was it twice? That last time was . . . confusing. I didn't know what to think of it so I tried not to think about it at all.

"I've watched you take time to talk with almost every person you've served," he pointed out. And, *shit*. I hadn't realized he'd been here long enough to see that. "So tell me, Bubbles, why not me?"

From the corner of my eye I saw Freddy's head turning back and forth like he was front and center at Wimbledon. "You two know each other?"

"No," I answered at the same time Beau replied, "We're old friends."

What the hell?

We were drawing attention, or more to the fact, Beau was drawing attention simply by existing. He was White-cap's very own celebrity. The hero football player. It was only a matter of time before he started to draw a crowd his way.

I leaned forward, lowering my voice so only he could hear me over Fleetwood Mac playing from the jukebox and the din of a million different conversations filtering through the air. "We aren't friends, Beau. We've never been friends, and we will never *be* friends. I don't know why you came in here, but if it was to screw with me, I'm going to have to ask you to leave my bar. I don't have the time to deal with your particular brand of shit tonight."

His brows went up infinitesimally, his eyes widening with curiosity. "Your bar? You own this place?"

"Not yet. But she's workin' on it," Freddy answered proudly, shooting a wink in my direction. "Our girl's a fighter." Poor guy didn't realize he'd given too much away to the enemy, but I loved him too much to get onto him about it.

"Let me go check on your food, Freddy. Be right back."

I scurried away from the bar without looking in Beau's direction. I stopped in the back hallway on my way to the kitchen, taking a moment to breathe, to shake off the effects of Beau Wade. Leaning against the wall, I closed my eyes and dropped my head back, focusing on my breathing. That was how Donovan caught me as he was returning from his break.

"Hey, boss. Everything okay?"

I pushed off the wall, standing tall and giving him a grin. "Yep. All good. Just taking a little breather. I have to grab Freddy's food, then I'll be right back out."

"You got it."

With Donovan back from his break, I was safe to escape that strange, almost intrusive pull to Beau. I made quick work of dropping Freddy's dinner off before heading onto the floor to help the waitstaff.

Beau had been right, though. It was impossible for me

to do my job without being personable. It was the kind of person I was. Not to mention, I knew most of the people here. And out of that group, actually liked at least three-quarters of them.

I was a nice person, damn it. There was nothing wrong with that, but it didn't mean I had to be nice to someone who hadn't earned it. I wasn't overly nice when Larissa or Anna came in. I just filled their orders and let them be. The same could work with Beau. It *would* work.

Only, as I moved around the busy bar, taking orders and clearing empties, I could feel that same tingle on the back of my neck that I used to feel back in high school, that persistent itch that traveled down my spine and centered between my shoulder blades, and every time I looked, Beau was watching me.

I passed a table of women—I'd clocked them as tourists the moment they walked in dressed more for a club than a small-town watering hole—and couldn't help but overhear their conversation. Of course, they were going on and on about Beau. Everything from how gorgeous he was to whether or not he was polite in person to what he was doing in a small town like Whitecap. One of them swirled the cocktail straw in her glass as she stared at his back like she was a jungle cat about to swoop in on her prey.

"I think I'm gonna go talk to him," she announced to her friends.

A strange sensation built in my chest at hearing that; it almost felt like heartburn.

"No, don't," one of the other women said as the table fell into a fit of giggles. "What if he doesn't want to be bothered?"

Yeah, I thought, *what if he just wants to relax without people all in his business.*

The truth was, I couldn't imagine what it was like to be him. It might have seemed glamorous to be rich and famous when I was younger, but now I couldn't imagine being able to stand the lack of privacy. I'd seen enough news coverage about Beau over the years to know it wasn't only the game that had people interested. Sure, he'd been the best quarterback in the league, but with looks like his, he'd drawn even more attention, and it seemed like the league had done everything they could to monetize that.

There had been cameras in his face all the time, every woman he was seen with was scrutinized and nitpicked. Every move he made—good or bad—was reported on, and if it was bad, he was raked over the coals. And God forbid he had an off game. People were downright brutal, everyone in this day and age thinking their opinions deserved to be thrust on complete strangers because they felt like being an asshole. It wasn't right, and I actually felt bad for the guy.

But it was more than that. Deeper. That burn in my chest was getting worse, and as ridiculous as it was, I disliked the woman for no apparent reason whatsoever.

The brunette, the one who'd decided to approach Beau and interrupt his evening, spoke again, this time adjusting her chest and pulling the front of her dress down lower to show more cleavage. "If he wanted to be alone, he wouldn't be sitting in the middle of a bar, would he?" she reasoned selfishly. "Twenty bucks says I can get him to come back to my hotel room with me tonight."

The other women at the table tittered with laughter as their friend rose to her feet, and something happened in that moment.

I wasn't sure what came over me. I just . . . reacted without a single thought. Holding up a partially full glass of red wine I'd cleared from an empty table, I spun around and walked right into the brunette, pretending to stumble as I dumped the contents of the glass down the front of her dress.

"Oh god. I'm so sorry."

"What the hell?" she shrieked, holding her arms out to her sides as she looked down at her ruined dress in shock.

"I think I slipped on a spilled drink or something. I'm so, so sorry. You know what? Your table's bill is on me."

Fortunately, they hadn't been there long, and I could cover the cost of three cosmos. "We have club soda in the back if you'd like to try and get that out before it sets."

The woman looked at me with open disdain as she snatched her beaded clutch off the table. "Forget it," she hissed as she waved her friends to their feet. "We're outta here. This place sucks anyway."

That didn't hurt my feelings a bit, and as the three of them stormed out, it took everything I had to keep from smiling.

And as I got back to work, I refused to question why I'd felt the need to take such drastic action in the first damn place.

Best to stuff it in that little box in the back of my head and seal it up tight, right along with what had happened that night back in college.

Thirteen

BEAU

THE SUN HAD BARELY RISEN past the horizon like a glowing orange ball rising from the water as I did my morning run along the beach. I tried not to take the same path more than three days in a row to keep things fresh, and the stretch of beach this morning was quiet. There was nothing and no one but me, the gulls, and the crashing waves. Usually I encountered other runners, people taking their dogs out for a walk, or early risers starting their day, but this morning, I basked in the solitude, letting my mind wander to the one person who seemed to consume my every thought.

I hadn't been able to stop thinking about what that guy at the bar the other night had said about Presley working to make Dropped Anchor hers and what exactly he'd been talking about. Why she needed to be a fighter.

I remembered her working there in college. She'd been a waitress back then, but it was obvious from watching her the other night that she played a much more pivotal role these days. Not only had I heard several of the staff refer to her as *boss*, but whenever someone needed an answer or had a problem, she was the one they deferred to. Clearly, she had a large hand in running the place, and from what I'd witnessed, she was doing a damn good job at it.

Watching her in her element like that, seeing how she was so open and warm and friendly with everyone, I would have been lying if I said it wasn't a massive turn-on. I'd never get tired of seeing that smile. But at the same time, seeing her give that smile to everyone but me was starting to weigh on me. Back in high school I'd been able to brush it off, but now that we were both adults, I couldn't let it go near as easily. I wanted that smile for myself. I wanted her to look at me and watch her expressive eyes light up and glow gold with happiness. I loved the spice too, don't get me wrong, but I wanted her to look at me like she looked at the people she cared about. Or hell, even the way she'd smiled at that Mike Perry asshole the night of the reunion.

She'd looked at me like that once, so I knew how addictive one of Presley Fields's smiles were. I knew that having it pointed at you hit you right in the goddamn chest like a sunbeam, warming you from the inside. Even from the deepest, darkest places you thought would never see the light.

That was all her. She was light. Pure and golden. For a split second in time, I'd had that in the palm of my hands. Then I'd gone and fucked it all up, and there hadn't been a day in all the years since that I didn't hate myself for it.

My lungs burned and beads of sweat slipped down the back of my neck and down my spine as I dug my feet into the sand and pumped my arms harder while cresting a sand dune. As soon as I made it to the other side I caught sight of someone in the distance. I couldn't make out who it was or what they were doing until I got closer and caught slow, rhythmic movements as the person adjusted their body from one yoga pose to another with such ease, they looked like they were flowing as smooth as the water sliding across the sand along the shoreline.

The closer I got, the better I could make out the person's features. Then, as if the low clouds in the sky parted just for me, a beam of sunlight cut through the early morning fog, clinging to the air and landing right on her like a spotlight, lighting up the cornsilk hair hanging down her back from the ponytail at the top of her head.

I would have known that particular shade of blonde anywhere, and at the sight of it, my body started moving faster of its own accord. I didn't have to tell it how to react when it came to that woman. It just knew. If she was near,

I wanted to be as close as possible. It was as though a tether had formed between us the first moment I'd spotted her at twelve years old, and despite the time and distance, it never snapped. It was still there between us, pulling me to her.

More of her came into better view, and I saw firsthand as Presley flowed from pose to pose, her long, lithe body moving with ease and precision. She was dressed in the shortest pair of fucking shorts I'd ever seen, the spandex material looking painted on and cupping her perfect peach of an ass, with a tight camisole that clung to her body, accentuating the dip in her waist and molding to her breasts. With more than thirty yards between us, she still managed to make me hard without even trying, not the most convenient thing to have to deal with while wearing athletic shorts.

As I closed in, slowing from a run to a jog, she folded herself onto the mat she had stretched out on the sand and sat facing the ocean, her long, toned legs crisscrossed in front of her, her palms resting on her knees. I slowed to a walk, not wanting to startle her, and noticed her eyes were closed. She wore the most serene expression, her face tilted slightly upward toward the rising sun. Even now, the tiniest smile graced her perfect rosy lips.

God, she was beautiful.

The last thing I wanted to do was ruin this moment, but I couldn't stand there watching her without her knowledge either. That was the kind of shit restraining orders were made of.

"Morning," I greeted, and the instant those brown eyes flipped open and landed on me, it felt like getting slammed in the chest by the biggest, baddest offensive tackle in the league.

Her full lips parted on a surprised breath, puckering into a pretty little *O* as she looked up at me. "Beau? What are you doing here?"

I wiped at the sweat that had built up on my forehead with the back of my hand before throwing a thumb over my shoulder. "Just out for my morning run."

I'd never been happier to have stripped my shirt off during the run than I was just then. It was obvious she was trying her hardest to keep her focus on my face, but I didn't miss the way her gaze kept darting down to my torso every few seconds, like she couldn't help herself.

"Oh, uh . . ." Her tongue came out, swiping across her bottom lip. "I've never seen you out here."

"I try to switch things up now and then, keep it from getting boring. What about you?" I pointed down at the mat. "Do you do yoga here every morning?" Because that would sure as hell play a role in me deciding where I'd run every morning from here on out.

"Not every morning. I like to sleep in on the nights I work until close at the bar. But other than that, yeah." She looked out at the water, her chest heaving on a deep breath, like staring out at the ocean brought her peace. "This is the kind of view you never get used to, you know? Takes my breath away each and every time."

"I know what you mean," I said as my gaze remained locked on her, my voice coming out low and deep. Her eyes darted back to me, blinking as her cheeks flushed that prettiest pink in the early morning light. She knew I wasn't talking about the ocean. Hell, we both did.

I pointed at a spot on the sand beside her. "Mind if I sit?" I asked before she could make an excuse to take off. It was just the two of us on this stretch of beach, and I wanted to keep her here with me as long as possible. Fuck the rest of my run.

She looked at the ground like she wanted to say no, make up some reason to send me away. She pulled her bottom lip between her teeth and bit down before finally answering, "Sure, I guess. I mean, it's a public beach."

It wasn't exactly the welcome I'd been hoping for, but it wasn't like I couldn't blame her for keeping her guard up. When we were younger, I'd given her no other choice but to build those sky-high, steel-reinforced walls.

It took everything in me not to plop down on the sand beside her and, instead, lower myself at a reasonable pace, but the longer I was in Whitecap and the more time I spent in her presence, the harder it was to keep from turning into a lovesick puppy that wanted to follow her around all day every day.

My conversation with Colbie earlier that week popped into my head, and I knew I needed to apologize. I didn't have the first fucking clue where to start. So I decided to kick things off with small talk, hoping the chance to tell her how sorry I was for treating her so shitty in the past would pop up organically.

"You know, I almost forgot what it was like, being so close to the water like this. It's funny how your mind tends to forget things the longer you're away from them." I was discovering that was true with most things—well, except for Presley, of course. I'd forgotten how it was, living in a small town, how it felt to be next to the ocean instead of the desert. But I never forgot how Presley made me feel. Not ever.

She surprised me by actually engaging in the conversation. "What was Arizona like?"

"Hot," I answered on a chuckle. "The days could be stifling, then the nights would nearly freeze you out. It definitely took some getting used to."

"I bet," she said, that tiny smile still on her lips as she continued to stare out at the horizon. I would have liked to have her eyes on me, but at this point, I'd take what I could get. "And you never came back? Not even once, just to visit?"

I shook my head, bending my knees toward the sky and draping my forearms over them. "Nope. Not until I moved back."

"Why did you? Move back, that is." Apparently, I was the only one struggling to find the courage to bring up the harder topics. Presley dove right in. "If you wanted out of this place so badly that you didn't come back once in ten years, why come back now?"

"My job—"

She gave me a look that let me know she thought I was full of it. "I get that OU is right around the corner, but you could have lived closer to the university." Leave it to the girl who never hesitated to challenge to call me on my bullshit.

There wasn't going to be a more perfect opportunity if I'd created it myself. Breathing deeply, pulling that fresh, salty air into my lungs, I answered her as honestly as possible.

"You don't live closer to the university." Her chest stuttered on a broken gasp as her head whipped around in my direction. "Truth is, I thought about living somewhere else, somewhere . . . not here. But I knew I couldn't set myself up one town over when I knew you'd be here."

Something flickered in her eyes, something almost sad, before she blinked it away and looked across the water. Her throat worked on a swallow. "Don't," she said hoarsely, like she had to drag that one word out.

"Presley—"

"Just stop, Beau," she said, almost pleading. "I don't know what game this is, but I don't want to play."

Christ, I was such an asshole. I took a deep breath, willing my heart to stop knocking so fucking hard against my ribs. We sat in silence, the air around us tense and full of static electricity, before it finally became too much for me. "You didn't tell Colbie about us."

Her eyes rounded, growing cartoonishly wide. "What?" she asked in bewilderment. "Of course I didn't. There's nothing to tell. It didn't mean anything." She pulled in a sharp breath. "Wait. You didn't say anything, did you?"

I shook my head, trying my best to ignore the stabbing ache in my chest. "No. I didn't tell her." Her whole body slumped on a sigh of relief that fucking killed me. "But it sure as hell meant something to me."

She shook her head, either in disgust or disappointment. "Well, you sure have a fucked-up way of showing it," she clipped, the brown of her eyes turning to cinnamon as her anger rose. "You know, you've got a lot of nerve showing up all these years later and bringing that night up, like it was something more than it was. Like it was somehow special."

My jaw ticked. "It was," I said on a low growl. "It *was* special."

She barked out an indignant laugh, shaking her head in shame. "I thought it was. At least until we woke up the next morning and you did what you always do." She reached up and tried dragging her hands through her hair in frustration before remembering it was tied up. She quickly yanked the elastic out, her movements jerky and agitated as she threw it back up, this time twisting it into a knot on the top of her head. "You know what? I'm not doing this."

I quickly shot to my feet when she did, my heart sinking into my stomach as she snatched the mat up and shook it out before she started rolling it up.

"Bubbles, I didn't—"

"Don't *call me that*!" she shouted, her words picked up and carried along the waves. "God, do you really get that much of a kick out of watching me suffer?" She threw her arms wide, dropping the mat in the process. "Oh, there's Presley, living her life," she said in a deep, mocking tone. "Wonder what I can do to ruin her day today."

"That's not what I'm trying to do. Presley, I know I fucked up, and I'm sorry."

"It's not you, it's me. I'm the idiot who let myself think there was actually more to you than what you'd shown me time and time again, year after year. I'm the dumbass who let myself be fooled. The poor, pathetic cliched college girl who lost her virginity to the hotshot football player." Her laugh was full of pain, and I felt it flay me open. "Honestly, what did I expect to happen?"

"That night meant something to me," I gritted out, my molars grinding together so hard I was afraid I might crack them all.

"You have a funny way of showing it," she said dryly. "I let you fool me twice, Beau. But you know what? It isn't going to happen again."

I was losing her, she was about to run away from me. The panic gripping my chest threw me into action, and I reacted without thinking. My arm shot out. My fingers wrapped around the back of her neck, and I did the one thing I'd wanted to do every day since walking into that reunion and seeing her for the first time in ten years.

I yanked her against me and slammed my mouth down on hers in a kiss that I'd been craving for more than a decade.

Fourteen

BEAU

PAST

I took my time in the showers, standing under the spray with my head hanging down for so long that by the time I toweled off and walked into the locker room, it had cleared out and I was the only one left.

I'd taken my time, moving as slow as possible on purpose because I didn't want to deal with what I knew was coming. I was in a shitty mood, and it didn't have a damn thing to do with our loss tonight. We were still eight and one with a clear path to the playoffs, but none of that was going to matter. Hell, the fact that we were still the number one ranked team, that no other school had a record as good as ours, wouldn't matter either. Not to him. Even with every game we won, my bastard of a father would still find a reason to bitch and belittle me. Tonight's loss was going to add fuel to that fire.

I dragged the towel through my hair, defeat sitting in my gut like a bowling ball as I finally dressed, nothing else to keep me in here, and the rest of my team had already taken off. I could hear Coach in his office, talking on the phone, but he'd said everything he needed to say to us before we hit the showers.

My shoulders sunk as I shouldered my gym bag and headed out of the locker room to face the firing squad that was Hank Wade.

Sure enough, the son of a bitch was waiting, leaned back against the brick wall right outside the field house exit, one foot propped up, arms crossed over his chest. As expected, my mom was nowhere in sight. She'd stopped coming to my games my sophomore year, making the excuse that she couldn't watch her baby boy get tackled, but I knew the truth. She couldn't stand listening to Dad berate me, however instead of saying something to him or making him stop, she removed herself from the situation.

Out of sight, out of mind, I guess.

"About goddamn time," were the first words he said to me. "You're slow as molasses today, boy. On *and* off the field, apparently."

An ember began to burn in my gut, growing hotter as

my rage built higher. Why couldn't he be supportive? Why couldn't he clap me on the shoulder and tell me I'd given it my best or that we'd get them next time, like my team-mates' fathers did? "Good to see you too, Dad."

He lifted a single brow as he pushed off the wall and started toward me. "You getting smart with me?" That was his favorite question to ask, and no matter what I said, he was always more than happy to take it as a *yes*, and a reason to, in his words, *teach me a lesson*.

My disdain for my old man had only gotten worse recently, which was really saying something, considering I already hated the bastard. A lifetime of being told I wasn't good enough had done that. The occasional smacks and punches when he thought I was being "unruly" had solidi-fied it. But what he said the day he found Presley Fields and me in my room had set it in stone.

The day we'd been working on the project for Spanish was the first day in longer than I could remember that I'd actually been happy. I'd seen it in her eyes, Presley was finally starting to see the real me. For the first time in years, she hadn't looked at me with hate, but like maybe she might actually like me. She'd laughed. She'd smiled, for god's sake. *At me*. I'd finally gotten one of those beautiful smiles for myself. And it had been the best feeling in the world.

I'd leaned in, unable to help myself. She was so pretty

and she smelled so freaking good. Having her sitting on my bed had been a freaking dream come true. My whole room smelled like honeysuckle and oranges—my favorite smell —and it was all because of her. Instead of pulling away, she'd leaned in too. Like she actually wanted me to kiss her. And, *god*, I wanted that too. It took a lot for me to summon the courage to kiss the girl I'd been obsessed with for nearly six years, but I'd finally managed.

Then he'd come home early, ruining everything.

The words he said that day still played in my mind, over and over, and each time I thought back to them, my hands would clench into fists and a fresh wave of rage would crash right over me.

"What the fuck do you think you're doing?"

"It's not a big deal, Dad. We're just working on a project for school."

He scoffed, and I could have sworn he saw right through me to everything I was thinking, everything I was feeling. He saw into my head and understood exactly what the girl sitting on my bed meant to me.

"Bullshit. What's the matter, Beau? You feel like slumming it with that girl in there?" He lifted his hand, tapping my forehead harshly. "Get this through your head, boy. Wades don't associate with white trash. You wanna get your dick wet, you call up that girl you been seeing. What's-her-name."

"*Larissa,*" *I gritted out, my chest rising and falling with each angry breath.*

"*That's the one. Her laugh might sound like nails on a chalkboard but at least her dad's a lawyer, not some pathetic handyman. They might not have as much money as we do, but at least being seen with her won't be a goddamn embarrassment.*"

My top lip curled up in a sneer. "Jesus, Dad. You sound like an asshole," I clipped, unable to stop myself. "You never seemed to have a problem with Mr. Fields when you had to call him to make a repair here."

"*Because that's his job. He knows his place,*" *he seethed, pointing at my bedroom door. "But that girl in there, she sees you as her meal ticket. Mark my words. If you don't watch yourself, she'll end up pregnant just to dig her claws in deeper. I won't let that happen. Not to my boy. You need to focus on football, not chasing tail. You've got the NFL to think about.*"

My hands curled into fists, and I felt the muscle in my jaw tick. "Presley's not like that," I growled, and for the first time in my life, I wanted to fight back. I wanted to defend her. I wanted to make him see how wrong he was, because maybe then I'd be able to keep her.

He laughed, a sound that grated along my spine. "Christ, I didn't raise you to be this fucking stupid. Of course she is! And I'm not gonna let you throw your future away.

Whatever the hell this is, it ends now. I better never see her in this house again."

My nostrils flared, and I felt like I was seconds away from breathing fire. "You can't tell me who I can date. I'm eighteen, Dad. I'll be out of here in a matter of months. If I want to date Presley, there's nothing you can do about it."

He smiled then, a slimy, evil smile that slithered beneath my skin and sank deep into my bones, freezing me from the inside and pushing out every bit of warmth my Bubbles had made me feel earlier.

"You think so, huh? Then how about this, hotshot? You either end it with that gutter trash in there, or I'll ruin her old man." I wasn't able to hide my reaction to that fast enough, and he chuckled in victory. "That's right. You either put a stop to this, or I'll make sure no one in this town hires Alan Fields ever again. How do you think that relationship'll work out when they have to pack up and move somewhere else because I saw to it he was blackballed?"

He'd do it too. Not because he was worried about me. But because he saw that Presley made me happy and he got a kick out of ripping that away from me.

My shoulders slumped in defeat. "Yeah, that's what I thought." He turned on his heel and started down the hall. "I want her out of here in five minutes, Beau. And I better never see her again."

I could still remember the sick, sour feeling that

creeped up in my gut at the sadness and betrayal I saw on her face the next day when I brushed her off like she meant nothing. I tried telling myself it was all right, that we still had the project. That I'd still get a chance to see her. But when I got to Spanish later that day, Ms. Garza informed me I had a new partner. I'd hurt Presley so bad, she'd gone to our teacher to get out of working with me. That freaking gutted me.

God, I hated him for making me do that to her. And I hated myself for hurting her.

But I couldn't think about that right now. After that day, I'd made damn sure to always keep my guard up. I reasoned that as long as he didn't know what my weaknesses were, he couldn't use them against me.

"It was a tough game, Dad. We did our best." I knew better than to defend myself by now. I just couldn't help it.

"Did your best my ass," he seethed. "You were throwing like a punk out there, and that sack in the third quarter should've never happened. You were slow, lazy. And that's why you lost."

My chest rose and fell as my breaths sawed in and out of my chest. Heat infused my cheeks, making them burn red. I stood in silence, doing my best to tune his voice out as he continued to criticize me, my fists clenched so tight I could feel my blunt nails cutting into the heels of my palms. I'd gotten pretty good at it over the years, and his voice faded out in my head, like he was shouting from the end on a long, dark, tunnel. It made it easier to stand there and take it so he'd burn himself out faster.

Only, just then I heard the sound of laughter over my father's voice, and for a moment, I forgot what I was supposed to be doing and accidentally let my mask slip. Because the one person I couldn't help myself around just happened to be coming around the corner at that very second.

My heart thudded against my sternum as the sight of her walking with a small group of friends. She was dressed in jeans and a baggy sweater, her long blonde hair pulled back into a ponytail. There wasn't a speck of makeup on her face, but she was still the prettiest girl I'd ever laid eyes on. And she was here. I didn't know she came to the games, but if I'd known she was in the stands tonight, maybe the outcome would have been different.

I couldn't take my eyes off her as she continued down the sidewalk, her eyes squinting as she laughed at something one of her friends said. That musical laugh, like wind chimes in the ocean breeze, made my chest feel hot and tight.

As if she could feel my gaze on her, she turned her head in my direction. Her lips parted in surprise, her smile falling away as her eyes widened, and as quickly as she'd looked at me, she ripped her gaze away, but not before I caught the way the apples of her cheeks turned the same rosy pink as her lips.

I watched her the whole way, completely lost in her, until she and her friends finally rounded the corner out of sight, making my heart sink.

It was the brutal smack upside my head that brought me back to the present and reminded me who I was standing in front of. Experience taught me I should have expected it, been better prepared, but I wasn't. The hit was hard enough that my head whipped to the side, sending a spark of pain through my neck.

"Get your goddamn head in the game, Beau," Dad stewed, turning to look over his shoulder in the direction Presley had just disappeared, his lip curled in derision. "You know I don't like repeating myself. What the hell did I tell you about that girl?"

"There's nothing going on," I said quickly. "We don't even talk anymore." He'd seen to that, hadn't he? "Anyway, she's nobody." The lie made me sick to my stomach, because the fact was, Presley Fields was *everything*.

"Good." He studied my expression for a lie, but I'd made sure to slam that mask back into place. "See it stays that way." Then, like he hadn't humiliated me out in the open where anyone could see, he turned and walked away from me like nothing had happened. "I'll see you at home. Don't be late. It makes your mother worry."

Fifteen

PRESLEY

As I walked along the dock to the adorable seaside restaurant that served the best brunches in Whitecap, I couldn't help but think I was making a mistake. Just like he'd promised, Mike had called a few days ago after he got back to town and asked me out. I'd said yes, but after my kiss with Beau on the beach two days ago, meeting another guy for a date felt . . . wrong. That was the only reason I could think why I'd called him the day before with a bullshit excuse about having to work so I could switch the date from an intimate dinner to a much more casual lunch.

I didn't know what the hell I was doing anymore. For the longest time, I'd been convinced that Mike was what I'd wanted, he was the perfect guy for me. The safe bet. Sweet, unassuming, pleasant to be around, and calm.

Mostly calm. The antithesis to the raging storm that was Beau Wade.

But then Beau kissed me.

And that *freaking* kiss. It had been screwing with my head since it happened and I didn't know how to make it stop. I couldn't make myself stop thinking about it. Just like in the past, Beau had managed to do something that consumed every single corner of my brain. *The bastard*.

In the past forty-eight hours I'd run the gamut of emotions. Everything from pissed as hell to so horny I could barely see straight. All because of Beau and that *damn, damn, damn* kiss!

It happened so fast I didn't have time to brace or prepare. One second I was yelling at him and the next his strong, hard, massive body pressed against me, his mouth sealed on mine. There was nothing slow or savoring about it. It was urgent and hungry. The way he wrapped his arms around me, one arm banded across my upper back, the other closer to my hips as he leaned over, surrounding me, felt almost possessive. His hold forced my back to arch slightly, pressing my breasts harder against the solid wall of his chest.

It was impossible not to react to the way he was kissing me, not to fall into it and get lost. His hands began to roam like he couldn't decide where he wanted to touch me most, like he was trying to commit every inch of me to memory. Sparks ignited in my blood and raced through my entire body as my heart pumped harder and faster, before centering between my thighs. My breasts suddenly felt heavy, my nipples so tight they could cut glass.

His tongue tangled with mine, thrusting like his hips would if he were to bury his cock deep inside me. And speaking of, I could feel the evidence of his arousal pressing like a steel rod against my belly as my hands molded to his chest. His incredible *chest.*

The man was built like something out of a romance novel. The first thing I thought when I opened my eyes and saw him standing over me was that he couldn't possibly be real. Rounded, defined pecs sat on top of stacks and stacks of ab muscles, the ridges between each one cutting deep. I counted silently, my jaw nearly dropping when I got to eight. If I thought his arms were sexy, they were nothing compared to the sight of him shirtless, all that golden bronzed skin glistening with sweat in the early morning sunlight creeping up.

He groaned into my mouth when my fingers curled, my nails digging into his flesh as I desperately tried to get closer. I couldn't stop the quiet noises of pleasure spilling past my lips and down his throat, and those sounds only seemed to spur him on. I'd never been kissed like this. I felt like I was coming out of my skin, and when he ripped his lips from mine to drag them down the sensitive cord of my neck, I couldn't stop my head from falling back or the needy whimper that dragged up my throat.

This was the kind of kiss you only saw in movies, where the hero plundered the heroine's mouth with an unfiltered need, consuming them both, the kind of kiss that only happened once in a lifetime, if you were lucky. It was as if my entire focus had shrunk to nothing but the two of us, my vision closing in around the edges so all that existed was the two of us.

"God, Bubbles," he groaned against my neck. "Your mouth's so fucking perfect. I've been dying for this longer than you could ever know."

Heat shot down my spine as a flood of arousal soaked my panties. I might have been embarrassed by the sounds I was making if I wasn't so freaking turned on. My fingers dragged up his body to tangle in his hair, holding him even closer, like I was afraid he'd stop.

"Say you want me too," he rasped against my neck, his voice pleading. "Tell me you've been thinking about me these past ten years like I've been thinking about you. Wanting you. Every goddamn day."

"I—"

His head came up to look at me, the vivid blue of his eyes nearly blinding, even with how they'd glazed over with want. His voice came out deep, craggy, when I stopped. "Presley."

My brain chose that moment to click back online, as if a bucket of ice water had just been dumped on me, snuffing out that inferno of want and need. My hands fell away from his body as I took a big step back, giving him no other choice but to release me.

My hand trembled as I brought it up to cover my mouth in shock, my lips swollen and puffy beneath my palm.

"Bubbles," he said in a voice that sounded an awful lot like he was about to beg as he reached for me. But I dodged him, moving back and holding my palms out to ward him off.

"You shouldn't have done that," I croaked, my chest rising and falling like I'd just run a marathon. The anger I'd needed earlier came swooping back in, filling me with indignation. "You had no right," I snapped loudly, my voice like the crack of a whip. "You can't just come back here and invade my life like this. It's not fair!"

I watched in bewilderment as his entire frame sagged with what looked a hell of a lot like sadness, his massive shoulders slumping and curling his spine. I'd never seen him look like that before. He'd always been so big, so imposing in a way that made him come off as unbreakable. That was all gone now, and I didn't like it one damn bit. But I couldn't focus on that.

"Everything's going so good. I'm happy. You have no right coming in and trying to fuck it all up!"

His expression fell like I'd slapped him, and a pang of regret shot through me but I refused to acknowledge it.

"That's not what I'm trying to do," he said so quietly the words were almost scattered away on the wind before they reached me.

Whether it was what he was trying to do or not, it was what always happened when it came to him, and I wasn't going down this road again. Fool me once, shame on you. Fool me twice, shame on me. I wasn't making the same mistake for a third time.

I bent forward and snatched my yoga mat out of the sand. "Do me a favor, Beau. Stay away from me." Then I whipped around and stormed off, unable to look back, because if I saw that sadness in his eyes again, I might cave, and I couldn't let myself.

I was shaken from the memory by a hand wrapping around my arm just above my elbow. I jerked back into the present, blinking up into Mike's kind, smiling eyes.

"Hey. You okay?"

A quick look around showed I was standing outside the restaurant where I was meeting Mike, the Sand Dollar. I'd been so lost in thought I didn't even remember making it here.

I smiled, doing my best to shake off the mood I'd been in for two days. "Yeah. Sorry. I must have spaced out. Long hours at the bar and not enough sleep, I guess."

More like, lack of sleep because every time I closed my eyes, the image of Beau popped into my head. Ever since that kiss, I couldn't stop picturing him moving on top of me. I'd had him only once, but everything about that night had been branded in my brain. I still remembered the look on his face when he came, the combination of bliss and agony. I couldn't help but wonder if he still looked like that.

He'd been impressive even back then, but he was bigger now, and I kept picturing those muscles flexing and bulging as he drove himself into me.

I shook my head, trying to rid myself of those thoughts. Beau Wade was the *last* man I should have been thinking about, especially when I was on a date with someone else.

Mike gave me a sympathetic grin. "You know, we can reschedule if you're too tired—"

"No, I'm good," I said quickly, giving my head a slightly frantic shake. I was determined to see this through. I could only pray that spending time with Mike would push a certain pain-in-the-ass former-football-star out of my head.

His grin widened. I stood there waiting to feel something: butterflies, bubbles, a sharp, insistent tug deep in my belly that felt like it was attached to my clit. All the things Beau made me feel. But I got nothing. Mike was sweet. But at the moment, sweet didn't seem to be working for me. I steeled my resolve, telling myself those feelings could build over time, I just had to give him a shot.

"Good, because I've been looking forward to this for a month." *God, so sweet.* He lifted an arm, guiding me toward the entrance before grabbing the door's handle and pulling it open for me. *And chivalrous too.* "Shall we?"

I nodded on a smile and preceded him into the restaurant. The hostess led us to a table in the center of the packed restaurant, and Mike waited behind my chair so he could push it in for me before rounding it and taking the seat across from me. The waitress came to take our drink order as soon as we were seated, and I ordered a Bloody Mary, the perfect brunch drink in my opinion, in the hopes that the alcohol would help loosen me up.

The smiling college-aged girl handling our table was back in no time, and I made a mental note to add to her tip for the speedy service.

"So how are things at the bar?" Mike asked once we'd placed our food order. "You've worked there for some time, right?"

I sipped my Bloody Mary, nodding. "Yeah, since my first year of college.

His eyes went wide. "Wow. That's a long time to work at one place."

"It is, but I love it. I can't imagine working anywhere else." I talked about my staff, about how lucky I was to have a boss like Diane, and how she'd turned us into a little family. I told him all about my favorite regulars, including Freddy, and as I talked, the smile on my face grew more genuine, the stiffness melting away.

"So your goal is to buy the place?" he asked after I told him how Diane wanted to sell Dropped Anchor so she and her wife could enjoy a nice, quiet retirement.

"That's the hope." I couldn't help the niggling kernel of worry in the belly that it might not work out. "I'm working with the bank on it." I hoped they'd eventually take pity on me and give me the freaking loan, already.

"That's great. I hope it all works out for you."

"Thanks. Me too." I smiled appreciatively as the waitress appeared and placed our plates down in front of us. I leaned forward and inhaled deeply, letting out a moan as my stomach grumbled. The ham and cheese Danish was nearly the size of the plate and had to have been one of my favorite things in the world to eat.

I snatched my knife and fork, not hesitating to cut right in, and when I finally looked back up, I noticed Mike had gone a little pale, his eyes pointed at something behind me. "Everything all right?"

That was when I felt it, that freaking, *freaking* tingle. And I knew without having to turn around who was behind me.

"Don't look now, but Beau Wade is a few tables back, and he's looking this way."

I knew. I felt it. And from the way my skin was heating, I imagined how pissed he must be to see me sitting with Mike.

"He doesn't look very happy," Mike mumbled, only confirming what I'd already guessed.

My cheeks felt stiff. "Just ignore him," I insisted as I took a bite of my food. Only, I couldn't enjoy it the way I normally would, not with Beau's gaze drilling into the back of my neck like a laser beam. "I'm sure he'll leave soon enough. Don't worry about it."

Mike let out an uncharacteristic snort. "Easy for you to say."

My brow pinched together. "What's that mean?"

He blew out a breath and shook his head, like he hadn't meant to say that last part out loud. "It's just, the guy's incredibly intense when it comes to you." He glanced over my shoulder again, his gaze flaring with panic like he'd been caught before he looked back at me. "Either he *really* hates you"—his expression turned knowing—"or he feels something else completely."

Ah hell.

My stomach bottomed out, and there was that freaking tug I'd tried so desperately to feel with Mike. "What—uh, what makes you say that?"

"I mean, there's the fact that he's looking at me right now like he wants to rip my head right off my shoulders. Then there's the whole thing in high school."

My fork froze midair. "What thing in high school?"

He let out a chuckle that was more like a humorless gust of air. "You know, I was going to ask you to prom senior year."

I was glad I hadn't taken a bite yet, because at that, I proceeded to choke on air. "What?" I croaked, picking up my water glass and drinking deeply.

"Yeah. I was going to ask you out. But Beau found out and warned me off."

My brows winged up so high they nearly kissed my hairline. I wasn't sure what I was feeling at that moment other than complete and total bafflement. "What do you mean, warned you off?"

A tinge of pink painted across his cheekbones as he admitted, "Well, he kind of threatened me."

My hands came down on the table hard enough to rattle the silverware and dishes. "He threatened to beat you up?"

"No . . . not exactly. He just said he'd make me pay if I asked you to prom. I don't know what he had in mind, but the dude was scary as hell when he said it."

I couldn't get my feelings in order. My head felt like it was spinning. It was a lot to try and process over brunch.

"Um, will you excuse me for a moment?" I said as I scooted my chair back and placed my napkin on the table beside my plate. "I need to use the restroom real quick."

His forehead pinched with concern as I rose from my seat, but I barely noticed as a million and one things swirled around inside my head. With my eyes pointed to the ground, I booked it to the back hall where the restrooms were, needing a few moments to myself.

Sixteen

BEAU

SAM WAS ALREADY SITTING at a table by the time I arrived at the Sand Dollar. He was scrolling through his phone and drinking a cup of coffee when I stopped at the table.

"Never took you for the brunch type, buddy," I said by way of greeting.

He looked up from his phone with a big, bright smile on his face and stood to his impressive height, pocketing the device before pulling me into a manly, back-smacking hug, nearly squeezing the breath from my lungs in the process.

"Usually wouldn't be. But Monica turned me on to this place. They've got the best bacon you'll ever eat." He did that chef's kiss thing with his fingers. "Cooked to perfection." He pulled back, looking at me with an expression like a proud father. "Hey, kid, good to see you. It's been too damn long."

I sucked air into my lungs and chuckled. "Good to see you too. But you know I'm thirty-four right," I teased. "And you're barely a decade older than me. What are the odds I can get you to stop calling me *kid*?"

He was still smiling as he answered, "Slim to none. And once you pass forty, everyone younger than you becomes *kid*, it's an unwritten rule of getting old, I guess."

I looked over the man who'd been my mentor and closest friend. He looked like he could get out on the field tomorrow and not have a problem keeping up with anyone. "Old my ass. You're in better shape at forty-five than most twenty-somethings I know."

He patted his non-existent stomach and waved me over to take the seat across from him before returning to his own. "It's the shit behind the curtain that's falling apart, believe me. I was at the gym the other day and when I stood from the bench press, both my knees creaked and rattled like they were full of loose change."

I threw my head back on a bark of laughter. It felt damn good to laugh, given the funk I'd been in the past two days. Ever since that morning on the beach—the morning of the best fucking kiss of my entire goddamn life —I hadn't been able to stop thinking about the look in Presley's eyes when she told me to stay away from her.

It had gutted me. Nothing compared to the burn I felt in my chest at the pain in her eyes. Not even when the doctors told me I'd never regain full mobility in my shoulder. Not even the day I retired from the NFL, the only job I'd ever had. The only fucking thing I knew how to do.

I'd put that pain there. She'd been right, I didn't have any business kissing her the way I did. But she was wrong to think I'd only come back to fuck up her life. That had never been my intention. I wasn't the same kid I'd been back when she'd known me. I'd done a hell of a lot of growing in these past ten years. But more importantly, I had more power than I'd ever had before. In the past, my father had been able to hold shit over my head to make me bend to his will.

Not anymore.

That was done. I was my own goddamn man, and I was here to claim what was mine. It might have been one of the hardest things I'd ever had to do, letting her walk away that morning on the beach, but I understood why she needed space. However, if she thought I'd let her run from me, she was dead wrong. I'd give her time to cool off, to wrap her head around the idea of us, but I'd be damned if I was going to do what she said and leave her alone.

A kiss like that didn't happen unless there was something incredibly profound behind it. She wanted me. I felt that down to my bones, and I wasn't letting her get away this time.

"So how are things?" Sam asked, pulling me back to the present. "I'm so glad we were finally able to do this."

A prickle of guilt crept along my spine. Sam had done so much for me, not just with the new job, but more than I'd ever be able to put into words. Despite being much closer to me in age, Sam was more of a father figure to me than my own had ever been. When I thought about what it took to be a good coach, I thought of Sam. Whenever I felt like I was failing, I'd ask myself *what would Sam do*? He was who I tried to emulate when it came to my team. I wanted them to look back on their time playing college ball and hold me in the same regard I held Sam Killborne.

The man had changed my life and he didn't even know it. He was the reason I'd gotten out. Why I'd been able to start over somewhere else without Hank Ward's boot pressing down on my neck, keeping me beneath him. It was because of him I had a shot that eventually led to the career most football players could only dream of.

I should have made more of an effort. I should have made time for him and Monica since I came back.

"I'm sorry. I've been a shitty friend. I let myself get so busy; it's been overwhelming."

"Don't worry about it. We get that you have a lot going on. You've basically started your life over. We're not taking it personally. Well, at least not yet. You might only have another week or two with Monica, so I suggest you take her up on the offer of the homemade dinner she gave me strict instructions to invite you to later this week. I think she's starting to worry you're working too hard and not getting out enough."

It had been a month and a half since my move back to Whitecap, and, honestly, other than the reunion and that one night out at Dropped Anchor, I hadn't done much else. Most of it was due to settling in while also preparing my team for the upcoming start of the season, but I had to admit, a small part of me hadn't ventured out too much because I wanted to avoid a run-in with my father for as long as possible. This brunch—or lunch, or whatever the hell—marked my third time out for something social.

"Tell her I'm there. Just text me the day and time, and I'll make it work."

"You got it." The waitress swung by to fill drinks and take our order as I told Sam all about the job at OU. I told him how I thought it was going so far, and about the one day I let my mood effect my coaching. If there was anyone I'd lean on for support or advice, it was Sam. I knew he'd never lead me astray.

He looked across the table at me, understanding in his sharp gaze. "Give yourself some grace, Beau. You're new to this. Not to mention, the stuff with your mom was heavy as hell. You're only human. You aren't going to be perfect. You know what you did wrong, and you corrected it. That's the makings of a good coach right there."

I lifted my water and took a drink, wishing it was a beer, but even though I didn't play professionally anymore, old habits were hard to break and I still found myself eating the same as I did when I had someone planning and prepping all my meals for me. "I hope you're right."

Sam gave me dry look. "I'm always right. Besides, the fact you're worrying means you care. As long as you care, you're good. Trust yourself. You've earned it."

Maybe I had. Or maybe he was just being kind. After all, it was hard to trust myself when I remembered what I'd done to Presley in the past to put that look in her eyes.

For all the good Sam saw in me, I still had Hank Wade's blood coursing through my veins, and I would have been lying if I said I didn't worry constantly that I'd turn out to be a miserable prick like him.

We dove into our meals, and damn if he wasn't right. The bacon was out-of-this-world good. I took a second bite of the BLT with avocado I'd ordered and moaned as my eyes rolled back in my head. Instead of plain mayo, they'd used a garlic aioli—whatever the hell that was—and the flavors, along with the crispiness of the bacon, the freshness of the vegetables, and the homemade bread, were outstanding. "Jesus," I muttered around a full mouth, "who knew a BLT could be so damn good?"

Sam nodded smugly, grinning around his own bite. "Told you."

"That you did, man. Looks like I just became a brunch person, also."

We didn't do much talking as we scarfed down our food like we were two pre-teens who'd been fasting for a week and were finally diving into our first meal, but I managed to tell him how I was coming along with the house and other light topics of conversation. The one thing we steered clear of was my parents. Sam never pushed me to talk about them, but always let me know the door was open if I ever wanted to confide in him.

He hated Hank Wade almost as much as I did. There were countless times when I was younger when Sam had wanted so badly to drag me into the sheriff's station and show them the bruises on my chest and stomach—my dad's favorite places to hit me—so they could arrest his ass. I would have loved to have seen that. But I knew it would have killed my mom, and I couldn't do that to her.

Even though he'd never once spoken poorly about my mother, I knew by the way his jaw would tense and the vein in his forehead would bulge, that he wasn't her biggest fan. He didn't like that she always defended her husband and kept pressuring me to talk to him.

I'd just popped the last bite of my sandwich into my mouth and was already contemplating ordering another as I chewed when I felt a shift in the atmosphere, like the air had become magnetized.

"Ah hell," Sam muttered behind his coffee mug, trying and failing to hide his grin as his eyes cast toward the entrance to the restaurant. "There goes the neighborhood."

I knew exactly who I would see the moment I turned around, but it was the person with her that sent my blood pressure through the roof, threatening to blow the top of my skull clean off.

My gaze followed them the entire way as the hostess seated them at a table not too far away. That asshole, Mike Perry, pulled out a chair for Presley—*my Presley*—taking the opportunity to glide his hand over the small of her back, and I saw red.

"Take a breath," Sam said, a warning in his tone, along with no small amount of humor. I'd never come right out and told him how I felt about her or what had happened between us in the past, but the man knew me better than anyone, and he'd seen right through me back in the day. "You grip that glass any tighter and it's going to shatter in your hand. I don't really feel up to a trip to the emergency room today."

I loosened my hold and set the glass down but couldn't

tear my eyes away from their table. Her back was to me, but that didn't matter. I couldn't stop watching the two of them together. Anger burned in the pit of my stomach, quickly growing out of control. Not two days ago I'd had my tongue in her goddamn mouth, thrusting in how I would if I was fucking her, and now she was out with another guy?

I didn't fucking think so.

Did she think he could make her feel like I did? That he'd kiss her so thoroughly she'd be clawing at his chest for more and pouring sexy little whimpers down his throat? No goddamn way. The starched collars and golf shirts that son of a bitch wore screamed that he didn't have the first fucking clue how to please someone the way a woman like Presley needed to be pleased.

A sense of satisfaction had my chest expanding when her back stiffened, because I knew damn good and well that she felt me. Just like I'd felt her the moment she walked it. She could fight it all she wanted, but we were two magnets being drawn together, ignoring that pull was impossible. She'd eventually give in.

The fucker at the table with her locked eyes on me a second later, and I grinned victoriously when the color drained from his face and he quickly looked away. Fucking coward. Presley deserved a hell of a lot better than some spineless asshole.

"You know you look psychotic right now, right? You look like you're about to commit homicide," Sam said, but I couldn't find it in me to care. Truth was, I felt like I could murder someone, and I knew exactly who I wanted it to be.

Presley moved then, standing woodenly from the table and moving in a fast clip toward the hall at the back of the restaurant where the restrooms were, and I felt myself rising to follow after her before I could give it a second thought.

"Be right back," I mumbled to Sam as I wiped my mouth with the cloth napkin before tossing it down.

"Sure you will," he said with a chuckle. He pulled his phone out, and a second later I heard a tinny, musical tune come from the devise as he pulled up a game to keep himself occupied.

The hallway was blessedly empty as I stopped in front of the ladies' room, bracing my back against the wall right across from it and waited. The seconds ticked by, feeling like an eternity, but in fact, it had only been maybe two minutes when the door opened and Presley walked back out, muttering to herself under her breath.

When she looked up, a startled gasp ripped from her throat and her eyes bulged out as she jerked to a stop. "Beau. What are you doing?" She looked around frantically, like a scared little bunny in front of an oncoming semi. She lowered her voice to a whisper and hissed, "You're following me now? That's really not cool."

Something in me snapped. I lost the tenuous grip I had on my self-control. My nerves were frayed, my mood in the gutter. It all snowballed, and I felt completely out of control, something I didn't handle well.

I pushed off the wall and moved toward her, no doubt looking exactly like the predator I felt lurking beneath my skin.

Her cheeks flushed, her lips parting ever so slightly as panic infused her pretty eyes. My voice came out as a low, rumbling growl. "You think *that's* not cool?" I asked menacingly as Presley inched backward with every forward step I took. We moved deeper down the hall, Presley the prey I was stalking, until I spotted an alcove off to the left. Placing my hand against her chest, I guided her into it, pressing her against the wall and surrounding her tight little body with mine so she couldn't get away.

Her nostrils flared, and I would have worried I was pushing her too far if not for the heat that creeped up her neck from her chest or the way her eyes had gone from wide to half-mast, the color turning into a molten gold honey I'd only seen twice before. That day so long ago in my bedroom when I'd nearly kissed her for the very first time. Then again back in college when I'd finally discovered what it was like to taste her, to tease her. When I fucking *finally* discovered that heaven really did exist; it was between her soft, silky thighs. Her breathing was ragged, but I read her like a book, it wasn't fear that had her breathing like that. It was arousal.

"Two fucking days ago you had my tongue down your goddamn throat, and now you're here on a *date*? If you ask me, *that's* not cool."

She placed her palm on my chest, and that simple touch was enough to have my dick standing at attention and pressing against my fly. "Beau. You need to back up."

I looked at where she was touching me before lifting my gaze back to hers and arching a brow. "You sure that's what you really want, Bubbles?"

Her eyes tilted to where she was fisting my shirt like she wanted to tear it off, and quickly released me as soon as she realized what she was doing.

"Admit it," I pushed, bracing my forearm on the wall and pulling in that honeysuckle and citrus scent. "He can't make you feel like I can, and you know it."

I lifted my other hand, dragging my fingers down the side of her neck with a feather-light touch. She trembled at my touch, goosebumps rising along her arms as her nipples tightened into stiff peaks beneath the thin material of her shirt. Her body's reaction spurred me on.

I leaned in, bringing my lips to her ear. "Do you think

he'd be able to touch you like I can? That he could make you tremble the way you are right now?"

"Beau." That one word came out as a breathy plea as her pupils dilated, the black taking over the gold as her desire grew and grew.

"If I were to slide my hand into your leggings right now, would I find you wet?" I whispered, forcing a whimper from deep in her chest. My lips brushed the shell of her ear as I asked, "I bet you're drenched right now, baby. Is that for me? Or for him?"

I pulled back on her stuttered breath. "You fucked up, showing up here with him. You're *mine*, Presley. And you fucking know it."

All that gorgeous amber fired as her anger rose, and goddamn, but it turned my blood to lava in my veins. I fucking loved it when she battled with me. "I'm not yours, Beau. I don't belong to anyone, but *especially* not you."

"You became mine when you let me be the first man to slide into your perfect body and proved that to be true again when you kissed me on the beach."

"God, I hate you," she argued, but her body was saying something else completely. Her eyelids narrowed viciously as she jabbed me in the chest with her finger. "I can't believe you! He just told me what you did when you found out he was going to ask me to prom. You scared him away!"

JESSICA PRINCE

Well, guess that particular cat's finally out of the bag.

I dug down deep, looking for a hint of shame or guilt for what I'd done, but there was nothing.

I straightened and crossed my arms over my chest. "Goddamn right I did," I answered unrepentantly. "And I'd do it again."

"You ruined my prom night! Because of you, I sat at home all night, feeling sorry for myself."

Okay, so I didn't like hearing that. Still . . . "Better than you going out with that fuckface. Besides, did you really want to go out with some limp dick chickenshit who'd let someone else scare him away?" I challenged, knowing her better than that. "I did what I did because I overheard him talking to one of his loser buddies about how he was going to try and get in your pants that night."

She slowly blinked. Obviously, she hadn't heard that part.

"You deserved better than that fucking asshole. I just made sure he knew it, and if I need to go out there right now and remind him, that's what I'll do."

Her hands shot out, wrapping around my forearm to hold me in place. "Don't you dare!" she squeaked. "So help me, Beau, if you go out there and embarrass me, I'll never speak to you again."

The two of us entered into a silent standoff that lasted until she huffed out a frustrated breath.

"I'm done with this. Move out of my way, I'm going back out there."

But I didn't move, instead, I kept her blocked as I warned, "This is the first and last date that fucker gets, Presley. When you go back out there, you better make sure he understands that."

If she didn't, I sure as hell would. And I'd let him know who she belonged to while I was at it.

With that, I turned on my heel and headed back to my table. I was going to get that second sandwich, and I was going to eat it while my Bubbles put that fucker in his place.

Seventeen

PRESLEY

I BANGED on Colbie's front door at a manic pace, the sound like rapid-fire gunshots against the white painted wood. My knuckles hurt, and I was actually worried I'd broken the skin, but I couldn't seem to make myself stop.

I'd been like this—keyed up and frantic—since I finally managed to drag myself out of that alcove and back down the hall on wobbly knees at the Sand Dollar. To say the rest of my lunch date had been awkward as hell would have been an understatement.

Mike hadn't missed Beau getting up and following me, he also hadn't missed the flush that covered my skin or the way my hands wouldn't stop trembling. But he hadn't done a damn thing to stop another man from charging after his date, and after that happened, he hadn't brought it up either, choosing instead to carry on awkwardly, like we didn't both know what happened.

As much as it pained me to admit, Beau was right. I'd really wanted to like Mike, but I couldn't get down with a guy like that, so at the end of the date—an ending that came only a few minutes after I returned to the table, I'd given him a friendly handshake instead of a hug, or even a kiss, and told him I'd see him around before he could do something like ask if we could do this again.

The disappointment on his face told me he'd gotten the hint, but he was polite about it, saying he'd see me around and hoped everything worked out with the bar. In the end, the date had been . . . mediocre at best, and something told me it would have been the same whether or not Beau had been there.

"Colbie!" I shouted as my other hand came up and I began to bang with both fists in earnest. "*Cooooooooool-bieeeeeee!*"

The door flew open so fast I almost accidentally punched my best friend in the face. She looked harried and disheveled. "Someone better be dead," she squeaked. "I was trying to pee! I had to pinch it off before I was finished. Do you have any idea how uncomfortable that is?"

I glanced down, and sure enough, the front seam of her leggings was twisted to the side like she'd had to yank them up quickly. I pushed past her as I dragged my hands through my hair. "I had sex with Beau," I blurted, the words spilling out as I paced the entryway of her home.

"*What?*" she cried so loud that the one word echoed off the floor and walls, bouncing back at me over and over.

"So, you know how I had that lunch date with Mike today?"

Colbie's jaw hinged open and her eyes nearly bugged right out of her skull. "You had sex with Beau at the Sand Dollar during your date?"

"What? No! God, no! I ran into him today. He just so happened to be at the same restaurant with Sam when I showed up with Mike, and he totally lost his shit after what happened at the beach two days ago."

Closing her eyes, she shook her head like she was trying to unscramble it. "Wait, so you had sex with him two days ago at the beach?"

"No!" I waved my hands in front of her in the negative. "No. We just kissed at the beach."

"Okay, I think maybe you need to start at the beginning."

Probably, because I wasn't only confusing her, I was starting to confuse myself too.

"Come on." She waved at me to follow her toward the kitchen at the back of her cozy little house. "I'll make you a cup of coffee"—she looked back over her shoulder, taking

JESSICA PRINCE

me in—"decaf, I think. After I finish peeing, you're going to tell me what the hell is going on."

I nodded like one of those ridiculous bobbleheads as I collapsed into one of the chairs at her kitchen table. "Yeah, okay. Yeah. You go do that. I'll wait here."

She gave me a bemused look. "You okay for just a minute? You're not going to lose your mind or something, are you?"

Now that some time—and distance—had passed, I felt myself starting to calm down. "I'm good. Go to the bathroom before you give yourself a bladder infection or something."

She scuttled off to take care of business, and I sat at her table, gnawing on my thumbnail as I replayed the whole thing with Beau.

"He can't make you feel like I can, and you know it."

"I bet you're drenched right now, baby. Is that for me? Or for him?"

"Do you think he'd be able to touch you like I can? That he could make you tremble the way you are right now?"

What the hell was wrong with me that I'd let him talk to me like that while I was on a date? And worse, what did it say that I actually found it incredibly *hot*?

The answer was a resounding *yes*; if he had put his hands down the front of my pants, he would have found me soaking wet. And it was all for him, because some sick,

198

twisted part of me actually got turned on at having him claim me as his own.

What the hell was that?

Colbie came back a minute later and headed for her Keurig to make me a cup of coffee before joining me at the table. She pulled in a breath, as if she were bracing herself, and said, "Okay, start from the beginning, and leave *nothing* out."

I took a deep breath before diving right in. "It happened back in college—the last year."

Poor Colbie was going to get rug burn on the bottom of her chin from all the bombs I was dropping today.

"Back in *college*," she shrieked like a deranged pelican. "That was ten years ago! And you're just now telling me?"

I massaged the front of my forehead, trying to ward off the tension headache I felt building inside my skull. "I know. I'm sorry. I wanted to tell you so many times, but I was embarrassed."

That admission had her changing her tune. Worry infused her expression as she leaned in to place her hand on my forearm. "Embarrassed about what? He didn't . . ." Her brows winged up. "He didn't hurt you, did he?"

"No, nothing like that," I said quietly as I wrapped my hands around the mug, letting its warmth seep into my skin. "It's just . . . That wasn't the first time something happened between us—or almost happened, I should say."

I told her all about that day in his bedroom so long ago, how we were working on a project for Spanish, and for the first time ever, we were actually getting along. How I actually fooled myself into thinking we could be friends. I told her how I was convinced he was about to kiss me before his father got home, and how he'd reverted right back to the boy I knew the very next day.

Colbie's face had gone hard as I talked. "God, what an asshole," she hissed once I'd finished. "I'm totally poisoning his coffee the next time he comes into the shop."

I gave her a tiny smile. I had the best friend in the whole world. "I love you for saying that, but I can't let you go to prison for me."

"Fine," she grumped, crossing her arms over her chest with a pout. "But at least let me put something in it that'll give him the shits or something. It's the least he deserves."

I let out a laugh and nodded. "I'll agree to that."

"Okay, so what happened in college?"

That story was going to be much harder to get through, but I did it anyway. "You know I lived with my parents the whole time so I didn't have to pay for housing and all that?" As it was, even with a job and the few grants and smaller scholarships I'd gotten, I'd still ended up having to take out student loans in order to cover the rest. "Well, I'd been at the library one night, studying for a midterm, and I lost track of time. By the time I left, it was already dark out. Anyway, you remember that piece of junk car I drove back then?"

She nodded. "I remember. That thing was a piece of shit."

"Yeah, well, it wouldn't start. My cell was dead, so I couldn't call anyone, so I did the only thing I could think of and started walking. I hadn't made it off campus when I ran into a group of guys who had been drinking and were in the mood to start some trouble."

I could still remember the fear I felt as I closed in on the three guys crowding the sidewalk, and it never failed to piss me off that men tended to think they had a right to do or say whatever they wanted to women simply because we're smaller and maybe not quite as strong. It was bullshit that we had to constantly be mindful of our surroundings, that we had to weigh the dangers of going somewhere by ourselves, even if it was somewhere as simple as a jog, or we needed to carry a means of protecting ourselves at all times, simply on the off-chance some raging prick might feel he had the right to touch us without our permission or make us uncomfortable.

Thinking about that night again made me all kinds of ragey as I went into detail about how one of those assholes tried to grab me, slipping his hand beneath my sweater to try and grab my breasts, and how his dickbag friends laughed and tried to get in on it.

"Oh my god! Please tell me you reported their asses to the school for assault and harassment."

A little grin pulled at my lips. "I didn't need to. Apparently, Beau was still on campus and saw it go down." In all the time we attended the same college, our paths would occasionally cross, but the university was so much bigger than our high school, so that was the first time in four years there'd been any interaction between us. I shook my head as I remembered the beating he'd given all three of them.

"He beat their asses, Colbs. I mean, *beat them.* One guy ended up with a fractured jaw, another with a concussion, and he actually broke the hand of the guy who'd tried to feel me up." Watching him do that and hearing them howl in pain was so much more satisfying than getting them kicked out of school."

"Holy shit," she breathed in awe. "He really did that?"

I nodded my head. "He really did. Then he drove me home. Obviously, the whole scene had really shaken me up. I don't know how he knew, but he must have sensed that the idea of walking around campus made me a little skittish, and all of a sudden, he just started showing up everywhere. We didn't talk about the attack, but he walked me to and from classes, even if his were all the way across campus. He walked me to my car regularly, and if I was studying late at the library, he'd be standing outside waiting when I finally left."

I looked into my mug, lowering my voice as I said, "Then one night, it just . . . happened. I let my guard down and ended up going back to his apartment with him."

I wouldn't admit it to her, but to this day, that was the best sex of my life. Not because it was actually *great sex*. I was a virgin, after all. That shit hurt like hell. But what made it the best was the absolute care and tenderness Beau had treated me with. That night, he'd made me feel like I was the most precious thing in the world to him. He'd done his best to make it good for me, and while I hadn't been able to orgasm—because *again,* it was my first time—it still ended up feeling good.

Colbie had leaned so far across the table as I told her the story that she was halfway draped across the thing, her chin propped in one of her hands, a rapt expression on her face. "Then what happened?"

I shrugged as a pit of sadness formed deep in my belly. "Then we woke up, and just like always, he went back to being the same jerk he'd always been."

Her whole upper body rocked back, her spine shooting straight. "Wait. What? Just like that? He had sex with you, and then went back to being the same asshole he always was?"

"Yep. Just like that. His father called that next morning

while we were still asleep, and I made the mistake of thinking the phone was mine and answered it." I lifted my shoulder in a shrug. "That set him off for some reason. After he got off the phone, he went total Ice King on me, and that was it. That was the last time I ever talked to him. He tried walking me a couple more times, but I started taking different routes or leaving class a few minutes early to miss him. I guess he eventually got the hint. He was drafted not long after, and that's it. That's all there is."

"That's"—Colbie's chest sank on a gush of breath— "so underwhelming! God, what a letdown. That wasn't a story, Pres. That was barely a store. It didn't even have a real ending. It just . . ." She waved her hand in the air between us, "petered out."

I chuckled, shaking my head at her ridiculousness. "I don't know what else to tell you, babe. That's what happened."

Her scowl was laced with suspicion. "But it's not, is it? I mean, not really. Because you showed up here freaking the ever-loving hell out."

Ah yes. That.

"I was doing yoga on the beach the other morning, and he was out for a jog."

Colbie let out a hum that surprised the hell out of me. It was almost dreamy. "What does Beau Wade look like when he's running? Asking for a friend."

I shot her a snide look. "Uh-huh. Sure you are. But to answer your question, good. *Damn* good. And he wasn't wearing a shirt either."

Her hand came down on the table with a slap. "I know we hate the guy and all, but can we be grownups here and admit that he's all kinds of gorgeous? I mean, if that man were a steak, he'd be the finest cut of Wagyu on the freaking planet."

I wish I could argue, but she spoke the truth. And the bastard had only gotten better with age.

"All right, so spill it. What happened at the beach?"

I told her about the conversation we'd had, how he told me he was back because of me before we inevitably got into a fight, because that was what we always did, and finally, how I was in the process of storming off when he kissed the freaking life right out of me.

By the end of it, Colbie was fanning her face, her cheeks having taken on a rosy glow. "Holy shit, Presley."

"I know."

"That was . . ."

"Insane," I said at the same time she sighed, "*hot.*"

I blinked in confusion. "Wait. What?"

"That was freaking hot! The man tells you he's come back because of you, then he kisses you stupid?"

"I never said he kissed me stupid," I countered, feeling

the need to argue simply because it was the easiest thing to do.

She gave me a look that said, *bitch, who you kiddin'*? "Okay, fine. How was the kiss, then?" My response was to curl my lips between my teeth to keep from admitting that she was right. "Uh-huh. That's what I thought. So, he kissed you, and let me guess, you ran off."

Ding, ding, ding, ding! And the prize goes to . . .

"What did you expect me to do? I mean, sure, it was hot, okay?" I admitted petulantly. "It was *freaking hot*. But I've let this guy in twice now, and *twice*, he's done a one eighty, hurting my feelings in the process."

She held her hands up. "Hey, I get it. And I don't blame you. Once burned, twice shy, and all that jazz. But now that he's back in town, I'm not so sure running is going to be an option."

"Tell me about it," I grumbled as I brought the mug to my lips and took a drink. I really wished there was booze in it. "He stared Mike down during our date like he wanted to set him on fire or something, freaking the poor guy out. Then he followed me when I got up to use the restroom, pinned me against the wall, and told me I messed up by going on a date with another man two days after he'd had his tongue down my throat. He said I was his, that I'd been his since I gave him my virginity, that the kiss at the beach only solidified that. And that Mike couldn't touch me the way he did."

"Jesus," Colbie whispered with big owl eyes. "I think I just had a mini-orgasm."

I slapped my hands over my face and let out a pained groan. "I know," I whined. "What's wrong with us that we think that domineering, bossy shit is hot?"

"Not a damn thing, if you ask me. There's nothing wrong with wanting to be treated like you're precious one moment, then have a man completely *destroy* you in the bedroom the next."

God, now I was turned on again. This was such a freaking mess.

"So, what do I do now?" I asked, panic laced through my words. I was desperate for her to tell me what to do.

"Honestly, babe, I don't know. All I can tell you to do is follow your gut, and I'll support whatever you decide. But from everything you've told me, this guy doesn't seem like one who backs down when he wants something, and I'm afraid, my beautiful little friend, he's got his sights set on you."

Eighteen

BEAU

I HEFTED the box marked *office* off the living room floor and carried it to the correct room. The process of unpacking was happening at a turtle's pace, but I was slowly getting there. Along with the kitchen, I'd also managed to unpack my bedroom and bathroom, a guest room, and was now working on the downstairs office.

Once I finished in here, I'd start on the living room. It would be nice to finally be able to hook my television up. My assistant had taken care of having the cable turned on before I'd even moved in, but with most of the boxes I wasn't sure what to do with piled in the living room, I hadn't been able to set everything up. I was the kind of guy who liked to have the television playing in the background, creating white noise for me as I went about whatever I was doing, and not being able to do that lately had made things pretty boring.

I could only watch *The Office* on my phone or laptop for so long before the small screens started to hurt my eyes.

My house was slowly starting to look like a home, as opposed to the nightmare maze from *The Shining*, only with cardboard boxes instead of hedges, and now that I could see everything coming together, I was starting to feel more settled. Like I belonged. There had been more times than I could count where I'd come home from a long day at work and cursed myself when I saw the mess still ready and waiting for me. My finger had hovered over the number for the company that came in and set your house up for you, but now that I could actually see the results of the long, tedious hours I'd put in, there was a sense of accomplishment I'd never felt before.

As embarrassing as it was to admit, I'd never actually done anything like this before. When I left for college, my mom had taken over packing my shit up when she didn't like how I'd been doing it, and the same thing happened when we got to my dorm room at OU. When I'd been drafted, the team had paid to move me out to Arizona and an interior decorator had come in and set my house up before I even got there. With flying back and forth for job interviews and campus visits, I hadn't had the time to pack myself this go-round, but I was determined to do the *un*packing without any help. I was a thirty-four-year-old man, for Christ's sake. It really was the little things that pointed out the fact a person was an entitled ass, wasn't it?

I dropped the box onto the desk and grabbed the box cutter, slicing through the tape that sealed it closed.

I removed a bunch of basic office supplies before my fingers brushed across the top of a spiral-bound notebook I hadn't seen in a very long time. My heart shot up, lodging itself in my throat as I gently lifted it from the box. I actually thought I'd lost it years ago. I didn't know where the packers had found it, but the relief that coursed through me now that I had it back in my hands was enough to make my shoulders sag.

Everything else was forgotten the moment I pulled my old sketchpad out of the box and flipped it open. I fell into the desk chair as soon as my eyes landed on that very first sketch of Presley, my fingers tracing over the pencil lines. It was crude and unpolished, the very start of my foray into sketching, but, like football, it was something that I had a knack for, and the more I practiced, the better I got.

And this tablet was filled with sketch after sketch of my favorite subject in the whole world. The one person who moved me beyond words with just a simple look. I flipped through the pages, watching as each one got a little better. Images I'd drawn from memory because I couldn't have anything else.

I couldn't possibly count the number of hours I spent trying to perfect these drawings until I was finally happy with them, until I felt like they captured the beauty that was Presley. As I reached the end of the sketchpad, I flipped to the pages that had been ripped out, frayed pieces of paper still clinging to the spiraled metal holding the book together.

I still remembered that day with perfect clarity. My father barging into my room and catching me working on another Presley sketch. The violent shade of red his face turned as he snatched the pad from my hands and began ripping the pages out, shredding them to pieces that littered my bedroom floor. Mostly I remembered the burning pain in my chest as I stared down at those tattered pieces of paper, feeling like I'd lost her all over again.

I'd hidden the sketchbook after that, never daring to draw in it again. I couldn't risk him catching me and taking even more of her away.

My phone rang, yanking me from the painful fog of memories. I pulled it from my back pocket and smiled at the name that flashed across the screen.

"Romero," I answered. "You missing me already?"

"Depends," my friend replied. "You gotten fat and lazy yet?"

I let out a hearty laugh. "Not yet, man. So, tell me, how's the slowest running back in NFL history doing?"

His rich chuckle carried through the line. Luis Romero and I had played together for five years before my retirement, hitting it off the moment he arrived, a trade all the way from Tampa, and, while I'd been friends with most everyone on the team, he was the one I'd always been closest to.

"I'm doing great, dickbag," he threw back. "Still making those millions, so I got no complaints."

"Glad to hear it. And Carmen?" I asked about his wife. They were high school sweethearts that were still going strong to this very day. I was convinced their relationship was as good as it was because she didn't put up with any of his shit, and loved to razz him even more than I did, keeping his ego in check. "She doing well?"

"Oh hell yeah. She's actually at a spa in Sedona with some of her girlfriends for a long weekend, so I got the place to myself. Figured I'd check in, see how you were doing. How's retired life treating you? Spending your days lounging on the beach, sippin' fruity cocktails?"

I shook my head good-naturedly. I really had missed this asshole, and it felt good to be able to give him shit again while he shoveled it right back. "You know it." I looked around at the mess of boxes still cluttering my office that needed to be gone through. If only he could see this place and the disaster it really was. "Living in the lap of luxury over here."

"Hey, I'm kind of jealous, man. I haven't been that close to water since I left Tampa. I've been missing it." Romero was a Florida native, and like me, moving to the Arizona desert had been a bit of an adjustment.

Grabbing the sketchbook, I tucked it under my arm and moved through the house and up the stairs to my bedroom as I talked. "Yeah, well, you're welcome here anytime, man. I'll get you your fix."

"Glad to hear that, 'cause I booked a charter this morning, actually."

I froze before tucking the sketchbook in the drawer of the nightstand on my side of the bed and rose to my full height. "What do you mean? You're in Oregon?"

"Sure am. Just landed about an hour ago. Got a couple days before preseason and figured you were probably missing me like crazy. I'm here to put you out of your misery, because I'm such a good friend. So, what do you say? You up for a visit?"

"Hell yeah, man."

"Excellent. GPS says I'm about an hour and a half out. You know your Podunk town isn't close to a single fucking airport? Had to rent a car."

I clicked back into motion, dropping the pad into the drawer and sliding it closed. "It's worth it, trust me."

"I'm taking your word for it. I just hope this place has some nightlife."

"We do," I assured him, a smile stretching across my face. "In fact, I know just where to take you."

It had been two days since that shit went down at the Sand Dollar, and it was high time I paid my pretty blonde bar manager a visit. Romero didn't know it yet, but he'd just given me the perfect excuse to make that happen.

"Wow." Romero's eyes traveled through the Dropped Anchor as he took it all in. "Okay, this place isn't half bad."

"You say that like you were expecting one of those rundown hole-in-the-wall joints we used to hit up after away games."

He chuckled, checking my good shoulder with his. "Christ. You remember that place in Michigan? The one with an ice-filled trough instead of urinals? I think that had to have been the worst place I ever set foot in."

It wasn't unusual for the team to go out to blow off steam after an away game. Sometimes we'd hit up a well-known joint if the single guys were looking to score. But if we weren't feeling the crowds and just wanted to relax, we'd find ourselves a ratty dive that not a lot of people went to. They served booze, which was good enough, and were usually relatively quiet. Some of my best memories with the guys from my team were in shit-hole bars all around the country.

I let out a bark of laughter as we moved deeper into the bar. "Jesus, I forgot about that place. I was so terrified of that thing I held it the whole damn night. Felt like my eyeballs were floating by the time we made it back to the hotel."

Romero clutched his stomach as he cracked up, placing a hand on my shoulder to keep his balance. "I remember that! You waddle-runnin' through the hallways with your legs pressed together, trying not to piss yourself." He finally stood to his full height, which was a couple inches shorter than me, and let out a fond *ahh* as we continued to make our way through the crowded tables and booths.

We bellied up to the bar and commandeered two barstools. I braced my forearms on the bar top, clasping my hands together, while Romero swiveled in a circle. "So this is Whitecap's local watering hole. Like the rest of the town, I'm pleasantly surprised."

"Told you I didn't live in some bum-fuck town, man. Whitecap's a tourist hotspot. Wouldn't be that way if it was a dump."

"True enough." His eyes were laser-focused, taking

everything in as he lifted a hand to scratch at his chin. "So where is she?"

My head jerked back in shock. "Where's who?"

He gave me a look that said *you damn well know who I'm talking about*. "The girl, man. Where is she?"

I lifted a hand to grab one of the bartenders' attention, getting the universal signal for *one second* in return. "I don't know what you're talking about. There's no girl."

And there certainly wasn't. Presley Fields was all fucking woman.

Romero spun back to face the bar just as the bartender stopped in front of us. "Two Buds, man. Thanks," he told the guy, who took off a second later to pull our drafts. As soon as we had our beers in front of us, my friend hit me with a no-bullshit stare. "Don't play, man. You know what I'm talking about. I barely set foot in your pad before you were hustling my ass out the door, talking about the bar I just *had* to check out."

I lifted my beer, drinking deep. It wasn't a local craft like I would have preferred, but it was ice cold and hit the spot. "That's just 'cause you're only here for a day and a half. There's not a lot of time to waste."

He barked out a laugh, clapping me on the back. The move jostled my shoulder, but I managed to keep the wince in check. "You act like I don't know you better than most. So quit screwing around already and point her out."

Truth was, I'd started scoping the place the moment we walked through the door, looking for Presley, but I hadn't seen any sign of her so far. Disappointment coated my skin like a gross, clammy sweat I couldn't manage to wipe off.

I opened my mouth, about to tell him she must have the night off, when I caught a flash of blonde hair coming around the corner.

She moved through the crowd on her way to the bar, stopping every few tables to check on customers and give them that beaming, sunny smile before finally making her way behind the bar.

I watched as she talked to one of the guys working back there, showing him something on the iPad she was carrying, unable to look away.

"Ah, so that's her."

I twisted my head to look back at my friend as he watched Presley with curiosity brimming in his eyes.

"What? How—"

"You've been staring since the moment she appeared, brother. Said your name three times, and you didn't hear me because you were all over watching that woman like she's your next meal. And I can't blame you." He nodded his head with approval. "She's shit hot. You got good taste. If I were single I'd be all over that."

A growl rumbled deep in my throat, the sound so feral

it even took me by surprise. "Talk about her like that again and I'll feed you your own dick."

For some inexplicable reason, that only made him laugh even harder.

"Shit, man." He pulled his phone from his back pocket and started messing around on the thing. "Carmen's gonna love this. I just thought maybe you needed to fuck the woman out of your system or something. I didn't realize you were sprung."

If only he knew how right he was.

Nineteen

PRESLEY

I FELT him the moment I exited the hallway into the main part of the bar. It felt like the air was charged with electricity, making the tiny hairs on my arms stand on end. It took a crazy amount of strength not to look in his direction when I could feel his eyes on me as I moved through the bar, doing my best to appear unaffected, even though my heart rate had kicked up, making the blood whoosh through my veins like a tidal wave.

I could feel his attention in the pull deep in my belly, in the way my nipples stiffened beneath my bra, and in the nearly uncontrollable desire to squeeze my thighs together against the dull throb building there.

I hadn't been able to stop thinking about him since our little showdown at the Sand Dollar a couple days ago, about the dirty words he'd whispered in my ear and the heat from his body as he caged me against the wall. As much as I didn't want to admit it, I'd been desperate for him to take it further. I'd wanted to know what it would have felt like to have him pick me up and pin me in place against that wall as he kissed me the same way he had on the beach, like he was *starving for me*. I wanted to know what kind of sound he'd make if I had wrapped my legs around his waist and ground myself against his erection.

My panties had been soaked through after that encounter, and every time I replayed it, a tingle built behind my clit, so insistent that I'd end up slipping my hands inside my panties as I lay in bed in the middle of the night, rubbing myself until I came on a silent cry with Beau's face on the backs of my eyelids.

I couldn't remember the last time a man had gotten to me to the point I had to touch myself to take the edge off, only for it to come raging back in no time. I felt out of control. Beau was the only person in the world who could do that to me. It was his gift. Or his super power.

I could feel the heat from my chest spreading upward, past my neck and into my cheeks, as I worked diligently to keep my gaze away from the barstool he occupied while I went over the schedule on my tablet with Donovan and showed him the distribution schedule I'd worked up.

I'd just finished that task and was about to whip around so I could spend the rest of my shift back in my office—*not* hiding—when a large, tanned hand shot out, right into my line of sight.

"Hi. Luis Romero. Nice to meet you."

I blinked up into a pair of smiling brown eyes, my brain taking a moment to click back online. I recognized the guy on the stool beside Beau. It was impossible not to. Since the whole town rallied behind Beau, his team had become the Whitecap favorite, their games being featured on the TVs hanging all around the bar. Everyone in this town knew who Luis Romero was. Myself included.

"Uh, hi," I responded, reaching out to his offered hand. His large palm engulfed mine, pumping up and down with such power I was afraid he'd pop my shoulder right out of socket. "Presley Fields."

His smiled got even wider. It was the kind of smile that was totally infectious. You couldn't possibly look at it without grinning in return.

"Jesus," Beau grumbled from behind his pint glass. "How about you don't try to rip her arm off, Rome?"

The guy chuckled, Beau's glower clearly rolling off him like water off a duck's back.

"Ah. Lovely Presley. It's great to meet you."

I let out a giggle. Something about this guy was so freaking *charming*. He was giving off massive golden retriever vibes. Unlike the man sitting next to him, scowling into his beer.

"Good to meet you too . . ."

"Call me Romero. Or Rome," he offered kindly. "Everyone else does."

"Well, good to meet you too, Romero. What brings you to Whitecap?"

He threw his thumb in Beau's direction. "Came for a quick visit. He's been whining and begging me to come see him, missin' me something fierce, so I'm here for a couple days to put the big guy out of his misery."

Like I said . . . charming.

Beau grumbled a few choice words behind the rim of his glass before downing the rest of it. "That's not how it happened, and you damn well know it," he grumped.

My gaze tracked to Beau, my smile broadening at the pout marring his handsome features. This was a side of him I hadn't seen before, and despite the way he was glaring daggers at his friend, I could tell there wasn't any heat behind it.

I couldn't help but join in, letting Romero's infectious energy rub off on me. "That was really nice of you."

He placed a hand on his chest, right over his heart, his expression growing solemn as he declared, "I'm an amazing friend."

"And humble," Beau deadpanned. "Keep it up and you'll be sleeping on the back deck, asshole."

I laughed, I couldn't help it, and at the sound, Beau's

gaze shot to mine, his eyes flaring wide for a second before he smiled back at me, looking like he'd just won the lottery or something.

That smile hit me in a place it had no business hitting, and I quickly looked away, clearing my throat awkwardly as I shifted my attention back to Romero, the much safer option.

"Well, then your next round's on me. Call it a great friend bonus."

"What about me, Bubbles? You just gonna leave me hanging?"

Romero's eyes pinballed between us with far too much glee. "Bubbles? That's your nickname? *Awww*. That's just the stinkin' cutest," he declared, propping his chin in the palm of his hand and batting his enviably long lashes.

How was it possible that these two men were such good friends? Romero seemed like the nicest guy in the freaking world. And Beau was, well . . . *Beau*. I wasn't sure how else to describe him other than not Romero.

I shot Beau a glare before turning back to the puppy in human form sitting at my bar. "It's not cute. He just calls me that because he knows it annoys me. It's an insult from way back in high school."

"No, it's not." Beau's brows pulled together, insult etched into his strong features like I'd just slapped him. "I call her Bubbles because she's got the sweetest, bubbliest personality," he informed his friend, rendering me speechless. "She's always had the biggest heart and is kind to everyone she meets." He looked back at me, one brow rising. "Well, almost everyone."

"Ah, okay, I get it now." Romero pointed between the two of us. "You two were high school sweethearts, weren't you? I can totally see it."

I blinked like a cartoon character, nearly choking on my own spit. "What? No! God no. Nothing like that."

His eyes narrowed with skepticism. "You sure about that? Because I'm totally getting a vibe here. *Something* had to have happened. As my wife would say, I'm shipping the two of you hard."

What the hell is happening right now?

"That's not—we aren't—" I looked to Beau, expecting him to argue just as vehemently as I was attempting to do before my tongue got uncomfortably thick all of a sudden, but instead of correcting his friend's assumptions, he was watching me like my face held the answers to solving world hunger or who killed JFK or something. He seemed expectant, like he was waiting for my reply before forming one of his own.

I looked away from him, unable to keep my gaze locked with those blue eyes that used to remind me of the coldest, most frigid day, because I was starting to realize, for the first time, that since he'd come back, the ice in those eyes was gone, and instead, they reminded me of the sky on a clear, sunny, cloudless day.

"We, uh. We weren't . . . like that." Those words tasted like an over-ripe lemon on my tongue, one that had passed its peak.

Romero looked genuinely confused as he turned to his friend. "For real?" He flicked his finger between us. "You two really weren't together?"

His eyes never wavered from my face as he answered in a low voice, "I never deserved her."

Talk about a direct hit. I wasn't sure how the hell I could survive a statement like that. Especially after the kiss we'd shared and the tempting things he'd said in that alcove.

Fortunately—at least, I thought it was fortunate— Freddy spoke up from his spot a little farther down the bar.

"Not a man on this earth good enough for a woman like our Presley. But she at least deserves a man who's willing to try. If you ask me, it's a crying shame someone as wonderful as her is still single. A travesty. Just waiting for the day when the man meant for her pulls his head outta his ass and realizes he needs to start pulling out all the stops."

My face was so red it was probably glowing as I grabbed a couple pint glasses and began filling them.

"All right now. Thank you for the sweet words, Freddy, but how about we stop discussing my love life while I'm at work, yeah?"

To my dismay, Freddy snorted into his Coke as I placed the fresh beers in front of Beau and Romero without meeting either of their gazes, despite feeling them waiting. "What love life? Girl, you're having a worse dry spell than the Sahara in middle of a sand storm."

I sent up a silent prayer that the ground would open up and swallow me whole, but it appeared as if luck wasn't on my side this evening.

On a laugh, Romero leaned over, hand extended to Freddy. "Luis Romero. And I feel like the two of us just became good friends."

Freddy tried to play it cool as they shook hands, but I didn't miss the way his cheeks went ruddy with excitement. "Freddy. I'm like, the unofficial security for this place."

The corner of my mouth hitched up slightly when I caught one of Beau's brows winging upward. "He's a regular," I explained. "He likes to stay close and walk the ladies to their cars when we're working late."

Beau's mouth pulled into a frown, and, if I didn't know any better, I would have said that he actually looked concerned. "How often do you work that late?"

"Well, I'm the manager," I answered, "so at least a few nights a week."

His frown only deepened. "And you don't have any kind of security?" He cast a look at Freddy. "*Real* security? That's dangerous as hell, Presley."

Heat started to rise in my belly as his words stoked that anger I always carried for him, bringing it just below the surface.

"And I'm more than capable of taking care of myself, *Beau*," I threw back childishly. "Besides, we look out for each other here. It's a safe place."

He grunted in response, bringing his beer to his lips as Romero laughed and clapped him on the shoulder.

"What he actually meant to say before going all caveman is that he's worried." He hit me with that charming puppy dog smile. "You'll have to forgive my friend here, He's got a heart of gold, just a terrible way of showing it."

He must have seen the look of disbelief on my face, because he leaned deeper into the bar, propping his elbows on it as he waved me closer. "Let me tell you the story of how I met my wife and how this man here helped me convince her to take a shot on me."

Well this ought to be interesting.

Nearly an hour later, I was keeled over, clutching my sides and howling with laughter as Romero regaled me and everyone close enough to hear stories of the things the two of them had gotten up to with the rest of their teammates back before Beau retired.

As much as I didn't want them to, Romero's stories had been like a battering ram to those walls I'd worked so diligently to keep up around myself where Beau was concerned. He was showing another side of the man I hadn't thought existed, a side I caught the very faintest glimmer of twice in my life, but convinced myself couldn't possibly be real.

Back in high school and college, it was hard to get a feel for Beau as a friend because the things we cared about as kids were a lot more shallow and self-satisfying. But hearing Romero talk about him and seeing the true, genuine affection he had for his friend, well, I was beginning to see Beau in a whole new light, and it was a disconcerting feeling to realize that side of him I thought was only a fluke was actually something real.

"So, I'm standing out there in the pouring rain, trench coat and everything, doing my best *Say Anything* at

Carmen's bedroom window, trying to get her to talk to me, but the goddamn Bluetooth speaker I was using stopped working mid-song, ruining the entire moment."

"Aw." I giggled, bending at the waist with an elbow propped on the bar top and my chin cradled in my hands, fully enraptured by Romero's story. "So what did you do?"

"Wasn't me." He flung his thumb at Beau. "This guy was hiding in the bushes with a couple of our teammates, you know, as moral support. He saw me panic when the speaker cut out, so he started singing 'In Your Eyes' at the top of his lungs. The rest of the guys joined in on the chorus."

I couldn't help but look in Beau's direction, my heart doing a weird sort of flip-flop in my chest.

The man shrugged like it was nothing as he sipped his beer. "You looked like a deer in the headlights. I felt sorry for you."

Romero elbowed him in the side with another hearty laugh, something he did a lot. "Anyway, Carmen finally comes to the window and says she's forgiven me as long as I can make Beau stop singing, then she agreed to marry me if I promised I'd never let him do it again."

For the life of me, I couldn't picture the Beau Wade I knew—or the one I *thought* I knew—crouched in shrubs, singing a Peter Gabriel song to help a friend win the love of his life. That was something I probably would have paid good money to see. If I'd had it, of course.

"That's really great, Romero. I'm so glad it worked out for you, and you have to be sure to come back with your wife. I'd like to meet her."

"I sent her pics of the beach earlier, and she's already planning our next trip."

I was glad to hear it, not only because I'd managed to be charmed stupid by this man, but because it had actually been nice to see Beau loosen up with someone he cared about. Someone good and kind, a true friend. I wasn't sure the boy I'd known all those years ago had ever had that, so it was nice to see he'd managed to find it as an adult.

I looked at Beau and saw him watching me with a tender look, a look that made me feel like I might have actually been important to him somehow.

At that look, the voice in the back of my mind reared its head, shouting at me that I was falling for it again. Only, this time, I wasn't so sure it was an act or a game. But it left me feeling off-kilter all the same, and I much preferred my feet to stay on solid ground.

I pushed up, knocking my knuckles against the bar as I pasted a smile on my face.

"As fun as this has been, I actually have a lot of work I should probably get to." I hiked my thumb over my shoulder. "It was lovely meeting you, Romero. We'll be rooting for you guys this season."

His chest puffed up proudly. "You better be. And it was awesome meeting you. Hope to see you soon, sweetheart."

Without giving Beau another look—because I wasn't sure I could handle it—I whipped around on my heel and bolted back to my office, not because I needed to work, but because I needed to hide from the man before I did something epically stupid, like let my guard down again.

Twenty

PRESLEY

I STRUGGLED to concentrate on my work, my thoughts trailing off to the man who I'd spent the better part of my life convinced I hated but was starting to question whether or not that was the case anymore. I didn't understand how he could piss me off so badly one moment, only to turn me on in a way no other man had ever been able to before.

We were oil and water.

No, that wasn't right. When it came to me and Beau, we were like fire and gasoline. A dangerous combination. Some might even argue lethal. So why was he the only man who could make me feel so . . . out of control and wild? I was levelheaded in all things in my life. I thought through every scenario or decision before I acted. Except where he was concerned. With him, I acted without thinking. He could make me impulsive and reckless. He could push my buttons like it was his sole purpose in life, eliciting a reaction from me that no one else could.

And what did it say about me that there was this part of me that actually enjoyed that unbridled feeling? I felt like I was sitting in the front car of a rollercoaster, steadily climbing to the highest drop, with my hands in the air and my heart in my throat. It was terrifying and thrilling all at the same time.

A knock on the door yanked me from my musings. I blinked, clearing my vision and bringing myself back to the present to find Donovan standing in the opened doorway leading into my office.

"Hey, Boss. Closing time."

"Already?" My head whipped back to my computer to check the time. It was five after midnight. I'd been so busy thinking about Beau that four hours had flown by without my notice. "I didn't realize."

I pushed out of my chair and had to brace myself against my desk when a pins-and-needles sensation shot through my legs and feet. Four hours of sitting made my knees stiff and put my thighs to sleep.

Donovan gave me a curious look. "You good?"

"Yeah." I smiled, shaking my legs out. "Just sat for too long, I guess. I'll meet you out front in a second."

I preferred to help my staff close out on the nights I worked to closing. Diane had always run a tight ship, but there had been managers in the past who sat back while the rest of us did the grunt work, and I found it was more of a struggle to respect them as my superiors if they weren't willing to get their hands dirty like the rest of us.

When I was promoted to this position, I told myself I wasn't going to work like that. Every night I helped wipe down tables and counters, close out the till, and stack chairs.

I walked past the kitchen, waving and issuing the staff back there a good night as they worked to clean and shut everything down for the next day, and headed to the front of the bar.

Sure enough, Freddy was parked in his usual spot, but what made me stop short was the sight of the man sitting beside him.

"What are you still doing here? And where's your friend?" I asked Beau once my feet came unglued from the floor. I rounded the bar, giving him a bewildered and suspicious look.

He tilted his head to the side. "Just hanging with my new pal, Fred, here. And Romero took an Uber back to my place. He caught a pretty early flight this morning, but I wasn't ready to leave just yet."

I grabbed a towel and got down to cleaning, spraying the countertop down and scrubbing it until all stickiness and streaks were gone, restoring it to its glossy shine. "Well, it's past close, so . . ." I trailed off, hoping he'd take the hint and leave on his own, but my favorite regular had something else in mind.

"The big guy and I were talking, and we had an idea," Freddy started. I had a feeling I wasn't going to like what he said next. "We decided we'd start splitting shifts."

I cast Beau a flat look, my eyes narrowing as he smiled in a way that clearly indicated the idea was all his. "Is that so?"

"Yep. I'll take Tuesdays, Thursdays, and Saturdays, and he'll handle Mondays, Wednesdays, and Fridays. We'll trade off Sundays."

Freddy looked so damn proud of himself, like he'd just come up with the best idea to ever be idea-ed in the whole wide world.

"Huh." I crossed my arms over my chest, popping a hip out. "Those just so happen to be the days I work to close," I stated with a glower in Beau's direction.

He smirked unrepentantly. "Well, would you look at that? Talk about a happy coincidence."

I was so sure.

"What about your day job?" I asked, raising my eyebrows. "This place doesn't close until ten on weeknights." Being a small town, we catered to different hours than a bar you might find in a larger city. Truth was, we didn't live in a place where people were cutting up until two or three in the morning. Weekdays we were open from eleven to ten while weekends were noon to midnight. "Don't you have to be up early?"

"I can manage, don't worry about that."

I wasn't prepared to roll over and play dead. "And once the season starts? How do you think you'll manage then?"

He lifted one massive shoulder. "We'll adjust as necessary." He patted Freddy on the back. "Right, Fred?"

Freddy nodded proudly, getting that same blush he had earlier when Romero told him they were best friends.

Son of a bitch! I'd lost Freddy to a couple football stars. So much for loyalty.

My head canted to the side as I took Beau in. *Really* took him in, trying to see if there was something deceitful or cruel motivating him. But I couldn't find it. "You aren't going to let this go, are you?"

His expression changed. The lightness went out and something hard and cold took its place as the muscle in his jaw ticked. "Senior year of college," he ground out, and I knew in an instant what he was referring to. He was thinking back to those boys who'd scared me, who'd tried to do worse than that. "Got that goddamn night burned into my memory, especially the look on your face when you thought there was no way out. So no, Bubbles, I'm not letting this go. It was sheer luck I was there that night to make sure you didn't get hurt. I'm not going to hope for luck this time. I'm making it my damn self."

The argument died on my lips. "All right."

His blue eyes flashed as they rounded in surprise. "All right?" he parroted back. "That's it? You aren't going to fight me on this?"

I went back to scrubbing, arching a brow at him. "Would it do me any good?"

"Not one damn bit."

I didn't think so.

I shrugged, blowing a strand of hair out of my face. "Then yeah. That's it. It's late and I'm tired. I just want to get this done so I can go home and climb into bed. So, no. I'm not going to fight you on this."

I went back to helping my team close down for the night while he and Freddy kept each other company. He even surprised me by helping flip chairs over and place them on the tables so the floor was cleared for the morning cleaning crew. Once everything had been tidied, locked, and the lights shut off, he took up the rear as we headed out the back of the bar to the staff parking.

A tingle formed low on my back and traveled up my spine as he stayed a step behind me, his hand on the small of my back, even after I'd called out goodnight to everyone else and moved to my car. I pulled the keys from my purse, my hand trembling to the point it took me three tries to get the damn thing in the lock. I let out a breath of relief once the lock clicked, and quickly pulled the door open, stepping into the opening it created and using it as a sort of barrier between us. "Well, as you can see, I'm safely to my car. Thank you for walking me. Have a good night."

"Jesus," he grunted, his top lip curling up as he scanned the length of my car. "This thing is just as bad as the piece of shit you drove in college."

I made a noise of affront, slamming my hands down on my hips as I scowled. "It's *not* a piece of shit."

His jaw hinged open. "It looks totally unreliable! It doesn't even have automatic locks, for Christ's sake."

"It's a perfectly fine car," I cried, feeling my ire rise again. I was cresting the top of that big drop, waiting for the feeling of free falling to hit and send my stomach up into my throat. "Excuse me for not wanting to blow money on a new one when this one is perfectly fine."

I patted the top of the door and, as if on cue, the window that had been giving me trouble for the past few weeks slipped off the tracks and slid down, leaving a two-inch opening.

His look said it all. "Perfectly fine, my ass," he grunted as he crossed his arms over his chest.

"This is nothing," I declared, ignoring the heat in my cheeks as I mashed at the button to roll the window back up, even though it wouldn't work until I turned the car on. Not that it would have mattered. The button had quit working some time ago. I had to brace my hands on either side of the glass and push it back up. I sent up a silent thank you to the universe when it actually stayed in place and didn't slide back down.

"See?" I chirped. "Good as new."

His expression remained hard, but I could tell by the way the corners of his mouth wobbled ever so slightly, he wanted to laugh.

I lifted my chin in an effort to look down my nose at him, an impossible feat, since the stupid man towered over me. "Now if you'll excuse me, my bed is calling."

I climbed into the car and slammed the door, letting out a stuttered breath at the nerves Beau had me feeling.

I jolted when the window slipped again, but it didn't only drop a couple inches. Oh no, it crashed all the way down, the sound of glass shattering inside the door panel echoing through the dark night.

As if that wasn't humiliating enough, Beau was still standing there, hands tucked in the pockets of his jeans like he was waiting for the opportunity to say *I told you so*.

I gripped the steering wheel in my hands, let out a long defeated breath, squeezed my eyes shut, and lowered my forehead to the cold, hard leather.

Son of a bitch. That was an expense I couldn't afford if I hoped to get that loan. I wanted it so badly, but it felt like no matter how hard I worked, my dreams were a little too far out of reach.

"Bubbles."

I let out a groan at the tenderness in Beau's voice, refusing to open my eyes and look at the man as he opened the door and stepped close enough that his signature scent of spice and the outdoors invaded the tiny cab.

"I don't suppose there's any chance you'll forget you witnessed that and leave me alone to stew in my humiliation?"

He reached out, and the feel of his fingers gently wrapping around my wrist gave me a jolt. I sat up, turning my head in his direction as he slowly worked to ease the death grip I had on the steering wheel. He was crouched down low enough to bring his face to mine, his strong thighs testing the tension on the seams of his jeans. God, it was criminal for a man to be as sexy as he was.

"There's nothing for you to be embarrassed about."

That was easy for him to say. I could only assume the guy was loaded.

"Come on, I'll take you home."

My brows slammed together in confusion. "What?"

"Bubbles, you can't drive this car. It's not safe. Hell, you don't even have a driver's side window anymore."

"It's fine. I'll just—"

He pinned me with a look that had me clamping my

mouth shut and curling my lips between my teeth. "I'll take you home," he repeated, dragging the words out as if to say *keep arguing and I'll put you over my knee.*

A delighted shiver rattled through me as he took my hand in his and stood to his full height, his grip giving me no choice but to follow after him and climb out from behind the wheel.

Having my hand in his took me back to that day in high school. The first and only time I'd ever been to his house, and just like that day, having his warm palm against mine as his large fingers engulfed my tiny hand, a flurry of butterflies took flight in my belly.

Twenty-One

WITH THE EXCEPTION of the GPS directing Beau to the address I'd given him, the ride to my house was made in silence. My mind was spinning, replaying every story Romero had told me and trying to associate the image with the boy I once knew.

I just didn't understand. To hear Romero tell it, Beau was a deeply loyal friend, not only to him, but to all the guys on the team. He was funny and kindhearted, always willing to go out on a limb. He'd even claimed the man would give the shirt off his back if a friend needed it.

The longer I thought on that, the hotter that coal deep in my belly grew, the one that fueled my anger toward the boy who'd tormented me for years. Toward the young man who made me think he was something special just to get me into bed, only to flip the switch back the following morning.

That heat burned hotter and hotter so by the time we pulled up in front of my house, I was well and truly pissed again. I couldn't claim it was rational, but at least I knew how to handle the anger. It was all the other emotions Beau made me feel that left me out of sorts and scrambling.

I gripped the door handle as he pulled the car to a stop at the curb, ready to issue a thanks and jump out, but instead of throwing the shiny, luxury SUV into park, he killed the engine.

I whipped around to face him as he opened his own door. "What are you doing?"

Confusion etched into the plains of his too-handsome face. "What does it look like? I'm walking you to your door."

A derisive snort scraped up my throat as I rolled my eyes. "That's totally unnecessary. I appreciate the ride and all, but I think I can handle it from here. Have a great night."

With that, I jumped out of the car and slammed the door harder than necessary before stomping up my front walk.

"Presley, wait," he called after me, followed by the sound of his own door closing, because of course he hadn't listened to me. I picked up the pace, my keys already clenched in my first, ready to unlock my front door. "Jesus, will you just wait?" He caught up to me on the front stoop. His hand wrapped around my elbow, pulling me to a stop before I could slide the key into place and spinning me around. "What's going on?"

I tilted my chin up and squared my shoulders, adopting an air of aloofness I sure as hell prayed was believable. "I don't know what you're talking about. I told you, I'm tired and want to go to bed."

I attempted to shake his hold off and twist back around toward the door, but he wouldn't let me. "Bullshit," he ground out. "Something changed. You were fine, and now you're . . ." he waved his free hand up and down my frame, "well, I don't know. But it sure as hell isn't fine. It's like you flipped a switch or something."

A sardonic laugh wrenched itself from deep in my chest. "Oh, that's really rich, coming from you."

His brows pinched together. "What the hell's that supposed to mean?"

Something in me snapped. The coal that had been burning grew so hot my insides felt like they were on fire, and I was itching for a fight. "It means that's the pot calling the kettle black, seeing as you're the freaking *king* of flipping switches!" I cried, throwing my arms wide. "Your mood changes so fast it gives me whiplash, so don't talk to me about mood changes, buddy. Because you take the cake!"

"Presley—"

"No!" I snapped, drilling my finger into his chest. "Don't you *Presley* me." I was on a roll, and a little bit out of control if using air quotes around my own name was any indication. We'd crested that highest peak of the roller-coaster, and now I was flying down at what felt like the speed of sound, so fast I couldn't even get a scream out. "What is all this, huh? What are you playing at? Did you ask your buddy to come to my bar tonight and feed me a bunch of bullshit so I'd let my guard down with you for a third time? Was this just another game to you? Because I've known you a long time, Beau, and I don't recognize the man he described. So tell me, was any of what he said real?"

"Yes!" he reached up, raking a hand through his hair, and the son of a bitch even made tousled hair look sexy. "I wouldn't do something like that. Not to you. I didn't tell him to say any of that shit."

I folded my arms over my chest to keep from hitting him as I barked out a loud, sarcastic laugh. "Ah, I see. So you're that guy with everyone else. That's it, isn't it? They all get Good Guy Beau. Meanwhile, I'm the designated punching bag. *I'm* the one you make feel like shit. Is that what you're saying?"

His face grew an unnatural shade of red. "Of course not!"

"Then what is it?" I shouted, too far gone to remember I was standing on my front porch in the dead of night, screaming like a maniac and probably waking up every one of my neighbors. "What was it about me that was so awful, I only got the worst sides of you? Why am I the only one you were so mean to!" Those last few words broke, my voice betraying me and revealing the pain I was feeling. A burn formed behind my eyes, my nose tingling with the need to cry, but I did my best to fight it back as the steam fueling me tapered out. "Why couldn't I ever get that side of you without you turning around and ruining it?"

Beau's hands came up and framed my cheeks, his long fingers threading through my hair as he tipped my face back to meet his. Fire flashed in those crystal blue eyes, along with something else I didn't understand until he started speaking.

"Presley, I'm so goddamn sorry." His voice was gravel, shattered and edged with more emotion than I'd ever seen or heard from him. "Out of every person in my life, you were the one I *never* wanted to hurt, and I fucking hate myself for what I put you through. I was a stupid kid. I didn't know what the fuck I was doing. All I knew was that I had these big, uncontrollable feelings for you that were so goddamn strong they terrified me. I wanted you so goddamn bad, but I couldn't have you. You were better off without me, so I pushed you away. But you have to believe me. There hasn't been a day, Presley, not a single fucking day where I haven't thought about you. Where I haven't missed you and wished I'd been good enough to deserve you. That's why I came back. When I left, I swore I'd never come back here. But in the back of my mind, I knew that was a lie, because as long as you were here, I could never break away from this place. Not completely. Because I could never bring myself to break away from you."

That reckless side of me breeched the surface. Only this time, I was doing it consciously. I *wanted* to say '*screw it*' and let myself act without thinking of the consequences. That was why I closed the distance between us on my front pouch with a lunge and wrapped my arms around Beau's neck so I could yank him down to my level, smashing my lips against his, pouring every ounce of anger and frustration and need and desire into a brutal, unforgiving kiss.

If he'd been surprised by my actions, he didn't show it, and the instant my mouth touched his, he was right there, fighting me for control. Our tongues tangled and thrust together. I pulled his bottom lip between my teeth and bit down hard enough to elicit a grunt from him right before he palmed my ass with both hands, squeezing hard enough to make me whimper as he hauled me up into his arms.

My legs wound around his trim waist, our hips lining up perfectly so the steel length of his erection pressed right against my core, where I wanted—no, *needed*—him most.

My back banged against the door as he pinned me in place with his massive frame, surrounding me completely. Heat poured from his body, sinking into mine and melting me from the inside until I was nothing more than a bundle of firing nerves, a live wire in water. Electricity coursed through me as the battle over who would control the kiss continued. My lips felt bruised, my nipples were hard, and I could feel the wetness between my thighs.

Beau growled against my mouth before scraping his teeth down the cord of my neck. "Invite me in." It wasn't a request, it was an order, and my whole body shivered with desire.

I dragged my nails through his hair, fisting it at the back of his head and giving it a jerk, forcing him to look at me. I grinned wickedly, feeling like a completely different woman as I dragged my tongue up his throat, right over where his pulse was pounding. "Now why would I do that?" My words were low, throaty, and dripping with sex.

He nipped my bottom lip at the same time he brought one hand up, giving my nipple a hard pinch that sent a bolt of lightning straight to my clit. "Because once we're inside, I'm going to fuck you so hard your neighbors will hear you screaming my name." He went in for another demanding kiss. "Because I want to fucking wreck your body, baby. And you want to let me."

Damn him, but I did. I *really* did. I wanted him to destroy me.

I wriggled in his grasp until he lowered me to my feet so I could spin around and unlock the door. The instant I had it thrown open, I reached out, fisting the front of his shirt in my hand, and yanked him across the threshold. "Get in here and fuck me."

He didn't have to be told twice. He gave the door a vicious kick, sending it slamming shut just before he grabbed me and pinned me against it.

"Fuck, Presley," he groaned against my skin as he peppered biting kisses down my neck and across my chest. He bent lower, his greedy mouth sucking the stiff peak of my nipple into his mouth through my shirt and bra hard enough to make me cry out. "You have no clue how long I've wanted this."

I pulled on his hair until his lips returned to mine. His massive thigh pushed between my thighs, applying pressure where I craved it most, making me whimper.

"Do you need to come, baby?"

My head fell back on a moan as my hips began to sway

and circle, rubbing my swollen, aching clit against him, desperate to get off.

"Jesus," he grunted, grabbing my hips and pulling me down harder against his thigh. "I can feel your heat through our clothes." I felt his smile against my skin as he licked and sucked along the top swells of my breasts. "You're going crazy, aren't you?"

"Beau," I ground out. "Stop teasing me."

His head came up, his forehead resting against mine. "Not teasing, baby. But if you want to come, you have to ask nicely."

Instead, I reached between us, gripping his erection as best I could through his pants. "Make me come."

I thought I'd won from the grunt my touch elicited, but apparently I'd underestimated the man's willpower, because instead of giving in, he grabbed hold of both my wrists and pinned them to the door above my head with one large hand.

"Ah, ah, ah. I said ask nicely." His voice was like velvet and sin, and all I wanted in that moment was to hear him lose control as he pounded inside me. "I'll make you come harder and longer than anyone who's come before me, but I want to hear you beg for it."

Twenty-Two

BEAU

MY HEART WAS in my throat as I locked eyes with her, seeing all that warm, sweet brown staring back at me through heavy lids, glazed over and glassy with need for me. I'd never wanted anything more than I wanted her, and the need to hear her beg was visceral. A living, breathing thing inside me.

Her lips parted, the tip of her tongue peeking out to swipe across her swollen cherry lips. "Beau," she whimpered almost as if she was in pain. "Please. Please make me come. I-I need it so bad. Please."

I could feel my cock leaking pre-cum at her sweet words. "Fuck, but you beg so pretty, baby." My hand skated down the front of her delectable body. Her chest stuttered, her whole body trembling as I flicked open the button of her jeans and lowered the zipper before dipping my hand inside. "You're such a good girl, aren't you?" A groan wrenched from my chest when my fingers slid between her thighs. "And look at that. You're already so wet for me. Hot and wet." I hissed as I slid two fingers through her slit, pushing them as deep inside her as I could. I ground my molars together as she cried out at the feel of me filling her. Christ, I couldn't fucking wait for it to be my cock stretching her so wide she'd feel me for a week. "And so goddamn tight."

Her eyes widened, locking with mine, that cinnamon I loved so much swirling with all that honey. "Oh fuck, Beau! I need—"

"Say it," I coaxed, pulling my fingers out and plunging them back in, curling them against that specific spot deep inside her that had her arching her back and pushing harder against me. "Tell me what you need and I'll give it to you. Fucking swear I will."

"I need . . . more."

I could most definitely give her that.

She let out a whine when I pulled my hand free, but it didn't last as I made quick work of stripping her completely naked, right there in her entryway. Her body was a goddamn work of art, all luscious curves and smooth, milky skin. Her nipples were the perfect rosebud pink, tight and straining, begging for my attention.

Ten long years had passed since I'd seen her like this,

and while she was still the only woman who made me lose all sense of reason, there were noticeable differences in the Presley I was staring at now. She'd grown, matured, and the self-consciousness that had been there the night she gave me her virginity was gone. Instead, the woman writhing against the door as I sucked nipples into my mouth until they were bright red and glistening beneath the overhead lights knew exactly what she wanted, and made no bones about getting it.

"Please," she continued to beg, driving me out of my mind. "Beau, please. Touch me. I need you."

And I needed her, more than she could ever possibly know. But that was a conversation for another time.

I lavished her body as I lowered myself to my knees. Kissing my way down the valley between her perfect tits, tracing a circle around her bellybutton with my tongue. There wasn't a single inch of her I didn't want to touch and lick and memorize until I could sketch her perfectly from memory alone.

Her eyes flared as she watched me lift one of her legs, throwing it over my shoulder. "What—what are you doing?"

"What's it look like?" I dragged my teeth along the inside of her thigh, looking up at her from the apex of her thighs. I could smell her arousal and see how slick her pretty pink pussy was, and my cock swelled even harder, desperate to feel her wrap around me. I'd get there, but first I wanted to savor her. I wanted her flavor on my tongue. I wanted to make her come until her arousal was dripping down my throat. The only regret I had from our night together was that I hadn't devoured her pussy, and for ten long years I'd dreamed of what she might taste like. Tonight, I was going to find out. "I'm worshipping you."

The red on the apples of her cheeks that I loved so goddamn much grew an even deeper crimson as she snagged her bottom lip between her teeth almost bashfully. "I've never—that is, I can't—I don't think—"

A sense of male pride shot right through me, puffing my chest. "Has anyone ever eaten your pussy before, Presley?"

Her nod was choppy and unsure. "But I didn't—you know. I don't think I can."

Christ, she was so goddamn perfect. "Then this is going to be another first you give me, baby, because I'm about to make you come so hard you won't be able to stay standing."

To prove my point, I dove in, burying my face between her legs and dragging the flat of my tongue through her drenched slit. "Goddamn," I grunted at that very first taste. "Knew you'd be sweet, baby. But this is fucking heaven between your thighs."

"Holy shit!" she cried out, her voice going high pitched. "Oh my god, *Beau!*"

Her body's reaction to me feeding on her pussy, the way her leg tightened over my shoulder and her hands fisted in my hair as her hips began to move, riding my face, was proof enough that the other assholes she'd been with didn't have the first fucking clue what they were doing. Because my woman was responsive as hell. Goosebumps spread across her arms and legs, as she undulated against my tongue. The noises that passed her lips were some of the sexiest I'd ever heard. She begged for *more* and *don't stop* and *god yes! Just like that*, not a single bit of shame or nerves when it came to voicing what worked best for her.

When I stuffed two fingers deep inside her and sucked her clit into my mouth, a fresh wave of arousal coated my tongue. Her pussy clenched tight, and I knew by the feel and the way her eyes widened in awe that she was about to come. She just needed to be pushed over that edge. Curling my fingers, I found her G-spot as I pulled her swollen clit between my lips and sucked hard, flicking it with the tip of my tongue. That combination was all it took, and she barreled over the ledge, those gorgeous amber eyes locked right on me as she came on a cry of my name, her grip on my hair so tight I thought she might rip it out, but fuck if that wasn't a turn on as well, just like everything she did. All the woman had to do was breathe and I was hard, but seeing her like this, her whole body flush from her orgasm . . . Christ, it was almost too much to handle.

I rode her though to the very end, until she did exactly as I'd said she would, her knee buckling and taking her down. If I hadn't been there to catch her, she would have melted right into the floor, but seeing as I wasn't anywhere near done with her, I couldn't let that happen.

I shot to my feet, my dick throbbing so hard behind my zipper I could feel my heartbeat in it.

"Beau, what—" she started, but before she could get her question out, I had her sexy little body tossed over my shoulder and was storming through her house, a man on a mission.

The laugh that bubbled out of her as I stomped down the hall, kicking open two doors before locating her bedroom, was like music to my ears, and if my dick didn't have a pulse of its own just then, I might have taken the time to really enjoy it. To watch her face light up as she made that sound for me again. But I needed to be inside her more than I needed my next breath. I was consumed with that need, nearly out of my mind with it.

I dropped her onto the middle of the bed and stripped down faster than I ever had before. From one frantic heart-beat to the next, I went from fully clothed to completely naked and crawling over the woman who enthralled me completely.

"Beau," she said on a whisper as I used my knee to spread her legs wide, lowering myself so they cradled my hips.

"Fuck me," I grunted as the underside of my stiff cock slid through the arousal that still coated her. The head bumped her clit, making her head fall back on a greedy moan as I dropped my forehead against the crook of her neck, lost in the feel of that slick heat coating me. "How the fuck do you make me want you so bad?"

Her legs wrapped around my hips and her nails sunk into my shoulders, dragging down my back as I continued to slip and slide, making sure to brush her clit on each upward stroke, building that fire back up in her all over again. I could have come just like this. In fact, I was embarrassingly close already.

"I don't know." She let out a sigh of pleasure as I dragged my teeth over the rapidly fluttering pulse in her neck. "But you make me feel the same way. I feel like I'm going crazy."

My head came up, and I took her in. *Really* took her in. All that flushed, creamy skin pressed against and around me. That golden hair draped over the pale mint comforter that covered her bed. Those gorgeous hooded eyes and that full, pouty bottom lip she kept biting as I moved against her and ramped up the need for me to reach the highest peak.

"I'm clean," I panted as pre-cum leaked from the head of my cock. "I've never gone bare before, but I need to feel you." Her teeth came back down on that lip, and, *Christ*, it drove me insane. "Are you protected?"

Her head moved up and down in a jerky nod as her hips began to rise and fall, meeting mine stroke for stroke. "I-IUD."

My chest squeezed almost painfully tight. "Tell me I can have you," I pleaded against her lips before taking another kiss, driving my tongue into her mouth the same way I wanted to drive my cock inside her. "Please, Bubbles." This time it was my turn to beg. "Tell me I can have you like this. Bare. Tell me I can come inside you, nothing between us."

She pulled in a shaky inhale, her eyes wide and pinned to mine. It felt like a lifetime passed before she finally let out a stuttered, "O-okay."

That one word was all it took for me to lose complete control. On the next slide, the head of my cock notched against her opening, and I drove in to the hilt, the sensation so intense we both cried out.

"Holy fuck," I groaned as her walls hugged me, fluttering just enough to tell me it wasn't going to take much to make her come again, and this time, I got to feel it around my cock. "Jesus, baby. You feel even better than I remember."

"Oh my god!" she shouted when I pulled nearly all the way out and powered back in. "Shit, Beau! Oh god! I'm so full."

Her nails raked down my back, and that small twinge of pain quickly morphed into a pleasure unlike anything I'd ever experienced.

A growl ripped from deep within my chest, primal satisfaction at its fullest. With one hand braced on the mattress, I gripped the headboard with my other, using it for leverage to pound into Presley with everything I had.

"Goddamn right you are," I gritted, losing myself in the sounds she made and the way her perfect tits bounced each time I drove into her. The way she clawed at my back and squeezed her thighs around me so tight, like she was scared as hell I'd disappear or something. "I fill you perfectly, baby. Don't you ever forget that." The tingle built at the base of my spine, my balls drew up, but I fought back my need to come, wanting to have my wits about me when she came so I could watch the entire beautiful thing. "No one else can make you feel like this, can they?"

"Mmm. No, Beau."

"Say it," I hissed. "Say I'm the only one who can fuck you this good."

Her eyes lost focus, her pussy began to squeeze tighter with her impending orgasm as the headboard banged loudly against the wall. "Only you, Beau. Only you can fuck me this good."

Fuck yes. "Tell me this pussy is mine. That it belongs to me."

She curled her lips between her teeth, like she was fighting the desire to let those words pour out. To me, that was a challenge I was more than willing to accept. I moved my hand down between our bodies, grazing my thumb across her nipple, drawing a gasp from her lips. "Say it and I'll let you come, baby. Tell me you're mine. That this pussy and everything else is *mine*."

She whimpered, her cunt closing around my cock like a vice, making it hard to slide in and out, but I didn't let up, determined to live up to my promise to destroy her body. "Oh shit. Beau, I'm—"

"*Fucking say it*," I growled, moving down to where we were connected in the most intimate way. "Goddamn it, Presley," I said, giving that swollen bundle of nerves a pinch. "Let me have you."

Her eyes rounded, her mouth fell open, and I felt her body crest that highest peak right before flying back down to the ground. "I'm yours!" she shouted as she came. "Oh god! I'm yours, Beau!"

"Goddamn right you are," I gritted right before

driving myself balls-deep and holding there as my own release slammed into me like a freight train. "Now take my cum like a good girl."

Her orgasm dragged out as I shot deep inside her, coating her walls with my cum. My head fell into the crook of her neck as her name passed my lips over and over, mingling with the loud, frantic sounds of her coming around me.

This was, hands down, the best I'd ever had. There was no coming back from this. My goal had been to make it so fucking good for her that no other man could ever compare, but it seemed my plan backfired, because as I collapsed on top of her, my body feeling completely wrung out, I knew I'd never be the same. She wasn't just under my skin, she was in my bones, a part of my marrow. Presley was soul-deep inside me, and after tonight, not having her was no longer an option.

This woman was mine in every single way.

Twenty-Three

PRESLEY

MY EYELIDS FLUTTERED OPEN, that fuzzy place between sleep and consciousness still clinging to me as I blinked my room into focus. The light peeking through the slit in my curtains was still faint, a muted purple-gray that indicated it was still early.

I wasn't sure what had woken me up until I tried twisting and the long heavy arm draped across my stomach clenched, reminding me I wasn't alone in my bed. I sucked a surprised gasp into my lungs as memories from the night before bombarded me. I clenched my thighs to be sure and had to curl my lips between my teeth and bite down to mask the whimper at the dull, delicious ache centralized there.

God, Beau had been something else last night. It was as if all that power that was him had been let off its leash. I'd never experienced anything like what he'd done to me. How incredibly he'd worked my body, like he was a musical prodigy and I was his instrument. I'd come so hard I'd actually seen stars.

My eyes slammed closed, but the image of him above me in all his glorious naked perfection was pinned to the backs of my eyelids. I could still recall how his muscles strained as he fucked me with everything he had, the bulge in his arms, the way his abdominals clenched. I could still hear the sounds he made when he buried himself inside me and—

"*Shit,*" I squeaked before slamming a hand over my mouth. I held my breath and turned my head slowly, taking in the man sleeping in my bed beside me.

Shit, shit, shit. I'd let him fuck me without a condom.

It wasn't that I was worried about pregnancy or anything. It was the power I'd handed to him by letting him come inside me bare. That was something I'd never done before. In my mind, that was a kind of intimacy a person only shared with someone they trusted implicitly, and I'd handed it over to him on a whim.

I'd gotten so swept up in feeling instead of thinking, that I'd done it again. I'd given this man even more of me to break into a million tiny pieces. I didn't know what the hell it was about him that had me throwing caution to the wind and doing things I'd sworn to myself over and over I'd never do again.

Being careful not to make a sound, I slipped from beneath Beau's iron grip and slid out of bed, padding across the floor as quickly and quietly as possible as I slipped the top drawer of my dresser opened and snatched out a pair of panties before tiptoeing to the bathroom and easing the door closed.

"God, Presley. You freaking idiot," I hissed at myself as I slipped the underwear up my legs and covered the rest of my body with the fuzzy robe hanging on the back of my bathroom door. Moving to the sink, I twisted the knob for the cold water and splashed it on my heated cheeks before bracing my palms on the vanity and taking in my reflection for the first time.

Mascara from the night before was smudged beneath my eyes. My lips were puffy and red from the volatile kisses, my cheeks still held a tinge of pink, and through the small gap in my robe, I noticed faint bruise-colored marks on my neck and chest.

"Holy shit," I whispered, grabbing the lapels and separating them farther. Sure enough, my chest was riddled with mouth-sized marks all the way down to my nipples.

My face heated as that persistent tug between my thighs returned because I knew exactly when he left those marks and how fucking *good* it felt.

"Jesus, Pres. Get your shit together," I warned into the mirror. The sex had been out of this world. So what? It didn't matter, because if the past had taught me anything, it was that the other shoe was currently dangling in the air, just waiting to drop. After all, that was what always happened.

Panic gripped my chest, squeezing it until it felt nearly impossible to pull in a full breath. What had happened last night was so much worse than all the other times. I'd let those goddamn walls down, even though I knew better, but what had happened after that wasn't just sex. It was so much more than that, and I knew when he flipped the switch on me, the fallout was going to be so much worse than the other times. There was no coming out of this unscathed. I only had one choice. Instead of waiting for that fucking shoe, I had to be the one to drop it.

I didn't know how I was going to do that. And I sure as hell wasn't ready for it. Unfortunately, when I slowly crept out of the bathroom a few minutes later, I discovered my time was up when I looked over to the bed and found Beau sitting up, his chest and stomach on full display. The covers were pooled at his waist and his knees were bent, arms propped on top of them.

But the real kicker was the smile stretched across his face the moment our eyes met. He looked so sleepy and rumpled, and . . . *God*! It was unfair how beautiful the man was.

"Come back to bed, Bubbles. It's too early."

"I, um . . ." I swallowed thickly, clutching my robe closed at my neck. I really wished his offer wasn't so damn tempting. "Sorry. Once I'm up, I'm up. I'd toss and turn, and you'd never get back to sleep."

He stretched his legs out, giving me an unobstructed view of those sexy stacks of ab muscles. "That's fine. Because I have no intention of letting you get back to sleep anyway."

My pussy throbbed like it had a heartbeat, but I gritted my teeth against the growing arousal and stood my ground. "Um, I-I—" I started, but before I could make an excuse, he threw the covers back and stood from the bed, completely comfortable with his nakedness as he prowled toward me. Though, in fairness, he had every right to be.

"God, I can still taste you," he rasped, his voice like gravel, low and rumbly and totally seductive. "Never felt anything like that last night, baby. That was . . . *fuck*," he hissed. "I'm addicted to you."

He stopped so close I could feel his heat seeping through the protective layer of my robe. His long, thick cock was already hard, straining toward me as he lifted his hands to cradle either side of my neck, tracing my jawline with his thumbs. "I need you again," he said quietly. "I'm going to take you back to bed and spend the entire day doing all the things to you I've dreamed of doing."

His mouth descended, and as much as I craved his kiss, I couldn't do it. I couldn't let myself go down that road again. I knew exactly how painfully things would end for me, and I refused to put myself in that position.

I turned my head at the last moment, causing his lips to graze along my cheek. "Beau, um . . ." I took a step back, wrapping my arms around my stomach protectively. "I don't—I'm not so sure that's a good idea."

"Really? Because I think it sounds like a fucking brilliant idea." He reached for me again, that smile of his nearly making me cave, but I moved out of his reach, causing his brow to furrow. He bent, grabbing his boxer briefs off the floor and sliding them up his tree-trunk thighs, concealing the hard-on he was still sporting behind the tight black fabric. "Baby, what is it? Are you sore? We can take it easy if that's what you need. I could make us some breakfast while you soak in a bath. How's that sound?"

It sounded perfect. Too good to be true, as the past had taught me.

"No, Beau. That's not—" I shook my head, struggling to piece my words together. "That's not what I mean. What I mean is, last night shouldn't have happened in the first place. We can't do this again."

"What the fuck? Presley, what's going on?" His hand came out for me again, and instead of moving backward another step, I rounded the bed, putting it and the whole space of the room between us. His arms fell to his sides, his hands clenching and flexing into fists. "What the hell is this? Why are you running from me?"

I let out a breath of frustration and anxiety. It felt like there was a war waging inside me, one side wanting to give in, to feel myself wrapped up and lost in him all over again, while the other side was sounding the warning signal so loud it sounded like a fog horn going off in my head. "Look, last night was . . . great—"

"Goddamn right it was," he gritted. "Best sex of my life, so why is it you won't let me touch you right now?"

I ignored his question and the warmth that bloomed in my belly at hearing him say it was the best. I kept telling myself it didn't matter, this was about self-preservation. "But it was a mistake."

He planted his hands on his hips, letting out a bark of incredulous laughter. "Are you kidding me? Like fuck it was a mistake," he barked so fiercely it made me jump.

"Beau, just listen—"

"Fuck that! I'm not going to listen to you downplay what happened between us last night and try to talk yourself out of this."

Just like that, the embers caught and that coal in my

belly ignited. "There's no *this* to be talked out of. It was just sex, Beau."

He stalked across the room, the ferocious predator coming out to play. I stumbled backward, trying to maintain distance between us, but he wasn't having any of it. He kept coming until my back slammed against the wall, his arms coming up to bracket either side of my head, trapping me in place. "What happened last night was so much more than sex, and you damn well know it. The game between us changed the moment you told me you were mine."

"I didn't—I wasn't—" I couldn't think straight, he was so damn close. The smell of him always managed to scramble my brain. "I'm not yours," I finally managed, my chest sinking with relief that those words actually came out stronger than I was feeling at that moment.

"You are," he argued, something like desperation flashing in those crystal-clear eyes. His voice went quiet, tender, almost sweet enough to make me forget myself. *Almost.* "Baby, please. Let's talk about this. I know there's a lot of history between us, but I can explain—"

I shook my head, ducking under his arm and moving away from him. I lifted a hand to stop him when he started in my direction. "I don't need an explanation, Beau." Truth was, I didn't want one, because a part of me was terrified to hear what he had to say. "That's all in the past."

"Obviously not, if you're holding it over my head right now."

"That's not what I'm doing." But a voice in the back of my head asked if that was really true.

He crossed his massive arms over his chest, his expression challenging as he asked, "Isn't it?"

"No," I shot back. "This is about me protecting myself. There's a reason people say the best indicator of future behavior is past behavior, Beau. I'm not trying to hold anything over your head, but I have to look out for myself, and every time you and I have gone down this road, I've ended up getting hurt, so excuse me for not wanting to stick around for the finale for a third time. I lived through the first two, and let me tell you, it wasn't fun."

His face fell, sadness sinking deep. "Baby, that's not going to happen this time, I swear."

I hugged myself tighter. "You're right. It's not. Because I'm not going to let it. You need to leave, Beau."

The look he gave me damn near flayed me open. He looked wrecked, like I'd shattered his world. "Bubbles, we can make this work. Last night was something I've wanted for so long—" He slammed his eyes closed and pulled in a deep breath before looking at me again, his eyes pleading. "I can't lose you. Not after last night."

God, he was killing me.

"Please," I whispered, feeling my resolve start to crumble. "Please, just go."

His frame deflated like a balloon being stuck with a pin. I watched in silence, willing my heart to slow down as I watched him pull on his clothes from the night before. My shoulders sagged as he moved toward the bedroom door, but at the last second, he turned and moved toward me, into me, pinning me against the wall again as his mouth came down on mine.

It wasn't the same hungry, frantic kiss as the night before. This one was slow and deep, like he was worshipping me.

When he finally pulled back, my vision was hazy, my breathing erratic. "I'm not giving up on this," he whispered against the shell of me ear. You're under my skin, right where I want you, and I'm going to prove that this time, everything will be different."

On that declaration, he pulled back, his eyes locking with mine. "I'll see you soon, baby." Then he was gone, and I was left with weak knees, a muddled brain, and a riot of emotions I couldn't begin to sort out.

The only thing I knew for sure was that I was in *big* trouble.

Twenty-Four

BEAU

A BEAD of sweat trailed down my back, seeping into my already sweat-soaked shirt as I pounded at the heavy bag hanging from the ceiling in my home gym. Heavy metal blared from my ear buds, drowning out all the other noises as I drove my taped fists into the stuffed leather harder and harder, doing what I could to work out the tension that had knotted up my shoulders and neck since I left Presley's house an hour and a half ago. Since I was *kicked out*.

With a grunt, I punched harder, sending the bag swinging, the blow ricocheting up my arm, right into my injured shoulder.

"*Fuck!*" I barked at the pain lancing through my shoulder like I'd been stabbed with a white-hot poker. I ripped my ear buds out and threw them across the room as anger, frustration, and pain all boiled together inside me, creating something toxic and combustible.

Romero's voice pulled me out of my downward spiral. "Jesus, man. Keep that shit up and you're gonna end up back under the knife. Jesus, I heard you beating the shit out of that thing all the way upstairs."

I shook out my shoulder as I looked to the entrance of the gym where he was standing, dressed in a pair of athletic shorts and serious bedhead. His jaw cracked open with a huge yawn as he scratched at his stomach. "Isn't it a little early for self-castigation? Christ, what time is it?"

"Just after eight." I unwound the tape from my hands and lifted one to massage my throbbing shoulder. "Sorry if I woke you."

"I'm surprised to see you here, honestly. When you weren't back by the time I crashed, I figured you'd scored with your pretty little Bubbles and slept over."

"I did. Or I was." I lifted my water bottle and sucked it back before folding myself down on the workout bench nearby, leaning forward and propping my elbows on my knees. "We hooked up last night. Then this morning everything turned to shit."

Romero leaned against the wall across from me, his arms folded over his chest. "You wanna talk about it or keep beating the hell out of yourself?"

I heaved out a sigh and drained the rest of the water

before crushing the bottle in my hand and tossing it in the trash a few feet away.

"I don't even know where to start."

"How about with what happened this morning?"

I went through everything from waking up and thinking things were fucking perfect, realizing Presley wasn't in the bed with me, then how everything took a wrong turn the moment she came out of the bathroom, and finally the fight that ensued before she inevitable kicked me out.

He rubbed at the back of his neck. "Jesus, man. That's brutal. I'm sorry."

"We've got history, and most of it's been pretty ugly," I admitted. "As much as I hate to say it, I get why she freaked out. I haven't exactly had the best track record where she's concerned."

"You know, if I'm being honest, I don't really understand the dynamics between you guys. I mean, it was clear from watching y'all that there's something between you, but when I mentioned it, she jumped at a denial. Were you two friends? Something a little more?"

I brought my hand up, rubbing at the ache that suddenly bloomed in my chest when I thought back to everything that had happened between us over the years. "She moved to town when I was twelve, and I swear to Christ, Rome, from the first moment I laid eyes on her, I wanted her. It was like something sprang into place between us, a tether that bound me to her and made it impossible to get her out of my head. I'll admit, I was a little shithead when I was a kid, and I did what all little shitheads did to the girls they crushed on."

"You tortured her."

"Yeah, basically." The tiniest smile tugged at my lips as I thought back to all the times her face would get red right before she'd rip into me for being a little twerp. "I had a gift for pushing her buttons, and I got off on it. She was just so goddamn sweet to everyone. But when I jabbed, she went off. She didn't cry or run to tell a teacher. She gave as good as she got." I gave my head a little shake. "Most of the time, she gave even better. She was better than me, smarter, stealthier. I forced myself to compete with her as often as I could to see if I could live up to her standards, if I could be good enough. But I would have been lying if that didn't come back to bite me in the ass a lot of the time."

Romero's brows winged up in curiosity. "How so?"

My heart beat hard, lodging itself in my throat as I thought back to one particular competition I hadn't even meant to force us into.

"I've told you about my dad."

Romero snorted, his top lip curling up in disgust. "That piece of shit? Yeah, on the rare occasion you got enough booze in you, you shared. Don't know the guy well, but I know enough from you that it's safe to say I hate the prick."

"The feeling's mutual. Believe me. Anyway, I knew if I had any chance of getting the hell away from him, I couldn't be beholden to him for anything. That included college. He wanted to dictate where I went, what I majored in. Hell, even who I hung out with. I couldn't stand the fucking thought of four more years under his thumb. His plan was for me to go to his alma mater, play ball where he did, where he was the big man on campus. Basically, he wanted me to live in his shadow. So I went behind his back and applied to OU. I ended up getting a sweet ride from OU. It wasn't far enough away, but I could deal."

It didn't hurt matters either that I knew Presley had already been accepted there. "But if I disobeyed him, I knew he'd cut me off. The scholarship was great, but I needed money to live on, so I started to apply for every grant I was eligible for."

His gaze lit with understanding. "Ah. And let me guess who else was going for those same grants."

"If I'd known, I would have backed out, but by the time I found out, it was too late. Her folks weren't as well off as mine. They couldn't afford to simply write a check for her to go to college." Christ, I still remember the day she got in my face about that one, how low I felt, how I wished I could make it all better for her.

"So that's the deal with you guys? A couple grants?"

I scrubbed at my face, a dry, humorless laugh pushing from my chest. "Christ, I wish. It would have been a hell of a lot easier."

I told him everything, from how I was finally building up the courage my senior year of high school to make a move before my father stepped in with his threats to ruin her father, basically taking a steaming shit on the only good thing I could have had in my sorry-ass life. I told him about college, how I fucking *finally* made her mine, and how goddamn happy I'd been. Then I told him how my old man managed to ruin that for me as well.

"Jesus," he grunted, rubbing at his temples like he was trying to sort through everything I'd dumped on him. "Talk about twisted." His eyes met mine, full of bewilderment. "This is some daytime soap opera shit, man."

"No shit," I grunted, pushing up and moving to the glass-fronted mini fridge I kept stocked with water. I tossed a bottle to Romero before taking another one for myself and twisting it open. "When Dad called and she answered my phone that morning in my dorm room, my heart fell right out of my chest."

"What did he do? He made another threat?"

If only.

I shook my head and forced down the lump that had formed in my throat as I thought back to that awful morning. "It started that way to get me to play ball. Threatened her parents again if I didn't get rid of her." Bitterness coated the words that came after that. "I did what that evil bastard wanted and made Presley feel like shit when I pushed her away, and you know what he did? That fucker went ahead and got her old man fired from the job he was on anyway. Just to prove he could. He didn't go full out, of course, didn't ruin his reputation completely, but he wanted me to see exactly what he was capable of if I didn't do as he said. I lost the only girl I'd ever cared about, the only one I wanted to be with, and he did it anyway. To prove a fucking point."

Romero blew out a "Fuck me," on a deep breath. "Jesus, Beau. I knew your dad was a piece of shit, but this is next level. She thinks you rejected her. She let her guard down, let you in, and thinks you had a change of heart."

All I could do was nod.

His back shot straight, indignation rolling off him in waves. "You have to tell her, brother. She needs to know the truth. She flipped out on you this morning because the past has shown her nothing good comes from letting her guard down, but that's not the case."

I let out a groan and dropped my head back. My chest hurt. My fucking shoulder hurt. I was pissed and didn't know where to direct it. I thought that, after last night, Presley and I had finally turned a corner. After wanting her for so goddamn long, I finally had her. Then, like every time before, she slipped right through my fingers.

I felt like breaking shit.

"You think I didn't try?" I shook my head, my chest feeling tight. "I tried to explain, but she cut me off. Didn't want to hear it."

"Then try again, man!" he shouted, throwing his arms out wide in a show of emotion that wasn't usually the norm for him. "I mean, if Carmen was here, she'd be dragging your ass out the door by your ear this very instant. As it is, when I get home and tell her this whole story, it'll be a miracle if I can keep her from jumping on a plane and flying here to try and fix this for you. But you can't give up."

I inhaled deeply, filling my lungs to the point of bursting as I remembered back to the night before, to what it felt like to have Presley beneath me, to hear her tell me she was mine.

"I don't intend to give up. This morning was only a setback."

Romero came over, clapping me on the back with a huge, cheesy grin. "That's my man. Fuck your dad, Beau. You deserve to be happy, and if she's the one who does that for you, I say go all out."

And that was exactly what I intended to do.

Twenty-Five

COLBIE'S MOUTH hung open so far she was going to catch a few flies if she wasn't careful. She'd was hanging with me at the bar before it opened to the public after giving me a ride to work because my car was currently in the shop, getting that stupid window fixed. I'd spilled everything that had happened with Beau the other night. The goal was to get her advice, but once I'd finished, she'd gone completely silent, gaping at me like a literal fish out of water, her wide eyes blinking slowly, like a cartoon character.

"Hello, Earth to Colbie." I waved my hand in front of her face, hoping to snap her out of it. "Are you just going to sit there with your jaw on the bar the rest of my shift, because that's not very helpful."

"I'm sorry." She shook her head like she was trying to

clear it. "I'm trying to wrap my head around the fact that you slept with a man you claim to hate, not once, but twice now."

I dropped my head onto the bar and gave it a couple bangs for good measure, hoping to rattle some sense into myself. Instead, all I did was give my team a reason to stare at me like they were worried for my sanity.

Welcome to the club, guys.

Colbie leaned forward, sliding her palm between my head and the wood to cushion the blow. Her brows rose high on her forehead when I finally looked up at her. "You know I have to ask."

I pointed my finger at her. "No you don't. You *don't* have to ask."

She nodded solemnly. "Oh, but I do, and you know it. It's girl code." She leaned across the bar and lowered her voice. "So? How was it?"

I shook my head frantically. "I'm not—I don't—it's —" I let out a groan. "It was . . . I don't even know how to describe it. Euphoric, maybe? It was out of this freaking world."

My best friend sucked in a sharp gasp before her face split into an ecstatic grin as she let out a delighted squeal.

"Shh," I hissed, clapping my hand over her mouth as she drew more of the attention of my staff. "God, crazy.

Will you relax already before people start asking questions?"

"Oh my god, you guys are so totally going to end up together," she chirped, completely ignoring everything I just said. "I'm calling it now. I mean, I totally get it. The two of you have been duking it out most of your lives. There's this rivalry that's always been there, that's kind of aggravating, but really hot at the same time. And it's basically in every enemies-to-lovers romantic comedy movie that chemistry like that eventually explodes, and the hero and heroine are helpless against it. Nora Ephron basically demands it."

"Can we maybe get our head out of the clouds and plant our feet back down here on Earth. This isn't a movie, Colbs."

"No, it's not. But you've now slept together twice, the last time being the best you've ever had."

I held up my hand to stop her. "I never said it was the best I've ever had."

She shot me a look that said, *bitch, please. Did you forget I know you?*

"Okay, so it was the best I've ever had," I relented on a grumble.

Her grin was almost triumphant. "So, like I was saying, the chemistry's already exploded between you two."

"Yes, but that doesn't mean it was right. The two of us

together, it's . . . so complicated. It always has been. Isn't this kind of thing supposed to be easy?"

She let out a scoff and reached into the bowl of mixed nuts I'd poured for her when she declared she was starving and tossed a handful into her mouth. "Sorry, babe, but my knowledge on this kind of thing is really limited. The last thing I'd claim to be is an expert in the matters of the heart over here. I mean, I'm a grown ass woman and still can't manage to keep my tongue from tangling up when the dude I've been crushing on walks into the room I'm in."

My heart broke at the defeat on my best friend's face as she slumped on her bar stool.

"Hey, knock that off." I reached across the counter to take her hand in mine. "You're amazing in every single way, and one day, that sexy sheriff is going to open his eyes and realize it. Mark my words."

She grumbled under her breath something that sounded an awful lot like *doubt it* before shoving another handful of nuts into her mouth.

"Stop it. It's going to happen," I assured her, mainly because I believed it down to my bones. It had to happen. Colbie was too good not to get what she's always wanted. She was kindness personified, the very best person I knew, and I refused to believe for a single second a man as smart and loyal as Kincade Michaels wouldn't see all the wonderful that was her and not want to make her his.

She waved me off. "This isn't about me. We're here to talk about you and the fact that you're now banging one of America's sexiest men alive."

Heat creeped into my cheeks and the ache that had been centered between my thighs for the past forty-eight hours throbbed again. The marks he'd left on my body had been covered by concealer and other makeup, but at the reminder of the other night . . . I could practically feel them pulsing.

"*Banged*," I stressed. "Past tense. As in, it's never going to happen again. That's the way it has to be."

Colbie's head canted to the side as her eyes narrowed, studying me closely, and as my best friend, more than likely seeing a hell of a lot more than I wished she could. "If that's how you really feel, then why do you seem so sad about it?"

And there it was. Damn her for knowing me so well.

I grabbed a towel and began scrubbing at a perfectly clean bar top because I needed something to do with my hands and a reason to not meet her knowing gaze. "I don't know what you're talking about. I'm not sad. I'm fine with it. It's the smart thing to do. It was my decision."

Her hand came down on mine to stop me. "Really? Then why are you scrubbing the varnish right off the bar?"

I let out a heavy sigh as my head dropped and my shoulders slumped. "Because I'm sad."

"Oh, honey." She flipped my hand over and laced her fingers through mine. "You know, there's no rule saying the two of you have to be enemies forever. What if you both put down your swords?"

I let out a snort. "You make it sound so easy."

She shrugged. "Well, I mean, it can be. If you like him, I say give it a shot."

That sounded really nice in theory, but the past wasn't so easy to let go. "I don't know. What if the other shoe eventually drops?"

"It very well might. But what if it doesn't?" She grabbed another handful of nuts and threw them into her mouth, mumbling around them as she said, "Just something to think about."

And I was still thinking about it a few hours later, after the bar opened and Colbie headed to work. I was still thinking about it as I sat back in my office going through invoices, when one of my servers, Rachel, knocked on my door and peeked her head inside.

"Hey, Pres. I know you're busy, but I think we may have a problem out here."

I could hear them as I followed her down the hall, and as soon as we turned the corner into the main part of the bar, I spotted the table of young, college-aged guys who were causing the problem Rachel referenced.

"Shit," I hissed, because I had a feeling I knew who

these kids were. And I knew exactly who I should call to come over here and put them in their place.

Beau

A growl worked its way up my throat as my phone rang again. Despite the fact I never answered, my old man had gone from calling once every few days to damn near blowing up my phone today. The only thing I could figure was what limited patience he had—and it was *incredibly limited*—had worn the hell out, and he was done being ignored.

Too fucking bad for him that I was done letting him dictate my life.

But the constant buzzing of my phone today had finally pushed me over the edge. Snatching the thing up, I swiped at the screen without looking and brought it up to my ear.

I growled through the line. "You know, when someone doesn't answer any of your dozens of calls, a person usually takes the goddamn hint and gives up."

"Uh, Beau?"

My back shot straight hearing the voice carrying through the line that most definitely didn't belong to Hank Wade. "Bubbles?"

"Um, yeah. Hey. Hi . . . Uh . . . I'm sorry to call if you're in the middle of something—"

"I'm not," I spit out quickly. "I'm not in the middle of anything." Well, that wasn't exactly true. I was actually in the middle of trying to install a mount to hang my television now that the living room was clearing up, but it was proving to be more difficult than I'd initially thought. I may have gotten frustrated once or twice and threw a screwdriver across the room, but no way was I admitting that to anyone.

"What's up?"

I listened as she blew a sigh though the line. "Well, we have a bit of a problem down at the bar." My skin began to prickle with concern, the need to rush to my car and blow through every safe driving regulation strong as hell. "It's not major. Just a few drunk kids making a scene, but, uh . . . I think they might be a couple of your boys."

"*Fuck*," I dragged out, bringing my hand up to pinch the bridge of my nose against the headache suddenly forming in my skull.

"Yeah. And I'm pretty sure a couple of them are underage. My staff didn't serve them, but apparently a few of the older ones kept slipping them drinks when no one was looking. I wanted to call you, see if you wanted to handle it or if I should maybe get the sheriff involved?"

"No. Thank you. I really appreciate you calling. If you wouldn't mind holding off on that, I'll be right down there."

"No problem. See you in a few."

I made what was usually a ten-minute drive in seven. I could hear my boys the instant I walked into Dropped Anchor, but the first person I had eyes on was Presley. It was *always* Presley.

She stood at the bar with one of her people, her eyes on the table of unruly college football players. At least until she felt me entering the bar. It was that invisible tether between us drawing our eyes together.

I stood in place, not wanting to reveal myself to my boys yet, as I watched her lean in to whisper something to the woman standing beside her before breaking away and heading in my direction. I didn't miss the way her eyes dropped to the floor before coming back up, her gaze almost bashful as she looked at me through the fan of her lashes, or how her cheeks went rosy. Her hand fluttered in front of her nervously before she caught herself and clutched them together in front of her.

"Hi," she said softly. "Thanks for coming."

"Thanks for calling me instead of the cops. I'm sorry about my guys."

She waved me off. "They're kids, Beau. I remember what it was like at that age."

If only I had the kind of life where I could relate. That was one of my concerns about being their coach. At their age, I was so focused on football and not fucking up because it was my only way out. I didn't cut up or get in trouble like all my buddies. I couldn't be a normal kid because I couldn't risk my future.

My chest tightened as I looked to the table full of kids I was supposed to be leading, supposed to be teaching to be better men. I couldn't worry that I was failing them. I couldn't get so tangled up in doubts that I dropped the ball with these guys. They deserved better. "I'll take care of it."

I'll leave you to it. Good luck." She took a step back, and I instantly hated the distance she put between us. But I could only handle one thing at a time. I'd take care of my boys, then I was coming for her.

Twenty-Six

PRESLEY

WATCHING Beau Wade handle his players was . . . really something.

"My god," Rachel breathed from beside me. "What is it about him reaming those kids out that's so damn sexy?"

I didn't have the answer. All I knew was it was. It really, *really* was. Something about seeing Beau exert his authority while still somehow managing to handle the kids with a level of care I hadn't thought him capable of was so freaking hot it made my insides feel like molten lava.

I wasn't above admitting I'd stealthily moved closer as he got on the kids so I could hear what he was saying.

"Martin, you're the captain of this team. That means, when it comes to the rest of these guys, you're supposed to lead. Not only on the field, but by example. What you did today didn't just let me down, it let them down as well."

The kid he'd been talking to lowered his head, shame washing through him. "Sorry, Coach. We wanted to bring the newbies out for a little fun, is all."

Beau planted his hands on his trim hips, his expression morphing into one my dad had used on multiple occasions whenever I did something stupid growing up. But even though his disappointment in the boys was clear as day, he never raised his voice. He didn't yell or curse to get his point across, he showed a level of patience I hadn't thought he was capable of, almost as though he was handling them with care. And I'd be damned, but it seemed he was getting through to them. That Martin kid especially.

"You thought bringing your underage teammates out and getting them wasted was fun? Coming here and drinking so much you made fools of yourselves, giving the team as a whole a bad name in the process, was all fun? This bar is someone's livelihood. You ever stop to think about that? These people, they came to have a good time, not to watch a bunch of immature kids make asses of themselves. You've been such a disruption, the manager had to call me to handle you. And you think that's fun?"

The whole lot of them shrunk under his disapproving glower.

"What do you think would have happened if she'd called the cops instead of me, huh? You think the tickets each and every one of you would have been slapped with for public intoxication, drunk and disorderly, and underage drinking would have been *fun*? Would that still have been fun when you were kicked off the team for breaking the school's code of ethics?"

"No, sir," they all grumbled miserably.

Beau let out a sigh, the disappointment weighing his shoulders down as he shook his head and took a step to the side, waving them up from the table. "I ordered an Uber to take you back to campus. Get out of here. Sleep off what you can tonight. I'll finish with you tomorrow at practice."

The five of them shuffled out of the bar. No doubt, what had seemed like a brilliant idea to blow off steam was now a decision they were seriously regretting.

I expected Beau to follow after them, having taken care of what he came to do, but instead of heading to the door, he looked up, his gaze landing on mine for a beat before he started in my direction.

My chest squeezed, panic and excitement mingling together and creating something inside my belly that felt an awful lot like what happened when you dropped a Mentos in a bottle of Coke.

"Hey." His voice was deep and velvety. "You got a minute to talk?"

I wasn't sure if being alone in a small, quiet room with him was a smart idea, but I could feel people looking at us and didn't want to start any gossip, so I nodded and led him back to my office. The room wasn't very big to begin with, but when Beau stepped inside, shutting the door behind him, it felt like the space shrank in half.

The things I'd told Colbie earlier about being sad replayed in my mind as I folded my arms over my chest and rested my behind on the edge of my desk. I tried to look casual, but tension and nerves poured off me, filling the room until the air felt thick and humid.

"Thanks for, you know, handling that whole thing out there."

He reached up and rubbed at the back of his neck. "You shouldn't be thanking me. I'm sorry it happened. I appreciate you not calling Cade in. I know tonight wasn't a good indicator, but they really are good kids."

"I don't doubt that, Beau. They made a stupid decision. One of many, I'm sure, because they're still young. But you handled the whole situation well. It's obvious they respect you."

"Yeah. Maybe." Judging from the look on his face, I wasn't sure he believed that, and seeing that concern lingering in his clear blue eyes tugged at something in me, made me soften toward him more than I already was.

I cleared my throat, giving my head a shake to try and erase those thoughts like my brain was an Etch A Sketch.

"So, um . . . what did you want to talk—"

He cut me off, moving so fast I didn't see it coming. One second he was standing near the door, and the next, he was cradling my face in his large hands and sealing his mouth over mine in a searing kiss that had my toes curling inside my shoes and my heart beating right between my thighs where I wanted him the most.

A whimper vibrated up my throat as Beau dragged his tongue across the seam of my lips, requesting entrance. I was helpless to resist. My lips parted, my tongue darting out to meet his, cranking up the kiss to a thousand.

When I moaned into his mouth and parted my thighs, giving him room to squeeze between them, he emitted a ferocious growl. One moment he had my hips pressed against the desk, and the next my legs were wrapped around his waist, his hands palming my ass, and he was moving us, pinning me against the wall beside the door.

I could feel his erection pressing insistently at his fly, that steel rod cradled in the apex of my thighs.

"Mmm, Beau," I moaned against his lips, fisting his hair in my hands when he rocked his hips, prodding at my aching clit with the rock-hard cock behind his jeans.

He pulled his mouth from mine, peppering kisses along my jaw and down my neck as he whispered against my skin. "To answer your question, *this* is what I wanted to talk to you about."

With a kiss, he'd managed to scramble my brain where I could barely think, let alone speak.

"I wanted to talk about the fact that you keep running away from me, even though the chemistry between us is hot enough to put the sun to shame."

"I don't—"

He lifted his head to lock eyes with me and wrapped one large hand around my throat. He didn't apply any pressure, but something about it being there, the weight of it collaring me, sent a flood of arousal between my thighs, soaking my panties through. His thumb scraped across my bottom lip before he pressed it to silence the words spilling out of my mouth.

"No lies," he ground out. "I don't want to hear lies about you not feeling what I *know* is between us, or that it was a mistake or wrong, or any of the other bullshit you're trying to convince yourself of because you're scared."

Something moved through me. A switch flipped at being called out, but this one was completely different from the ones of the past. He'd pressed a button, but instead of triggering rage, he triggered something altogether different.

My lips parted around his thumb, drawing it into my mouth and sucking before scraping my bottom teeth across the pad of it.

My eyes dropped to half-mast as his own flared, a rumble rattling from deep in his chest.

"Don't tell me there's nothing between us when I know if I were to slide my hand inside your panties right now, I'd find you dripping for me."

I sucked his thumb even harder as a wave of need crashed into me.

He leaned in, dragging the top of his nose across my neck to the shell of my ear before nipping on the lobe. "I'm right, aren't I?"

A jerky exhale escaped my lungs as my head bounced on a frantic nod.

"You want to come, baby?"

"Yes, Beau," I breathed out, wanting a release in that moment more than I wanted my next breath.

He hummed in my ear, rolling his hips to press his erection harder against me. "Then be a good girl for me. You know what to do."

A tremor wracked through my whole body. "Please," I begged, my voice nearly a whine. "Please, Beau. Make me come."

A sound of satisfaction worked its way up his throat as he released my throat and slid his hand down my body. In the blink of an eye, he had the button popped and the zipper lowered on my jeans, his fingertips teasing the waistband of my lacy pink thong.

"If I give you this, are you going to run from me again?"

I shook my head, but apparently that wasn't good enough. "I need the words, Bubbles. Are you going to run from me?"

"No," I breathed as his hand dipped inside my panties and slid deeper to cup my aching pussy.

A growl rattled in his chest. "Fucking knew it. So goddamn soaked you're drenching my palm. You want to come on my fingers?"

"I do. God, so bad. *Please.*"

"Jesus," he hissed. "You beg so fucking good, baby." With that, he stuffed two fingers inside me at the same time he slammed his mouth down on mine, swallowing the cry that poured out as my pussy clamped down around the long, thick digits.

"Ask me to fuck you with my fingers, Presley."

I didn't hesitate to do as he ordered. "Please, Beau. Fuck me with your fingers."

As soon as the request left my mouth, he drove those digits in and out. The sound of my pussy trying to suck him back in with every outward stroke filled my office, along with his ragged breathing and the moans I muffled by dropping my head and biting down on his shoulder.

"Christ, I can feel how close you already are. No one else can do this for you, can they?" he asked, curling his fingers to brush against that hidden spot deep inside me that no other man had ever found before him, the one guaranteed to set me off.

"No one," I told him as my thighs clenched his hips tighter and I began to rock against his touch, desperate to meet the release barreling head-on at lightning speed. "No one makes me feel like you do," I admitted, the words spilling out of their own accord. But I would have been lying if I claimed they weren't the truth. No one had ever affected me the way Beau did, on every single level.

"That's right, baby. No one can do for you what I can. So tell me, baby, who does this pussy belong to?"

I wasn't sure what it was about his need to claim me and for me to validate that claim that turned me on so fucking much, but I was done trying to deny it. "You, baby," I panted as pressure and heat built deep in my core.

"Goddamn right. Ride my hand. Take what you want. It's yours." He picked up the pace, fucking his fingers harder into me, brushing against my G-spot every single time. When his thumb came into the mix, pressing hard against my clit, stars exploded across my vision.

"You're mine, Presley. You have been longer than either of us was willing to admit, and I'm done letting you run from me." He dragged his teeth up the column of my neck as he worked me to near oblivion. "Now that I finally have you, I'm not letting go. Now come for me, baby."

On that order, I exploded, the tingle in my core sank in on itself before exploding outward, blasting me into a million pieces. I came so hard I felt it in my toes, all the way up to the ends of my hair. My whole body vibrated.

Beau silenced my cries of his name with his mouth, driving his tongue against mine in the same way his fingers plunged inside me.

He worked me until the very end, until there was nothing left and I collapsed against him on a tremulous exhale.

"Oh my god," I breathed once I returned to consciousness. "That was . . . *incredible*."

Beau slipped his hand from my pants, his gaze staying pinned to mine as he lifted his drenched fingers to his lips and sucked them into his mouth, licking my arousal off as his eyes rolled back in his head.

"Christ," he grunted. "No, baby, what's incredible is how fucking delicious you taste."

My cheeks heated and I ducked my head in his neck to hide the sudden flush of shyness that crashed into me. His body shook on a quiet chuckle. "My new favorite flavor is Presley Fields," he declared, his voice sounding awfully joyful for a man who was still poking me with a massive iron rod that hadn't gone down.

I lifted my head, catching my bottom lip between my

teeth as I looked at him. His gaze turned tender as he leaned in to press a quick, sweet kiss against my lips.

"What now?" I managed to ask through my nerves. I couldn't shake the feeling there was still that other freaking shoe, but I was done letting the fear of it falling dictate my life.

"Well, now you get back to work and I go out and sit at the bar since it's my agreed upon night that Freddy and I worked out."

I batted my lashes as a slow smile tugged at my lips. I really liked the thought of that.

"Mmm," he hummed pleasurably. "Then I'll help you close up and drive you back to my house, where I'm going to spend the rest of the night fucking you until you can't move and memorizing every inch of this body that I've been obsessed with since I was old enough to realize cooties didn't matter for shit."

I let out a giggle that he quickly kissed from my lips, like he wanted to keep it for himself. "That sound good to you?"

It really freaking did. "I think I can work with that. But even if you don't eat or drink anything, you still have to tip the bartenders handsomely," I bartered. "You can afford it, and they depend on those tips."

"Deal."

With one last lingering kiss, he lowered me back to my

feet and reached into his pants to adjust himself before leaving my office. And by the time I got myself cleaned up and headed to the front of the bar, he was already sitting on the stool next to Freddy, a Coke in front of each of them as they chatted like they were longtime buds.

Twenty-Seven

I WASN'T SURE WHY, but as Beau turned the car into his driveway, a rush of butterflies woke up in my stomach and took flight. I felt like a high school girl on her prom night who was finally planning on giving it up to her boyfriend. Which was ironic, considering I could still feel Beau's ministrations from earlier every time I moved. It had caused me to squirm all night long, keeping me in a constant state of arousal. I was pretty sure from the heated looks and smiles Beau kept throwing my way, he knew exactly how crazy he'd been driving me without having to do a damn thing.

"Wow," I breathed as I leaned forward in my seat to get a better view of his house through the windshield. "This is some place you got here."

On the level of ostentatious, it was nowhere near his

parents' house, but it was still leaps and bounds from my older, much smaller home. Now that I saw where he was living, I couldn't help but feel a little embarrassed of my own. "Man, my place must have felt like a shoe box in comparison."

He stopped in the center of the circular drive, right in front of the door. Throwing his SUV into park, he killed the engine and turned my way. "I liked your house."

I snorted and rolled my eyes. "Sure you did."

"Hey." He reached out, taking my chin between his fingers and turning my head so I was facing him. "Don't do that. When I say something, you need to know I mean it. I liked your house. I didn't even think about the size. I just thought about the fact that it smelled like you, about how it felt warm and homey because of the way you decorated it. How I could see you in every corner of the place, because you made it yours. So, baby, I liked your house." He stressed that last part slowly, leaning in so I could see the sincerity in his gaze before he gave me another of those quick pecks, like he couldn't be close and *not* kiss me.

"Come on. It's late and you're probably tired."

He hopped out of the car, leaving me confused as he rounded the hood and came to my door, pulling it open for me and taking me by the hand. But he didn't just hold it, he laced his long fingers through mine in a way that felt much more intimate, like, to him, I was something to be cherished.

"What's with the face?" he asked, looking at me over his shoulder as he led me to the front door and unlocked it.

"It's just . . . I thought you said we were gonna . . ." I lifted my shoulder in a shy shrug as I bit the corner of my lip. "You know."

"Ah, yes. That I was going to fuck you until you couldn't move?"

My cheeks caught fire as I ducked my head. "Yeah. That."

He threw the door open, a huge grin on his face as he led me inside. "Well, I was going to, but then you yawned at least five times on the drive here. I want you to be able to enjoy our night together, not go catatonic on me because you're exhausted."

He started flipping light switches, illuminating the place.

"Oh." I paused, looking around the big open space. "Wow. How—Beau, you've been here several weeks now, how do you still have this many boxes left to unpack?"

He looked around, his face pinched in offense. "Excuse you, but I've been busy."

I snorted then curled my lips between my teeth to keep

from laughing. "Busy? Or just hate unpacking so you're finding any excuse not to do it."

He grinned and continued pulling me through the house and down the hall. "Maybe a little of both."

"Hey, slow down, would you?" I had to hop-skip just to keep up with his long strides. "You aren't giving me a chance to scope the place out."

"You can do all the scoping you want another time. After you get a full eight hours." It was as if he were excited about the prospect of the two of us sharing a bed together. It was actually kind of . . . sweet. Okay, there was no kind of about it. It was incredibly sweet.

We entered what I could only assume was his bedroom, and I had to admit, I was impressed. There were no boxes in here—at least none I could see—and the décor was dark and masculine without crossing the line into gaudy or dreary. The furniture was a rich, dark wood with navy bedding and the walls were slate gray. Pops of complementing colors were with the accents, and put all together like it was, it really worked, making the room feel like a comforting embrace rather than moody and claustrophobic. The large picture window overlooking the ocean probably filled the room with natural light during the day, but the only thing it was letting in right now was a bit of silvery moonlight.

"Here." Beau stepped in front of me, extending the

shirt he was holding. "I don't know what you usually sleep in, but I thought this might work. The bathroom's right through there. There's an extra toothbrush in the middle drawer. Help yourself to anything else you might need."

I took the shirt from his hand and smiled up at him through my lashes as I whispered my thanks and headed for the bathroom.

I could have changed in front of him. It wasn't like he hadn't seen me naked. Hell, he'd been up close and extremely personal with the most intimate part of me, but for some reason, getting dressed to go to bed with him— just to sleep—held a different level of intimacy, and I needed a bit of privacy, just for a moment, as I wrapped my head around the shift that had taken place in our relationship over the past few hours.

Talk about a massive turn of the tides.

This wasn't a drop from the top of a rollercoaster or an unexpected reaction to the turmoil he stirred up in me. What I was about to do was a conscious decision to step out from behind those walls that had been guarding my heart for a very long time. It was me choosing him— choosing *us*—even though I still had uncertainties. Instead of letting my guard down in the heat of the moment, I was doing it purposely.

I stripped out of my clothes, leaving on my underwear,

before shaking out the shirt Beau had given me and sliding it over my head and down my body.

It was a shirt for his former football team, and despite me being five seven, Beau was still so much bigger I swam in the thing. It smelled just like him, and in the privacy of the bathroom, I gave in to the desire to pull the shirt over my nose and sniff deeply as a ridiculous smile split my face in half. The soft, faded cotton felt like it had been washed a million times giving it that perfect worn-in feel.

When I stepped out of the bathroom a couple minutes later, all the lights were off except for a golden glow coming from the lamp on Beau's bedside table. The man in question was currently sitting beneath the covers on the left side of the bed. His back was resting against the headboard, the sheet pooling at his waist, revealing all those delicious muscles, and I had the deep, yearning desire to trace all those deep ridges with my tongue as soon as possible.

"Fuck me, Bubbles," he grunted as soon as he looked up and saw me standing there. "I love you in my shirt. In fact, I think that's all you should wear from here on out. All day, every day, my shirts only."

I giggled as I moved toward the bed. "Might be a little uncomfortable come winter."

His smile was downright wicked. "Oh, don't worry about that. I promise to keep you plenty warm."

I just bet he did.

The muscles in his torso clenched as he threw the covers back and patted the mattress beside him, silently telling me to climb in.

He might have thought I looked good in his shirt, but it was nothing compared to the sight of him *without* one. The man was mouthwatering, and I couldn't help but lick my lips as I dragged my gaze over his strong, drool-worthy body while climbing onto the bed on my knees.

Beau let out a groan that sounded almost pained. "Baby, you can't look at me like that. You keep that up, I'm gonna stay hard all goddamn night, then neither of us will get any sleep."

I opened my mouth to tell him I was more than okay with that when a big, jaw-cracking yawn cut me off.

He chuckled, reached across the mattress to snag me around my waist, and pulled me all the way across onto his side.

"Yeah, that's what I thought." He moved me easily enough, curling me so that my back was pressed into his chest, our legs tangled together beneath the covers. He switched off the lamp, bathing the room in darkness before settling in behind me, draping his heavy arm over my waist, and holding on tight.

I wasn't sure how I'd expected him to sleep, but in all

my years, I never would have imagined Beau Wade to be a spooner.

"I can hear your brain spinning," he said quietly into the dark, his words whispering across the back of my neck before he lowered his head and pressed the sweetest, most tender kiss to my shoulder. "What are you thinking about?"

"Nothing important." I bit down on my bottom lip. "I guess I'm just surprised that you're a cuddler."

I felt him stiffen behind me, but he didn't let me go. "Do you not like it?"

"No. I do! I mean, I'm totally fine with it." To prove my point, I wriggled even deeper into him, the warmth he was throwing off was like a heated blanket, and it was comfortable as hell. "I just didn't think it would be something you're into."

He was silent for a moment as he gave my statement some thought. "I guess I never really thought about it, but, no, I don't think I've ever really been a big cuddler. Until now."

Something warm bloomed to life deep in my belly. "Oh?" I asked into the darkness. "What's so special about now?"

"It's you," he answered simply, without a moment of hesitation. And damn if I didn't love hearing that.

I snuggled even deeper into him, loving the way his

arm clenched tighter around me as he brushed more kisses on my shoulder and neck. The biggest, goofiest smile overtook my face as I burrowed into the softest pillow I'd ever laid my head on. In fact, the whole bed felt like being nested in a cloud.

"I find that reason to be acceptable," I said, trying to play cool even though I was sure he could hear the giddiness in my voice.

Beau's body shook against mine. "Glad you approve, baby. Now get some sleep."

I wasn't sure that would be possible. The excitement he'd shown earlier when it came to us sharing a bed had suddenly rubbed off. It felt like my tummy was full of champagne bubbles. I was certain there was no way I was going to get to sleep. But not even two minutes later, I was dead to world, sleeping the deepest, most peaceful sleep I'd had in a very long time.

Twenty-Eight

BEAU

I BLINKED MY EYES OPEN, taking in the pale purple of the sky outside the bedroom window as the sun slowly began rising over the sand and ocean beyond the glass. It was the kind of view I didn't think I'd ever get tired of waking up to and a large reason why I had no issue offering full asking price after my assistant showed me the pictures of this place.

I was usually up by now, heading out for my morning run on the beach, but after the best night's sleep of my life, the last thing I wanted to do was drag my ass out of this bed for an early morning run. I had a much better idea of how to get my heart rate up this morning, and I intended on doing it with the woman who had spent the entire night in my arms.

Speaking of . . . I reached across the bed for Presley,

planning to wake her up with my face between her thighs, but instead of finding her, my hand landed on cold sheets.

"Bubbles?" My voice was rough with sleep as I sat up and looked toward the bathroom, thinking she might be in there, but the door was open and the light was off.

Panic shot through me as I strained my ears, listening for any sounds coming from somewhere else in my house. "Presley."

There was nothing.

Throwing the covers off, my feet hit the floor and I bolted for the door in nothing but my underwear, not even stopping to throw on some sweats as I booked it out of the room and down the hall. So help me god, if she got freaked and ran again, I was going to track her down, drag her ass back here, and tie her to my goddamn bed until she finally accepted that this was happened.

"Presley!" I shouted, dread dripping from my voice as my heart started beating dangerously fast.

Then I heard it. Her sweet, melodic voice echoing down the hallway. "In the kitchen."

My entire body sagged with relief as I rounded the corner and spotted Presley in front of my fridge, the door open as she peered inside. Her hair hung down her back in long, golden sheets, the strands slightly wavy from sleep. She was still wearing the shirt I'd given her the night before, looking like a goddamn vision. The cotton hit her at mid-thigh, showing off long, smooth, toned legs that I couldn't wait to have wrapped around me again.

She turned to look back at me, smiling in a way that slammed right into my chest and filled me with warmth.

"Hey." Her face had that soft, sleepy quality to it but lit up when she saw me in a way it never had before. It was a look I'd never seen on her, but now that I had, I wanted to see it every morning for the rest of my life. "Good morning. I was going to make some breakfast, but did you know you don't have any food in this place?" My feet came unglued and headed right for her as she continued. "The best I could do was some coffee. But we have to drink it black." Her smile fell, her expression growing concerned as I closed in on her. "Are you okay? What's—"

I kept moving, forcing her backward until her back hit the wall, then I removed the mug from her hand and placed it on the counter so I could take her face in my hands and press deep against her as I sealed my mouth over hers in a kiss that was charged with everything I was feeling, from the relief that she was still here to the need that seemed to grow stronger with each passing day. By the time I pulled back, lowering my forehead to hers as I dragged my thumbs along her silky jawline, we were both breathing heavily.

"Morning, baby." My voice came out rough and craggy, dripping with every emotion swirling inside of me.

Her hands came up, her fingers combing softly through my hair, and my eyes closed at the gentle, soothing touch as I leaned into it. I couldn't get enough of touching her, and the only thing better was when she touched me back.

"You okay?"

After one last kiss, I pulled back just enough to smile down at her. "I'm perfect now that I know you didn't take off on me."

Her lips parted in surprise. "Oh. No. I wasn't going to—"

"I know. I just panicked for a moment." Christ, it felt good waking up to her, knowing she was still under my roof, walking around in nothing but my shirt and—I caught sight of her feet and arched my brow. "Are those my winter socks?" They were way too big for her and slouched down around her ankles, the toes flopping well past her own. They looked absolutely ridiculous on her, but also cute as hell.

She held a foot out and pointed her toe. "My feet got cold, so I went rummaging. Hope you don't mind."

I didn't mind one damn bit. I slid my fingers through her long silky hair. Now that I could touch her all I wanted, I couldn't seem to make myself stop. "Bubbles, what's mine is yours. You never have to ask."

She got a soft, dreamy look in her eyes as she lifted up

on those toes and pressed a kiss to my lips. "Good to know. But I actually do have one question I've been meaning to ask you."

I dragged my nose along the column of her neck. "Shoot."

"Why do you always do this?"

I brought my head up, my brows furrowing at her question. "Do what?"

"This." She waved her hand in the air, circling where we were pressed together. "You always push me up against a nearby wall and hold me there. Don't get me wrong, I'm not complaining." Her cheeks turned that pink I loved so much as her tongue slid across her bottom lip. "It's actually really hot. I'm just wondering why."

"I guess it's because I'm still struggling to believe this is real," I said in a low, quiet voice. "You've slipped through my fingers so many times in the past, I feel like I need to hold on to you so it doesn't happen again."

Those eyes of hers were pure gold, looking back and forth between my own without a hint of worry or animosity or anger. She was looking at me the same way she looked at all the other people she cared about.

No, that wasn't right. There was actually more to it. So much more. I'd wanted that smile and those honey eyes I'd seen her give others for so long, but what she was giving me was a look I'd never seen her give anyone else.

I brushed her hair back, tucking it behind her ear and sliding my fingers down to caress her neck. "What are you thinking right now?"

Her tongue came out to wet her lips as she looked down at my own. "I'm thinking . . ." She stopped and pulled in a deep breath. "I'm thinking that I really liked that answer," she finally whispered. "And I'm thinking that I really, *really* want you to keep your word on what you promised me last night." Those eyes returned to mine, the honey going dark as her pupils expanded. "After I taste you, though, because I've been dying to suck your cock for longer than I can remember."

A growl ripped from my throat as I pushed back, leaning against the counter behind me. My dick was already hard as stone, straining the front of my boxer briefs like it was trying to bust through.

She inched toward me, her pace slow and seductive as she bit that goddamn bottom lip of hers, her eyelids going half-mast as she let her gaze slide up and down, taking me all in.

"Shirt off," I ordered gruffly. "I want to see you while you're on your knees with my cock stretching your lips."

Her smile was pure temptation as she reached down to toy with the hem of the shirt. "You mean this?" she teased, lifting it just enough to give me a peek of pink lace beneath. "You want me to take this off?"

My hands fisted the edge of the counter so tight it was a wonder I didn't crush the porcelain in my grip. "You know goddamn well I do."

She finally put me out of my misery, whipping the material over her head and extending her arm to the side to drop it on the floor as she continued slinking to me. She placed her palms on my chest, curling her fingers just enough for her nails to scratch lightly as she dragged them across my pecs and down the valleys of my abdominals. "Is this how you want me?" she asked in a breathy voice as she pressed those fucking perfect tits against me and rose up to brush her lips against mine.

I released the counter and reached around to grab her ass, moaning when I encountered skin. That sexy piece of fabric between her thighs was a thong, and as embarrassing as it was to admit, the realization that she spent the night with her ass cradled against my dick, nothing but a flimsy little string to separate us, was almost enough to make me lose it.

Leaning in, I deepened the kiss before taking her bottom lip between my teeth and tugging it. "Presley, I want you any fucking way I can have you. But right now, I want you on your knees and swallowing my cock until it bumps the back of your throat." I fisted her hair and tilted her head back. "I want to hear you gag on it."

Her eyes went glassy, then she was lowering herself to

the floor in front of me. The globes of her ass were on perfect display, that sexy pink lace stretching around her hips just beneath the two dimples at the small of her back. That, combined with the way she licked her lips and stared up at me through that thick fan of lashes as she reached for the waistband of my underwear, pulling it low so my cock could spring free, was one of the hottest fucking things I'd seen in my life.

She let out a hum just before darting her tongue out to swipe the bead of pre-cum that had formed there, forcing a hiss from between my clenched teeth.

"Mmm, Beau. Have I told you lately that you have the most beautiful cock?" she asked, that flush on the apples of her cheeks extending all the way down her chest to her tits, making her nipples pucker. "I never thought I would describe a dick as beautiful, but yours is. I can't get enough of it."

"Presley," I ground out.

"I want you to do something for me," she continued. "I want you to fuck my mouth. Don't be soft with me, baby. I want you to fuck it like you can't get enough of me."

I fisted my hand in her hair, wrapping it around my wrist and pulling her head back, causing her lips to part. "That's not going to be a problem, because I already can't get enough of you. Now open your pretty mouth so I can stuff it full."

She flattened her tongue, sticking it out in invitation, and, holding her head steady, I slid my cock right in, groaning at the feel of her warm, wet mouth closing around my length.

"God*damn*," I grunted as I pulled out and shoved back in. "Fuck, baby. *Fuck*! Your mouth feels so good."

She held my cock at the base with one hand while reaching around with the other and grabbing hold of my ass, digging her nails into my flesh in a silent order to do as she'd asked.

I drove in harder, a sharp bark falling past my lips when I bumped the back of her throat. I felt her gag just before she swallowed around the crown, the muscles in her throat squeezing tight. I picked up the pace, my hands tightening in her hair, my thumbs brushing against her hollowed cheeks so she could suck me hard each time I pulled out. It was the best goddamn blowjob of my life. Nothing else came close to comparing. I was already on the brink, and she hadn't even been at it all that long.

I could feel my balls draw up as my hips snapped forward and back. Saliva dripped from the sides of her mouth as she hummed, gripping the base of my shaft tighter and plunging the other hand into her panties.

Her eyes rolled back as her fingers moved between her

thighs. She fucked herself with her fingers as I fucked her throat, the sight of it driving me out of my mind.

"Does having your lips stretched around my cock make you wet?"

She hummed again, nodding as she looked up at me with those hazy eyes.

My lips pulled back from my teeth as I fought my body's need to come, to blow down her throat, forcing her to swallow every single drop. I wasn't ready yet. I didn't want this to end. And as enticing as the thought of spraying my cum on her tits or ass was, that could wait for another time. I wanted to be inside her when I came. I wanted to coat her walls with my release.

"Show me."

On a needy whimper, she pulled her hand free and lifted it, showing me the slick digits. I bent forward, grabbing her wrist and sucking those fingers into my mouth, my eyes rolling back at her flavor bursting on my tongue. And that was all I could take.

One moment I was in her mouth, and the next I was hauling her off the floor, whipping us around, and depositing her on the counter I'd been leaning against.

"I wasn't done," she said with a cheeky pout through swollen lips, but I cut her objection off when I reached between us and pushed her thong aside. I grabbed my cock and lined it up with her opening, then in one thrust, I buried myself balls deep.

Presley screamed my name, her walls clamping down around me already. Christ, she really had been turned on from sucking me off, because she was already close.

"I'll let you finish me off next time," I grunted as I powered in and out of her perfect cunt, my cock glistening with her arousal. "I'll blow my load wherever you want. But I needed to be inside you more than I needed my next breath."

"Oh shit, Beau!" she cried out, arching her back so deep her hair hung nearly to the counter. I leaned forward, sucking one of those candy pink nipples into my mouth as I fucked her hard and fast, my cock plunging into her so hard the kitchen filled with the sounds of skin slapping skin. "Yes, baby. Just like that. Oh my god, you always fuck me so good."

A sound of animalistic pride tore through my chest as I placed my palm between her breasts and pushed so she was spread out on the counter in front of me like the most delicious feast.

Her tits bounced with each punishing thrust, her hair hung over the counter, and I had the perfect view of my fat cock sliding in and out of heaven.

Christ, I was so close, between her mouth and her cunt gripping me, I wasn't going to last much longer. Palming one breast, I plucked and pinched at her nipple as I braced my other hand right above her mound so I could circle her clit with my thumb. "Fucking come for me, Presley. Don't hold back. I want you to scream my name as you drench my cock."

Her walls clamped down and every muscle in her body locked tight, her back arching off the counter as she screamed my name like I'd ordered.

"That's it, baby. Fuck, such a good girl. Look at you. Jesus, so goddamn beautiful when you come for me."

I buried myself deep and threw my head back, roaring out my own release so strong I thought the back of my skull had been blown clean off. I collapsed on top of Presley, wrapping my arms between her and the counter and holding her as close to me as possible while still deep inside her as we worked to regulate our breathing.

She gently played with my hair as I peppered her chest with kisses, both of us content to be quiet as we came down from the highest high I'd ever experienced.

"Beau?" she finally asked after a few minutes had passed.

I lifted my head and smiled drunkenly down at her—at the woman I had fallen head first into love with. "Yeah, Bubbles?"

"That was fantastic. Every bit of it from start to finish. But as perfect as your dick is, it doesn't count as breakfast, so I'm going to need you to feed me."

I blinked, my mind absorbing what she'd just said. Then my head fell back in a long, deep belly laugh.

Could my girl possibly get any more perfect?

Twenty-Nine

BEAU

STANDING ON THE SIDELINES, I gave my whistle a sharp burst and set the five boys still on the field off to running. Practice was technically over, but after doing some thinking on it, I'd decided on the perfect punishment for the guys who'd gone to Dropped Anchor the night before and acted like asses.

That was why, after a long, grueling practice, complete with a bitch of a hangover for all of them, they were now doing shuttle runs after a brutal set of gassers and wind sprints, followed by up-downs.

Brad chuckled beside me, his arms crossed over his chest. Sunglasses shielding his face as he watched the torture continue. "Twenty on Ramirez being the first to hurl."

Ramirez was one of the freshmen new to the team. He was one hell of a cornerback.

I studied the kids as they slugged their way through their punishment. "Nah. My money's on Johnson. Kid's looking a little green."

Just then, our outside linebacker, Derek Sanders, bent at the waist and lost his breakfast right there on the field.

"Oh!" Brad let out a laugh, punching a fist into his hand. "Looks like we were both wrong."

Sanders puking kicked off a chain reaction, and in no time, all five of them where hurling, making noises like they were expelling the devil himself from their bodies.

"Jesus." My defensive coordinator, Matt Anderson, curled his top lip in disgust, but it didn't stop him from popping a handful of sunflower seeds into his mouth, the man's snack of choice. "Think we need a priest out here to perform an exorcism?"

I smiled and shook my head. "Nah. Think they've gotten it out of their systems."

Matt nodded. "Well, I think it's safe to say these boys won't be fucking up any time soon."

I blew my whistle again and waved them over, putting them out of their misery. "Think you learned your lesson?"

Five heads nodded miserably.

"Fu—I mean, hell yeah, Coach," Sanders answered. "Don't think I'll ever drink again."

I chuckled, knowing better. Famous last words.

Ramirez looked at me with a hangdog expression. "We're really sorry we caused trouble at your girl's bar."

I lifted my brows and rocked back on my heels. "What makes you think she's my girl?"

That got a smile out of the young kid. "You mean besides the fact you couldn't stop staring at her when you walked in?"

Johnson piped up then. "She's a freakin' smoke show, Coach. I'd high-five you if I didn't think I'd puke on your shoes."

Matt and Brad laughed under their breaths.

"Thanks for the restraint," I told them. "Now hit the showers."

They took off for the field house, but Martin hung back, still looking like he'd been put through the wringer, but there was something else in his expression as well. "You got something you want to add?" I asked the kid, giving him the opportunity to get off what was obviously weighing on his chest.

I had to hand it to him, he met my gaze head-on and didn't waver as he said, "I screwed up last night, Coach. Everything you said about me being a leader hit really hard, and I just want you to know, I take that position seriously. I know I let you down. I let myself and my team-mates down as well. I wanted to give you my word that it won't happen again."

I gave my chin a jerk in acknowledgement and watched him take off after the rest of the guys. And for the first time since taking this position, I started to think that maybe I could do this after all. Maybe I could make a difference with these kids. Maybe the faith Sam had in me wasn't misplaced after all.

I was about to dismiss the rest of the coaching staff when something caught Brad's attention, making him groan.

"Christ, not this shit. The season hasn't even started yet, and administration is letting people in to watch our practices?"

Matt grunted in agreement. "Last thing I'm up for is a schmooze fest with whoever the fuck that is."

I turned to see who they were talking about, and despite the warm temps, felt my body temperature drop at least ten degrees as the blood in my veins turned to ice.

"That's not someone whose ass you have to kiss," I grumbled as my hands clenched into fists.

"Yeah? You know that guy?"

I did. Unfortunately.

"Yeah. That's my father." *Fuck me.* "You guys can head out. I've got this."

Matt chuckled and bumped my shoulder. "What? You don't want us to meet your pops? You embarrassed of us or something?"

I gave him a hard look. "Not of you."

They read my meaning loud and clear, each of them clapping me on the shoulder before taking off.

The woman who'd been escorting my old man pointed me out, giving him a polite smile before turning and heading back to the offices.

This was the last fucking thing I wanted to do, especially when I'd had such a spectacular start to my day. But I should have known better. Things with my Bubbles were finally on the path I'd wanted to be on for so goddamn long. I should have known Hank Wade would appear to try and fuck it up. But I'd be damned if I let him this time.

I started in his direction, meeting him near the twenty-yard line. Stopping a couple feet away, I braced my feet shoulder-width apart and folded my arms across my chest. Nothing about my demeanor was inviting in the slightest.

"What are you doing here?"

He shoved his hands in the pockets of his perfectly-ironed slacks. It was clear the man had come from work, I just didn't know why he'd wasted his time. "Is that any way to talk to your old man, boy?"

This fucking guy. "It is when the old man in question is a piece of shit. And I haven't been a boy in a long fucking time." I got a sick sense of pleasure at the fact that I now topped the man by at least two inches and several pounds of muscle. He was still in decent shape, but there was no stopping time, and age was starting to make the man a little soft around the middle. "Now say why you're here then get the hell off my field."

"You haven't been answering my calls."

"Yeah. That's by design. I was hoping you'd take the hint, but apparently, I'm not that lucky."

His cheeks went ruddy with anger, his nostrils flaring like a pissed-off bull, but despite the man's incredibly inflated ego and narcissistic tendencies, he no longer had the power he once wielded. "I suggest you watch how you speak to me—"

"Call me boy one more time, and I'll frog march your ass right out of here myself."

"Where the hell's your respect, huh? I'm still your father."

Christ, talk about laughable.

I took a step closer, taking immense pleasure in the tiniest little flinch that pulled at his features before he masked it. "You're my father, sure. But as far as I'm concerned, that label means nothing. You haven't done a goddamn thing in my entire life to earn it, or my respect, except get Mom pregnant. As far as I'm concerned, you don't even exist, old man. This is my field, and as of this moment, you're not welcome here. And you can bet your ass I'll be letting administration know."

I pushed past him, more than ready to put him in my rear view when he spoke again.

"Heard through the grapevine that you and that gutter trash were looking awfully cozy last night."

I whipped around and was in his face in the blink of an eye, my vision painted red as I bared my teeth. "You watch how you talk about her. You hear me?"

"I told you to stay the hell away from that girl. Warned you what would happen if you defied me. Looks like you didn't listen."

I let out a bark of caustic laughter. He was unbelievable. "You really are pathetic," I said, shaking my head in disbelief. "Christ, you really think you still hold all the cards. I've got news for you. You stopped having any sort of power a long time ago. You think you're the big man in this town? Push me, and I'll show you who's bigger. Your money and status don't mean shit anymore. You go after Presley's parents, I'll show you who really has the power. Don't test me."

The smile that stretched across his face was enough to send a chill through the bright, sunny day. "Who said anything about going after her parents?"

A growl ripped from my throat. "You stay the fuck away from her. You hear me?"

"Oh, I don't need to go anywhere near her to crush her dreams, son. Just remember that."

On that note, he turned on his loafers and walked off the field like he didn't have a care in the world.

I didn't know what the hell he was planning, but there was no way I was going to let that bastard win. I was finally fucking happy, and I'd be damned if I let him take that away from me . . . again.

Thirty

PRESLEY

EVERYTHING IN MY BODY TIGHTENED, my impending release threatening to overtake me, swallow me whole. Beau looked up at me from where he was stretched out on the bed, his hand holding my hips in a near bruising grip as he snapped his hips upward, driving his cock deeper inside me from below.

I'd been riding him up until a second ago when he'd lost all control and took over, fucking into me with the kind of brutal power that only made me burn hotter. Every time with him was as good as the last, if not better. We'd officially been together for a week now, and I still couldn't get enough of him. I wasn't sure I ever would, and that was fine with me.

I never knew it could be like this. Not with Beau, at least. Not given our past history. But every time the man walked into a room, a fresh wave of butterflies took over my belly. Just thinking about him made me smile.

I'd been nervous as hell to tell my parents what was going on between us, but once they'd seen how happy I was, they'd given in. Joyfully on my mom's part, but with a lot of hesitance and threats of dismemberment on my father's if Beau were to ever hurt me.

When I'd informed Beau he was expected at the next Sunday dinner, instead of being scared or intimidated like I thought he'd be, he'd actually smiled.

"Can't wait to show your folks how much you mean to me, Bubbles," he'd assured me when I asked him why he wasn't worried. "I'm sure once they see how good I intend to treat you, they'll give me their blessing."

I admired his confidence.

"Jesus, *fuck*," Beau grunted from beneath me.

I stared down at him, at his gorgeous face contorted like he was in the very best kind of pain, as my hands braced on his firm pecs, my fingers curled to dig my nails in as his thick cock stroked against my G-spot. The little crescent shaped indents I left behind on his skin made my clit pulse as I rode him harder, faster, while he fucked himself up into me. It was like I'd marked him, branded him as mine.

Ladies and gentlemen, I've licked Beau Wade, so he's mine. Move along.

His abs bunched as he gripped me even harder, and there was nothing in the world like watching my man lose control.

"Fuck, fuck, *fuck*! Gonna come, baby."

That first hot spurt of his release painting my walls set me off. My head fell back as my body writhed on top of him, the noises that left my mouth so loud they made my throat burn, but I couldn't stop. It was just so. *Damn. Good*! Every single time.

I collapsed on top of him in a sweaty, boneless heap, nuzzling his chest and peppering kisses along my marks as he wrapped his arms around me and held me against him.

I could feel his heart beating against my chest, and it felt like it was in tandem with my own.

"Christ," he grunted before letting out a chuckle. "Now that's how you start a day. This is how every morning should be."

I giggled as I shifted so his softening dick slipped out and I could slide down his side, cuddling against him. I traced random patterns on his chest, agreeing wholeheartedly about starting each day with knee-shaking, earth-moving sex. These were my favorite moments. The ones that came *after*. When it was just us, lying in bed wrapped in each other.

We might not have been together for very long, but it didn't feel new to me. It was as though our past, our turbulent history, created a bond stronger than most other new relationships.

He'd come to the bar every night I worked and sat there, cutting up with Freddy and the rest of my staff, enjoying a Coke while he waited for me to get off. Then he'd take me home, but instead of my place, I'd ended up every night in his bed, and I had to say, I didn't mind in the slightest. The nights I'd spent next to Beau, wrapped in his embrace, were some of the best sleep I'd ever gotten, and I was quickly coming to love his house, cluttered boxes and all.

The size might have intimidated me at first, but I was getting used to it. I could see that, once it was finished, it would feel just as homey as my place. I loved waking up to the view of the sun breaking over the rolling waves just beyond the window. More than once, I'd taken my yoga mat out there, and while Beau took his morning run along the beach, I started my day with a pleasant flow.

Beau's fingers combed through my hair as he let out a deep, contented sigh. "What are you thinking about, baby?"

I really loved that he asked me that.

"At the moment I'm thinking that you need to shower and get to practice, but that I really don't want to get out of this bed."

"Then don't."

I hummed, brushing a kiss to his ribs and grinning when he jolted and let out a grunt. I'd discovered his most ticklish spot the other night, and I wasn't above using it to my advantage. "If only."

"No, I'm serious." He rolled to his side, bracing his head in his hand as he stared down at me with such tender affection, still toying with my hair. "Stay. I want you to. It's your day off, and, honestly, I like the idea of you being in my home when I'm not here. I'll give you the spare key. It's yours, baby. To keep."

I blinked, nibbling on my lower lip as a slow smile stretched across my face. "You want me to have a key to your place? Isn't it a little soon?" I teased.

"I don't give a shit if it's soon or not. I want you here. Hell, if I could, I'd move all your things in tomorrow."

The air whooshed from my lungs with that declaration. My heart flipped over in my chest as Beau collared my neck with his hand, something he'd been doing more and more, and something I really freaking liked.

"Beau," I whispered, my throat suddenly feeling tight.

"I haven't exactly hidden how I feel about you, Bubbles. I've wanted this—*you*—longer than I can remember. All those years were a waste. Now that I have you, I can't imagine my life without you. I get you're probably a bit further behind in this than I am. That's my fault. While my feelings for you were growing, you spent the past several years hating me. But I'm willing to wait for you to catch up. Just as long as you're mine."

"I am," I breathed. "I'm yours, Beau."

He smiled, and my chest squeezed. "That's all I care about."

He sat up, grabbing me beneath my arms and hauling me up so fast I let out a squealed giggle as he climbed out of the bed, holding me in a way that I had to wrap around him like a koala to keep from falling.

"Come on. I want to fuck you in the shower before I have to leave for work."

Colbie: *Gah! I'm so jealous of you right now! All dicked up and blissfully in love.*

I let out a laugh as I fell to my back on Beau's couch. After a round of shower sex that left me momentarily unable to walk, I made a quick breakfast with the groceries Beau and I bought at the store the other day so he had *something* in the house, kissed my man goodbye, and sent him off to work. Then, mainly because I'd never been all that good at lying around and doing nothing, I'd done a bit of yoga, then started tackling the boxes that still needed to be unpacked.

Was I overstepping? Potentially. But I knew Beau well enough to know he was going to make one excuse after another, and I was tired of looking at cardboard boxes with his messy chicken-scratch handwriting, so I was doing it my damn self, and he could just deal.

I'd taken a break after the third one to have a little text session with my bestie.

Me: *All dicked up? Classy, Colbs.*

Colbie: *Why thank you.*

Me: *And I never said anything about being in love.*

Colbie: *You didn't have to. It's that BFF ESP I have.*

I let out a snort as I typed back.

Me: *I don't even know what that means.*

Colbie: *It's like that weird mind-meld thing that twins have, but for bestest friends.*

God, my friend was ridiculous.

Colbie: *Just admit it. You heart the guy. There's nothing wrong with that.*

I sat up, staring down at the text thread as I chewed on my thumbnail nervously.

Me: *Don't you think it's a little too soon?*

Those three little dots appeared, blinking on and off on my screen for a solid minute before her reply came through.

Colbie: *Are you kidding? You guys have been circling each other since you were twelve years old. I told you there was something more than hate there. And the only people who have the right to decide what's too soon are you and Beau. Are you happy?*

I pulled in a deep breath, holding it in my lungs for five seconds before slowly letting it out. Then I replied, *Insanely.*

Colbie: *Then that's all that matters. Oh, crap. Gotta go. A murder of high schoolers just came in for an after-school fix. About to be slammed.*

I let out a laugh, feeling lighter now that I'd talked everything through with Colbie.

Me: *Isn't it a murder supposed to be for crows?*

Colbie: *You ever been stuck in the middle of a group of teenagers, all jonesing for caffeine? Well I have, and murder is more than accurate. Talk later. Love ya!*

I tossed my phone aside and looked around the bright, airy living room. I really did love Beau's place. And the fact that he wanted me here only made me that much more comfortable in his space.

With nothing else to do, I got back to unpacking. A couple hours later, his office was set up, and all that was left were things like miscellaneous phone and computer chargers and random keys, the kind of stuff every person in America had tucked into the weirdest places in their homes. I was pretty sure I had chargers for phones I hadn't had since my early twenties tossed away in my nightstand.

And that was exactly where this stuff was going to go. Out of sight, out of mind. Then Beau would well and truly be unpacked.

I slid the drawer open on the nightstand on his side of the bed and was about to toss the junk in when I spotted a spiral-bound notebook sitting in the drawer. I knew it wasn't my place to snoop, but my curiosity got the best of me when one of the pages inside slipped out partially, and couldn't help myself.

Sitting down on the bed, I flipped the cover back and lost my breath, because staring back at me was page after page of my own face.

Thirty-One

BEAU

MY MOTHER HAD BEEN BLOWING my phone up all day. But with work and practice and meetings with the athletic department to discuss the season opener next week, I hadn't had time to take her calls. I told myself I'd call her back, but now that my work day was over, all I could think about was that Presley would be there when I got home from work and how fucking much I loved that.

All damn day I'd thought about her, not that I didn't do that every single day already, but it was different, knowing she was spending her day off at my house by herself. I loved the thought of her relaxing on my couch or maybe taking a nap in my bed. I could just picture her walking around barefooted, humming quietly the way she always did. I wanted her to be comfortable, for my place to feel like hers. I wanted her to make my home her own, because she was mine, and I was never letting her go.

I wasn't delusional enough to think I'd ever be good enough for her, but I wasn't going to let that stop me from wanting to build a life with her. I might not deserve her, but there was one thing I knew for a fact. No one would ever love her like I would. I'd give everything I had to my name for a chance to make her smile. But patience was key. I told her I was perfectly happy to wait for her to catch up, so that was what I intended to do.

A grin split my face in two when I pulled into my driveway and spotted her car sitting there. Right where it belonged.

"Bubbles," I called the instant I pushed through the door. "I'm home."

I stepped into the living room and stopped in my tracks, my feet rooted to the floor. When I'd left this morning, boxes had crowded the space. Now they were gone. Everything looked absolutely perfect. I was officially unpacked, and it was all thanks to Presley. My Bubbles.

"I see you've been busy," I said with a laugh as I headed down the hall toward the bedroom I soon hoped to share with her full-time. "I'd tell you I had every intention of getting to that myself, but I think we both know that would be a lie—"

The words died on my tongue when I turned and

stepped across the threshold into the bedroom. Presley was there, sitting in the very center of the bed with her legs folded crisscross and my sketchbook stretched out in front of her.

She looked up, her eyes connecting with mine, and my chest tightened when I couldn't place what I was seeing on her face. There was surprise there, for sure, but I wasn't sure what else. Was she bothered by finding a book of drawings that were all of her? Did it creep her out? Was it too much for her, knowing I had those because I needed a piece of her with me? Christ, I wish I could tell, but her expression was giving me nothing.

"How did—"

"I was unpacking the last of your stuff. I went to put some things in the drawer and saw this." She placed her fingertips flat on the image in front of her. "Beau, what is this?"

I swallowed thickly, trying to force down the knot that had formed in my throat. "That—it's, um, my sketchbook."

Her eyes rounded. "You drew these?" All I could do was nod. "Beau, these are . . . they're beautiful."

It took a moment for my brain to comprehend what she'd said, but as soon as it did, my shoulders sagged with relief. She wasn't disgusted or weirded out. She looked at those sketches and saw what I saw: raw, unfiltered beauty.

"How long—" She let the sentence hang, waiting for me to answer.

"It started freshman year of high school. I took an art class for an easy credit and figured out I was pretty good at it."

"God," she breathed, awe in her voice as she flipped through the pages. "This is so much more than just being *good at it*. But . . . these are all me." Her curious gaze returned to me. "Why me, Beau?"

My head tilted to the side in disbelief that she hadn't figured it out by now. "You really don't know?" She shook her head. "They're all you because I've been in love with you since I was a kid, baby."

She sucked in a sharp gasp, her lips parting, eyes widening. "You—you love me?"

"Of course I do." I moved closer to the bed, coming to a stop at the foot. I stared down, hoping every ounce of what I felt for her came through in my gaze. "You're it for me, Presley. I've known that since we were kids." I pointed down at the notebook on the bed. "That sketchpad is full of four years' worth of it."

She shook her head, her brows pulling together as sadness darkened her amber eyes. "I don't understand. If that was the case, if you really had feelings for me . . ." She stopped and shook her head like she couldn't get the words out. But I knew what she was asking. If I loved her, even back then, why did I ruin us?

It was a conversation I hadn't been looking forward to, and one I'd hoped to avoid for longer, but it appeared my time had run out. On a heavy sigh, I sat on the edge of the bed, rubbing anxiously at the back of my neck.

"It started because I was the only one you gave attitude to, and in my own twisted way, that made me feel special. I could push your buttons and set you off in a way no one else could. You were always so sweet—"

"So *bubbly*?" she tacked on, lifting a brow in a sarcastic way that made me smile.

"Exactly. You were like that with everyone but me. I got the fire you had down deep. You didn't care that I was popular or my family had money. You didn't kiss my ass like all the other kids in school did. When I pushed, you pushed back, and it didn't take me long to discover that I loved fighting with you more than I loved getting along with anyone else. You made me feel alive, and I didn't have much in my life back then that could make me feel that way."

Concern laced through her features as she asked, "What do you mean?"

"Things at home weren't exactly . . . cheerful. My dad was a miserable bastard. He'd dreamed of being a bigshot football player, but he didn't have the skill to go pro.

When his dreams didn't pan out, he decided to make them my dreams. From as far back as I can remember, he rode my ass to be the perfect football player, only problem was, when he realized I was better than him, that I actually had a shot at *his* dream, he resented me for it."

I shook my head, the laugh that rasped up my throat didn't hold an ounce of humor. "You know, I've tried remembering if there was ever a time when I thought he actually cared about me, and I can't come up with a single instance where he actually behaved like a father. How fucking sad is that?"

"Beau," she whispered, sadness laced heavily through that one word.

"I love my mom, and I'm as close to her as I can be, but it's hard, because no matter what I said, or what he did, she always chose him over me. To this day, she's still trying to guilt me into having a relationship with the man who went out of his way to destroy my life."

I looked over at her, my light through the darkest storms. "I know I was a shit when we were kids, and it's not an excuse. I didn't know what the fuck to do with how I felt about you. Then our senior year rolled around and I finally got up the nerve to act on it."

Her brow furrowed, but only for a second before understanding dawned across her face. "The project in Ms. Garza's Spanish class."

A smile tugged at my lips as I nodded. "That was the first time I saw what it would be like to have you, and I knew I had to make my move."

She reared back, sucking in a large gasp. "I knew it! I knew you were going to kiss me. Wait. You were going to kiss me, right?"

"I was," I admitted, my face falling into a frown. "Then my father came home." Christ, this was going to be the hardest part, but I had to get it out there. "He told me that whatever was happening between us, it had to end."

"Is that why you acted the way you did the next day? Why you and Larissa . . ." I saw the pain in her eyes before she tucked it away, and it was like a knife to the gut.

"I'm so goddamn sorry," I rasped. "I didn't know what to do. He said if I didn't cut you off, he'd start spreading rumors about your dad, cause him to lose business. I didn't want to be the reason your family suffered. I was young and dumb, and I did the only thing I could think of to push you away."

She shook her head like she was trying to clear it, and I could see those wheels turning as she tried to make sense of it all. "But why? I don't understand."

She didn't understand because she was a good person, and it was hard for good people to wrap their minds around the actions of the assholes of the world. "Because he's a bastard?" I speculated, lifting my shoulder in a shrug. "Because he saw that I cared for you and wanted to take that away? Saw that you made me happy and wanted to ruin it? I stopped trying to understand his reasoning a long time ago."

"But . . . Beau, he's your dad. He wouldn't rather you be miserable. That's . . . that's just insane."

I flipped through the sketchpad to the tattered pages. "He did this. He came into my room one day and saw me drawing you and tore the pages to shreds. I couldn't have you, so this was the best I could get. But even that was too much in his eyes."

She reached out, tracing the frayed edges of the torn paper. "I can't believe it," she whispered sadly. "He destroyed something so beautiful, something you created. Just to hurt you?" Those warm brown eyes came to mine, tears swimming in them. "What kind of father does that?"

"The one I was cursed with."

She sniffled, lowering her head and wiping at her cheek with the back of her hand. "That morning in your dorm room," she said a minute later, finally piecing everything else together. "He called. I answered, so he knew I was there."

I nodded, hating the sadness washing over her, even if it was for me. I probably didn't deserve it, but she had too big of a heart to not hurt over what I went through.

"He reminded me of his original threat, so I did the

only thing I could think to do. Unfortunately, your father was working a job for my dad, and to prove a point, the son of a bitch fired him anyway."

"I remember that. God," she said in quiet disbelief, her eyes going distant as she thought back to that time ten years earlier. "My dad was so angry. Kept going on and on that he was let go for no good reason."

"It's true. Your father suffered because mine wanted to keep me under his thumb, and I've always blamed myself for that."

"Hey. Stop that." She moved then, swinging a leg over my lap to straddle my thighs. She took my face in her small, delicate hands and tilted it up to hers. That honey brown was gone now, replaced with that heat, only this time, the angry fire was for me, not because of me, and I loved it even more. That was her instinct to fight right there, and it was coming out for me. "What happened wasn't your fault. It was his. A father is supposed to protect his children. He's supposed to love them unconditionally and teach them right from wrong, raise them to be good people. Your father failed you, over and over, and I'm so sorry you had to suffer through that." She lowered her forehead to mine, squeezing her eyes closed as she spoke again, her voice quivering. "I wish I could go back in time and make it all better for you."

I banded my arms around her, holding her to me and

pressing her heart against my own. This was where she belonged, in my home and right here in my arms, and I'd spend the rest of my life proving that to her if I had to.

"You have to know, you were the one good thing I had back then. Even if I didn't act like it, you were all that mattered. I spent too long hurting you, even if it was the last thing I ever wanted to do, and I swear, baby, I'm going to spend the rest of my life making it up to you."

She smiled, combing her fingers through my hair before wrapping her arms around my neck. "The rest of your life, huh? That's a pretty bold claim."

I lifted my shoulder in a shrug. "Not to me. I've loved you for more than half my life, Presley, why the hell would I want to stop now?"

Her giggle took those broken pieces of me and put them back together again. "Well that's a relief to hear. Makes the fact that I love you too all the easier."

My arms clenched tight around her at those words as a growl rumbled from my chest. "Say it again," I ordered, fisting her hair and bringing her lips to mine. "I want to hear it again."

"I love you, Beau. Turns out, it took a lot less time to catch up with you than I thought."

She let out a shriek that turned to a giggle as I rose to my feet and started moving.

"Where are we going?" she asked, her smile so

goddamn bright and beautiful it lit up even the deepest, darkest corners of my heart.

"Bathroom," I answered on a grunt, finding it hard to communicate now that all the blood in my body had rushed to my dick. "I'm going to fuck you in front of the mirror so we can both watch as you come around me. Then I'm going to take you into my newly unpacked office and do it again so that every time I sit at that desk, I'll remember you being stretched out naked across it."

She leaned down, taking my bottom lip between her teeth and tugging before licking the sting away. "Sounds like you've got it all planned out."

I pulled back, giving her a cocky smile. "You have any objections?"

She shook her head, all that golden hair brushing against my arms. "Not a single one."

Thirty-Two

PRESLEY

It was actually a lot of fun to see the man who'd been so confident he could win my parents over, no problem, lose all that cocky swagger as he followed me up their front walkway on the way to Sunday dinner.

I stopped at the front door and looked back at him over my shoulder, trying my best not to laugh. "Will you stop fidgeting? What is wrong with you?"

He tugged at the collar of his button-down and scratched at his neck as he scowled at me. "We should have stopped to get your mom flowers. I *told* you we should have brought flowers."

It took everything I had not to burst into laughter. He was so damn cute when he was panicking over whether or not my parents would like him. I already knew they would, especially after I'd shared what he told me about his own

361

father. My mother had gotten all sniffly and weepy during that phone call. Even my dad's voice had taken on a much gruffer tone as he said, "Damn shame a kid had to grow up like that. Damn shame."

Even still, I knew my dad would put him through his paces, at least at the beginning, because when it came to his baby girl, he didn't feel he was doing his job as a parent if he didn't scare the living hell out of all my boyfriends before finally taking pity on them.

My mom would be another story. She'd probably spend the entire time doting on him, pouring him a fresh glass of whatever, whether he wanted it or not, until his bladder was damn near full to bursting, then she'd basically force food down his throat until he couldn't possibly eat any more. It was like her love language, stuffing the people she cared for like she was preparing us to go into hibernation and wanted to make sure we didn't wake up hungry.

Of course, I hadn't given Beau a heads-up on any of this. I could have, sure. It probably would have been the girlfriendly thing to do. But he'd spent the better part of the week acting all arrogant that he'd win my folks over no problem that I couldn't help but want to teach him a little lesson.

Yes, we were in love and all, but some habits die hard, and one thing Beau and I had gotten really good at over the years was sticking it to each other. I couldn't resist.

"And I told you flowers were a bad idea. My dad's allergic and my mom can't keep anything alive and always ends up getting all sad when her plants die."

"We could have gotten something hypoallergenic," he insisted. "That's a thing, right? Hypoallergenic flowers? I'm pretty sure it's a thing."

I threw my arms out. "I don't know. They're flowers, not a dog whose breed ends in the word doodle. Allergic is allergic."

His eyes flared. "Should I have gotten them a doodle dog? Is that something they'd like?"

Oh, for the love of god. This had officially entered ri-damn-diculous territory.

"Do *not* buy my parents a dog. Doodle or otherwise. Now come on."

I reached for the knob, but he grabbed my hand to stop me. "Wait. You're not going to knock?"

The humor I was feeling a moment ago flew away in a puff of smoke at the realization that he never had the kind of home you could just walk into because you were always welcome no matter what. I wanted to give him that. Almost as much as I wanted to punch his father in the trachea and rip his mom a new one for not protecting her son as she should have.

Instead of giving into my rage at the Wades the way I wanted to, I grabbed Beau by the front of his shirt and pulled him down until I could reach his mouth for a kiss. Like always, the moment our lips met he took over, swiping his tongue past my lips to take it deeper, burning me up from the inside the way he always did. It was official, I was never, *ever* going to get tired of kissing Beau Wade.

I was so into it that I didn't hear the front door open until it was too late.

"What kind of impression do you think you're making, shoving your tongue down my daughter's throat on my front porch?"

And here we go.

Beau

At the sound of Presley's father's voice, my balls shriveled into raisins and burrowed right up into my stomach for protection. I didn't think, I just reacted and shoved Presley away from me like her touch set my skin on fire.

"For the love of—" she sputtered as she righted herself, gaping at me with a perplexed expression.

"Shit. Sorry. Shit! I didn't mean to say shit! I mean—damn! Sorry, I'm sorry!"

Christ, I was making a fucking mess of this whole thing, and I hadn't even made it into the goddamn house yet. Meanwhile, her father stood across the threshold with a shit-eating grin on his face.

I pulled in a breath, trying to calm my frayed nerves as I reached out for Presley and pulled her against me. "I'm really sorry. He just startled me is all."

"Damn it, Dad." She hit her old man with a disapproving glare and batted him in the chest. "I told you, no hazing."

Alan Fields's chest puffed out as he planted his hands on his hips. "It's my right as a father to see if the man my baby girl brings home is up to snuff."

"Presley?" Presley's mom appeared then, hip-checking her husband out of the way to get to her daughter. "Oh, sweetie, you're here! What are you guys still doing outside? Come in. Come in. I didn't hear you pull up."

The two of them embraced, and it was so much more affectionate and warmer than anything my mom and I had ever shared. "Hey, Mom. Dad just about gave Beau a heart attack before we could even make it inside."

Pride had me wanting to object, to insist that I was fine, he'd barely fazed me. But . . . why lie?

"Damn it, Alan!" She shot her husband a murderous

look. "What did I tell you about giving Presley's gentleman friend a hard time? Do you *want* to sleep on the couch tonight? Is that what this is about?"

He held his chin high, the face of the women in his life glowering at him full on. "Just exercising my right as her father."

"Yeah, well, you're about two seconds from exercising my foot up your rear if you don't knock it off." After that threat, she turned to me, going from pissed to smiley in half a second. "Beau," she said affectionately before jerking me into a hug so tight I worried my lungs might collapse. She pulled back, grabbing my hand and leading me inside. "We're so happy to have you."

"I'm happy to be here. Thank you for including me, Mrs. Fields."

"Please, call me Shirley. And I hope you brought your appetite."

And just like that, I stepped into a home full of warmth and love and acceptance. A stark contrast to my own. And I'd never felt more welcome in my life.

I was miserable.

It felt like I had a rock sitting in my stomach. The weight of all the food Shirley had served me was going to take days to digest. But it was all worth it, because despite the rocky start, things had taken a major turn for the better over dinner. If it took eating my body weight in roasted chicken and au gratin potatoes to win their approval, I gladly would have done it a hundred times over. Just as long as Presley didn't mind me getting a gut, developing high cholesterol, and nursing me back to health after my first heart attack.

Shirley was easy to win over, and it took no time at all to see just who my Bubbles got her kind heart from. Alan wasn't quite as easy, but we eventually found common ground with football. Most specifically, college football. He was an OU fan, so we spent most of the time talking about my coaching strategy going into this season. When he asked if I thought I could get my boys to the playoffs this year, I'd answered with a resounding "Hell yes." Apparently that was the right way to go instead of being humble about it. After all, there was no room for humility in football. It was all about visualizing the outcome you wanted and busting your ass to get there.

Alan took a sip of his water as he studied me across the table. It took everything I had not to fidget under his scrutinizing gaze, but the longer he stared in silence, the more I started to feel like a specimen under a microscope. "Hmm. Maybe you aren't so bad after all."

As far as I was concerned, that was stellar praise in Alan Fields's book, and apparently Presley felt the same way. She placed her hand on my thigh beneath the table, and when I turned to look at her, she was smiling at me with so much love and affection I forgot all about the food pains in my stomach. There wasn't anything I wouldn't do for this woman, any lengths I wouldn't go to in order to ensure her happiness. Including eating twenty pounds of food in one sitting.

She was worth everything.

She was even worth stuffing down a slice of the chocolate silk pie Shirley had just carried out from the kitchen after announcing it was time for dessert.

It was official, I was going to be spending my night hugging the toilet in misery as my body tried to expel everything I'd forced into it.

Presley's hand on my thigh clenched, drawing my focus back to her so she could lean in and gently brush her lips against mine.

Worth it.

Her mother was in the middle of plating slices for everyone when Presley's phone rang from her back pocket. She pulled it out and looked at the screen with a frown.

"Hey. Everything good?"

She gave me a distracted grin as she pushed her chair back and stood up. "Yeah. Sorry. It's Diane. Probably something with the bar. I'll be right back."

Shirley shuffled off into the kitchen for something, leaving me alone with Alan.

"*Psst.*" He waved me closer when I looked over at him, leaning in deep and lowering his voice to a whisper. "There's a potted ficus behind you. You can stash the pie in there. I'll get it after you guys leave and toss it out so Shirl'll be none the wiser."

What the . . . Was this some sort of test? I had to assume the wrong response here was make or break.

"Oh, no. That's okay." I offered him a smile as warning sirens began blaring in my head. "I'm actually still a little hung—"

"This isn't some kind of test or demented game, son," he insisted, his expression nothing but genuine. "I've been where you are. I know your pain. I love the woman with all my heart, but if I ate everything she put in front of me I'd have had at least three massive coronaries by now." He looked over his shoulder to make sure the coast was still clear. "We have to stick together. I'll do you a favor this time and you return it come the holidays. You think she's bad now, just you wait."

I wasn't sure I'd survive it. To get through a Thanksgiving at the Fields house, I may actually need to fast for a week.

It was a no brainer. I sat back and extended my arm across to table "Deal." He gave my hand a shake then played lookout as I dumped the pie in the plant he'd indicated.

Shirley returned to the dining room and took her seat as Alan shot me a wink behind her back. We were partners in crime now, and as ridiculous as the whole thing was, I actually felt like this was a sort of bonding moment between us. We had a shared secret.

I was starting to think that this evening couldn't have possibly gone any better when Presley walked back into the dining room. I came to my feet the moment I saw how pale she was. The usual flush on the apples of her cheeks was long gone. Her eyes were wide and distant, filled with worry.

"Bubbles, what's wrong?"

"It's—" She shook her head and did her best to clear her expression, but it didn't work. "It's nothing," she tried to reassure me, but I knew better. That call had rattled her in a serious way.

"Puddin' pop, you're white as a sheet," he father pointed out. "Clearly it's not nothing."

She cleared her throat and let me lead her back to her seat. I sat down in my own, pulling it closer to hers.

She raked her fingers through her hair, something she only did when she was agitated. "Um, well . . . Diane wanted to give me a heads up that—that there's been an offer to buy the bar."

"What?" Shirley shook her head, confusion on her face clear as day. "But, how is that possible? She hasn't announced to anyone but you that she's planning on retiring." My stomach dropped like a bolder being tossed into the ocean. "Who could have possibly known?"

Presley's gaze lifted to mine, and I knew what was coming from the sadness swimming in her eyes. "It was your father," she admitted quietly.

Thirty-Three

I HATED Hank Wade more than I'd ever hated anyone in my entire life. Not because of what he was trying to do to me, but because of the devastation on Beau's face. I hated telling him the truth and had actually considered keeping the whole thing to myself, because I knew what would happen. But in the end, I knew he'd figure it out. Owning that bar was my dream. My future, and I knew I wouldn't have been able to hide what was happening for long.

Now he was taking what his piece-of-shit father was doing and internalizing it, adding it to the weight already stacked on his shoulders. But this wasn't his weight to carry.

"This is my fault."

And there it was.

His voice was low, devoid of all emotion. He was shut-

373

ting down. I'd seen it twice before, and I couldn't let it happen again.

"He's doing this because of me."

"No." I twisted in my seat and reached out, taking his face in my hands. "No, baby. This isn't your fault."

He shook his head, the pain in his eyes almost too much for me to bear. "It is. You know it is. He's trying to hurt you because of me. I can't let him do that, Bubbles. I—"

"He won't," I insisted quickly. "He's not going to hurt me, and he's not going to win, Beau. I don't know how he found out Diane and I were talking about selling the bar to me, but it doesn't matter. She told him no."

The fact that she'd turned down his offer of ten percent over Dropped Anchor's current estimated value only made me love the woman even more. It was a ridiculous amount of money. Obscene, actually. But that didn't matter to her. To her, we were a family. And she wanted to keep her legacy going.

"She promised me the only way she's selling the bar is if it's me she's selling to, so he can try throwing all the money he wants at her, but in the end, it's not going to matter. I'll get that loan and the bar will be mine."

I'd hoped that would help to ease his concerns, but his features didn't change. "It doesn't matter. Presley, if she refuses to sell to him, he'll try something else. It's never going to stop. This is because of me—"

"No, son."

Beau and I turned to face my father, his expression full of anger as he clutched Mom's hand on top of the table. It was the very same look I got whenever Beau pushed my buttons. I might have gotten my sunny disposition from my mother, but my rage was all Alan Fields. He looked like he was about ready to rip someone's head off. Meanwhile, my mom was nibbling anxiously on her bottom lip, her skin sallow.

"This isn't on you, Beau," Dad assured him. "The truth is, your old man's doing this because of me."

"What?" My brows pulled together in confusion. "What does it have to do with you? I mean, you guys barely know each other."

My mom spoke next. "That's true, but Hank and I grew up with each other." She let out a sigh before turning to my father and giving him a tiny smile. He squeezed her hand as though to silently communicate he was right there, and he had her back.

"Presley, sweetheart. You know I grew up here before I moved away for college." I nodded, having heard the story of how she got into college in Idaho and how she met my father not long after. The two of them had fallen in love, gotten married, and started a life in Boise. That was where

I'd been raised until my grandfather got sick and they decided to move to Mom's hometown.

"Well, Hank and I went to school together." She made a noise of disgust as she shook her head. "No offense intended, sweetheart," she said to Beau, "but your father was a selfish, self-centered ass even back then."

Instead of taking offense, Beau snorted, humor laced through his words as he told her, "That sounds on brand for the old man."

"He was always causing trouble, just because he could. Always picking fights with the kids he thought he was better than. It's my nature to always give a person the benefit of the doubt, but Hank Wade was mean down to his bones. And unfortunately, he had an eye for me."

The air whooshed right out of my lungs. "You—you mean he liked you?"

"As much as a narcissist can like anyone, I suppose. Mainly, he liked the way I looked. And since he was convinced he should have everything he wanted, he expected to win me, like I was something to be possessed, another pretty thing he wanted for himself so he could show it off to everyone else. Unfortunately for him, I wasn't interested."

"Because your mother's got good taste," Dad stated proudly, running a hand down his puffed-out chest. "Always has."

Mom gave an affectionate roll of her eyes. "Let's just say, he didn't take too kindly to being rebuffed." From what I knew of the man, I wasn't at all surprised by that. "He became obsessed after that. Pursued me relentlessly. When that didn't work he tried making things difficult in the hopes I'd cave. Leaving for college was a relief." She flipped her hand over beneath my father's and laced her fingers through his in the very same way Beau always laced his through mine. "Then I met your father and forgot all about Hank. I left him in the past where he belonged."

She let out a sigh, so my father picked the story up. "She was the only one who let it go, though. Guess he'd been stewing in that rejection all those years your mom was gone, and the moment she came back, all that old resentment came flooding back."

I leaned forward, bracing my elbows on the table as I tried to wrap my head around everything I'd just heard. "But . . . I don't understand. You did work for him."

"I took those jobs because I'm not the kind of man to let my pride get in the way of taking care of my family," my dad announced. "Didn't mean I was happy about it. He hired me off and on as a way of trying to remind me he was better off, tried to make me feel like I was less than him because I didn't have his money. But I knew the truth. Money without happiness doesn't equal a good life. He wanted to try and keep me down by rubbing that in my face."

"But you got to go home every day to a wife and daughter you loved," Beau finished for him. Understanding dawning in his eyes. "And that probably only added fuel to his bitterness."

My father tapped the tip of his nose in a silent *bingo*. "I guess that's when he decided it wasn't worth trying to mess with me anymore. I didn't give him what he wanted, because I had a damn good life and knew it. So he moved on to you kids."

Beau took my hand under the table as my mom sniffled, dabbing at the corners of her eyes with her napkin. "I'm so sorry he set his sights on you."

"Mom, it's not your fault." Emotion made my throat tight, the words coming out painfully as I reached across the table with my free hand and grabbed hold of hers, giving it a squeeze. "It's not yours or Dad's or Beau's. It's his. There's something deeply wrong with that man, and that problem doesn't fall on a single one of us to fix."

I sat up straight and turned back to Beau. "I'm not letting you take this on," I declared. "He doesn't get to win this time. I know the truth now, and I'll be damned if I let that man take your happiness again."

"That's right," my father agreed. "Family looks out for

each other, son, and now that Presley's claimed you, you're part of ours. We have your back."

Beau

I stood out on the balcony that faced the ocean, listening to the waves crash in the darkness as I thought over everything that had come to light earlier. The bad, sure, because when Hank Wade was your father, bad was a fucking guarantee, but also the good.

I thought about how it felt to have Alan call me son. The only other person in my life who had given me that was Sam, and hearing that from Presley's father felt just as important as it did when my oldest and dearest friend said it.

The words had landed in my chest, nearly rendering me speechless. But when he referred to me as family, hell, that one almost took me to my knees. They'd accepted me so readily, so wholly, all because their daughter loved me. Simple as that.

I'd never experienced anything like that before. They

had my back. And my own father was going out of his way to make things miserable for them. I didn't know what to do.

"I can hear those wheels spinning in your head from all the way inside."

I squeezed my eyes closed at the sound of her voice and breathed deeply. She was light and sunshine, and the only person in the world who'd ever dimmed that magnificent glow of hers was me.

"Hey." She came up, placing her palm on my back and trailing it across my shoulder as she circled me, squeezing her way between me and the railing. Those eyes, all sweetness and honey, glowed in the faint porch light. "Talk to me. You're always asking me what I'm thinking, now it's your turn to fess up. Tell me what's on your mind, Beau."

If walking away from her in the past was hard, it was going to fucking gut me this time. Now that I knew what it was like to have her in my life, to wake up to her in the mornings, to be loved by her . . . losing all of that was going to destroy me.

I grabbed her hips, pulling her to me and lowering my forehead to hers. "You already know what I'm thinking."

Her chest rose on a deep inhale as she slid her palms up my chest, circling her arms around my neck and playing with the hair at the nape of my neck. "You're right, I do.

That's why I came out here. To tell you it's not going to happen."

"Bubbles—" I tried to pull away, but she wouldn't let me. "You aren't pushing me away this time, and I'm certainly not going to leave you. This is it, Beau. *We're* it. You and me. That asshole doesn't get his way this time. Not anymore."

"Baby." God, just holding her made everything better. But if walking away meant I'd spare her a lifetime of Hank Wade, I'd do it. I'd do anything for her, including breaking my own heart.

She shook her head before I could finish. "This isn't the end of our story, Beau," she demanded, that fire sparking to life behind her eyes, turning those brown eyes cinnamon. "This is the beginning. I spent so long convinced I couldn't stand you, that you would always be my enemy. But now I know you were the one thing I was missing all along. I'm not going to lose you now that I finally have you. And I'm not going to let you lose me. This is *not* how we end. You understand?"

If she was willing to fight, then I'd fight. I'd bend over backward and bleed myself dry. Presley Fields was my happiness, and if she said we were endgame, goddamn it, we were endgame.

"Okay," I finally relented, unable to deny this amazing woman anything she wanted. "I understand."

Her face lit up with a smile that never failed to repair the tiny tears in my heart. "Okay, good. Now that your head's screwed on straight again, I have a plan for how we're going to beat your father at his own game." She arched a brow and bit down on her bottom lip. "You in?"

For a chance to take that bastard down? To protect my family? To keep the girl once and for all? It was a no-brainer.

"Hell yeah, I'm in."

Thirty-Four

BEAU

PRESLEY SAT in the passenger seat next to me as I stared up at the imposing, ostentatious house through the windshield. It had taken a few weeks to get everything in her plan squared away, but now that it was, we were here, sitting in front of my parents' house, so I could go in there and pull the rug out from under him.

Sensing the tension knotting my shoulders and making my neck stiff, Presley reached across the center console and placed her hand on my thigh, giving it an affectionate squeeze. "You know, we don't have to do this if you don't want to."

She made everything better without even trying.

"No, I want to." I looked back to the house and heaved out a breath. "Let's get this over with already. Once it's done, we can move forward."

"Exactly." She smiled brilliantly, and if it was possible, I fell more in love with her. "You can put him out of your head once and for all, and we can start planning our lives together. How's that sound?"

Like heaven.

"Sounds perfect." I leaned over, hooking my hand around the back of her neck and pulling her forward so I could press my lips to hers. Just like every time we kissed, I easily got lost in her, forgetting where I was and what I was supposed to be doing. She had that effect on me. "Christ, I can't wait to get you back home. I want to spend the rest of the day fucking you so hard you'll feel me between your thighs for a week."

Her body trembled, her lids lowering to half-mast. "Then I suggest we make this quick."

She waited in her seat for me to round my SUV and open her door, then, hand in hand, we marched up the front porch steps of my childhood home.

It didn't take long after I knocked for my mother to answer, and as soon as she pulled the door open, her face lit up at the sight of me. "Beau! What a surprise. It's so good to see you."

I leaned in and pressed a kiss to her cheek. "Hi, Mom."

"Oh, I'm so glad you're here. I wish I had known you were coming, I could have put something on for dinner."

"That's all right. We aren't staying long." On that, I

pulled Presley up beside me and looped my arm over her shoulder. "You know Presley Fields, right? My girlfriend?"

Some of the excitement drained from my mother's expression. She knew Presley, all right. Just like she knew the games my father played with us in the past. She caught herself before the concern swallowed her features and pinned her smile back into place, but this time, it wasn't nearly as bright. "Yes, of course. It's nice to officially meet you."

My Bubbles hadn't exactly hidden the fact that she wasn't the biggest fan of my mother's. She didn't like that my mom didn't protect me from my father's bullshit, and was downright pissed at the fact she continued to try and get me to build a relationship with the man, after knowing everything he'd done.

But even with that animosity, Presley was too kind-hearted to be outright rude. Smiling politely, she extended her hand to my mom. "Nice to meet you too, Mrs. Wade."

I didn't miss the way my mother didn't insist Presley use her first name like Shirley had for me, but I put that on the back burner for the time being. I had bigger things to deal with at the moment.

"Is Dad here?"

My mother's eyes widened with surprise at my question. "Oh, um, yes." She threw a thumb over her shoulder awkwardly. "He's—he's in his study."

"Great, thanks."

With Presley's hand held tightly in mine, I guided us through the massive house without taking a single thing in. I didn't bother to look to see if any changes had been made since I left the place fifteen years ago, because I didn't care. I'd hated this place back then, and that feeling hadn't faded over time. Truth was, my skin was beginning to crawl, being back in here. I only wanted to get this over with so we could get the hell out and never have to look back.

"Um, Beau, sweetheart." My mother trailed behind us, her footsteps a quick shuffle in order to keep up. "I think he's on a call. Maybe you could come back another time."

Not fucking likely.

I didn't slow my pace or look back at her. "That's all right, this won't take but a minute. He can call whoever it is back."

I grabbed the knob as soon as I reached the door to his study and threw the thing open without a single knock. Sure enough, my old mad was sitting behind the desk, his phone to his ear. His head shot up at the interruption, his expression momentarily confused before he registered exactly who was standing in the middle of his private space.

"Leonard, I'll have to call you back. Something's come up." He hung up the phone and tossed it aside before slowly, menacingly, rising to his feet and bracing the pads of his fingers on the top of his desk. "Have you lost your mind, barging in here? That was a business call." He threw his finger toward Presley, who only lifted her chin higher and narrowed her eyes into vicious slits under his angry gaze. My girl was a fighter and she wasn't here today to take any shit. "And I thought I made myself clear about bringing *that girl* into my house."

"Oh, you made yourself perfectly clear," I said back, my voice low and threatening. "I just don't give a shit. You came to my place of work to issue your threat the last time, so I figured I'd meet you on your turf to let you know how this is going to go down."

"Threat?" My mother's confused voice rang through the room. "Hank? What is he talking about?"

Instead of answering her, my father waved her off, silently telling her to be quiet.

"Your plan to try and buy the Dropped Anchor out from under Presley isn't going to work," I informed him, cutting right to the chase. "We know that you called the owner with a ridiculous offer to buy it, and we know that you've been going out of your way to prevent her from getting that loan with the bank she's been trying so hard to obtain." I couldn't help but grin when the bastard lost a bit of his bluster. He hadn't counted on me being able to find out his golfing buddy, who also happened to be the bank manager, had been throwing up roadblocks with Presley's loan at my father's request. The fact of it was, she was more than qualified for it, and should have gotten it a long time ago.

"Your old buddy Phil's in the market for a new job. Turns out, the bank doesn't take too kindly to their managers taking bribes. Something tells me he's going to have a hell of a time finding another job."

He squared his shoulders and folded his arms over his chest in an attempt to look imposing, but it didn't do him any good. "That doesn't matter. One way or another, I'll stop your little whore from getting that bar."

One moment I was standing next to Presley and the next I was across the room, fisting my father's collar so tight it compromised his air supply. "You don't *ever* talk about her like that. Do you understand me?" I gave him a violent shake, his cheeks turning ruddy as he struggled to pull in a breath. "Call her a whore again, or, hell, just *look* at her in a way I don't like and I'll make it my life's mission to ruin you. And I can do it too. Don't test me, old man. If there's anything you taught me, it was to always make sure you had more power than the man you were going after. And I took that lesson to heart."

He sputtered, slapping at my wrists as my mother cried out, begging me to stop. But it was Presley that managed to clear the haze of red that had crept across my vision. She remained completely calm as she walked up beside me and placed her hand on my arm.

"That's enough, Beau," she said gently, her eyes a combination of amber and cinnamon as she smiled at me.

I let him go, hooking my arm over her shoulders and holding her to me as my father sputtered and sucked in huge, gulping breaths.

She stared the man down like he was nothing more than a bug beneath her shoe. "There's nothing you can do to stop me from buying that bar because it's already done. And I didn't even need the loan to do it." She cast me a quick glance, her grin turning downright wicked as she lowered the boom. "Since Beau and I decided I'd be moving in with him, there was really no reason for me to keep my house. It sold in record time, and as it turned out, I had quite a bit of equity built up in the place. Diane sold the bar to me outright."

"I guess I should actually be thanking you," I said. "Turns out, your threat only pushed us closer together. It'll only be a matter of time before she has my ring on her finger too."

His face went red again, only for a whole different reason this time. He'd spent so long trying to keep Presley and me apart, but it was all in vain. I was going to make this woman my wife one day, and I was going to spend the rest of my life loving her exactly how she deserved.

"I might live in the same town as you, but as far as I'm concerned, you don't exist. The last words I'll ever speak to you are to warn you if you ever try to come between me and Presley again or harm her in any way, it'll be the biggest mistake of your life."

And there it was. I'd said what I wanted to say, and I was officially done. Tilting my head down to Presley, I smiled and asked, "You ready to go home?" Because that was exactly what it was now—*our* home.

"Absolutely."

We turned as one and started toward the door, only stopping when we reached my mom. She'd gone pale and was staring at my father with wide, disbelieving eyes.

"Mom." She blinked, bringing her attention back to me. "I love you, that's never been in question, but our relationship needs to change." She sniffled, tears forming in her eyes before sliding down her cheeks. "I'm willing to put in the work if you are, but you have to accept that he will never, ever be a part of my life. Nothing you say or do will ever change that. And if you continue trying to guilt me into having a relationship with him, the one you and I have will suffer."

She let out a little whimper as I leaned in to press a kiss to her cheek, and while it killed me to know she was hurting, I couldn't go back on my word. The only way she and I could move forward was if he wasn't a part of it.

I led Presley to the door, but right before we crossed the threshold, she pulled me to a stop and looked back over her shoulder at my old man, her eyes pure cinnamon as she smiled at him and said, "My mom and dad say hi."

With that parting shot, she laced her fingers through mine and led the way to our new lives.

Epilogue

PRESLEY

DROPPED Anchor was closed to the public for a private event that was filled with all my family, closest friends, and the bar staff who had officially become mine when I signed the papers, taking ownership from Diane.

We were celebrating not only my purchase of the bar, but also my former boss's retirement. Their RV was packed up and Diane had shown me the route she and her wife were taking when they left for their cross-country road trip in a few days.

As always, Freddy was sitting on his designated stool, enjoying a Coke as he talked all things football with my dad, Beau, and Sam Killborne.

Beau's mom was standing with mine, the two of them tipsy and red-cheeked on wine and giggling every other minute. After Beau's confrontation with his father, something rattled loose for Catherine. She realized how wrong she'd been and made quick work of trying to fix it. She'd hired a divorce lawyer, was seeing a therapist, and she and Beau were working hard to repair their relationship. She'd also started joining us for Sunday dinner at my parents' house, and since then, she and my mother had become close.

Donovan was behind the bar, slinging drinks, even though I'd told him twice now to take a load off. He was too excited to sit idle. When I'd become the new owner and vacated the manager position, I couldn't think of anyone better to fill it than him. He reminded me a lot of myself. He'd started as a busser and quickly moved his way up, knowing he was destined for bigger and better things. When I'd offered him the job, he'd hugged me so hard and so long that Beau had eventually stepped in to separate us, shooting the poor guy a glare that made Donovan's spine curl in on itself before he tucked me under his arm protectively.

Turned out, my man had a bit of a jealous streak. And I didn't hate it. In fact, I'd gotten endless pleasure out of teasing him mercilessly about it.

I took a private moment to stand in the corner and gaze over my dream. For as long as I could remember, I'd wanted this bar, and now it was mine. Not only that, but it was filled with all the people I loved and cared about the most.

As though he felt my gaze land on him, Beau lifted his head and turned to look at me, gracing me with a smile that made my insides all soft and melty. He broke away from the group and started in my direction, taking my face in his hands as soon as he was close enough and brushing a tender kiss against my lips.

The two of us had had our own private celebration the night before. After closing everything up, we'd spent *hours* christening the place.

"Hey, Bubbles," he said softly once he ended the kiss. "What are you thinking right now?"

"You mean aside from the fact that I'm the luckiest woman in the world?"

His clear blue gaze heated. "Yeah, aside from that."

"I was thinking if you'd told me a year ago I would be running my own bar and be blissfully in love with the boy who tormented me all through school, I would have laughed in your face and called you a dirty liar."

He hummed, the corner of his mouth trembling with a suppressed smile. "Is that so?"

"Mm-hmm." I lifted up on my toes for another kiss. "And I'm also thinking I'm so damn grateful the tides turned for us. That you came back and put it all on the line for me, because I can't imagine my life without you in it. I love you, Beau."

His nostrils flared on a deep inhale, his pupils dilating as he stared down at me. "I love you too, Bubbles. Have since I was a kid and will until my last breath."

The sound of breaking glass broke our little moment, but that was okay, we had a lifetime of them ahead of us.

When I turned to see what happened, my brows slammed together in a worried frown. Colbie was standing in the middle of the bar, shattered glass all around her feet from where she'd dropped her cocktail, but she wasn't paying any attention to that. She was too busy staring at the person who'd just walked through the door.

Sheriff Kincade Michaels.

And he was staring right back at her. In fact, it seemed she was the only one he had eyes for at the moment. I waited with bated breath to see what would happen, then my heart sank into my stomach when Colbie's face went white as a sheet right before she whipped around on heels and bolted for the back of the bar.

"What's going on there?" Beau asked, his concerned gaze trailing off after my best friend.

I let out a weary sigh and shook my head. "Colbie had a little too much liquid courage the other night and decided it was high time she made a move on the man she's been crushing on for years."

He looked down at me, his brows winging up toward his hairline. "She finally made a move?"

I winced, pulling my bottom lip between my teeth. "Yeah, but it didn't exactly work out. He shot her down. Apparently, he's not interested."

And he'd crushed her in the process. I'd been trying to pick up the pieces of my friend's shattered pride for days now, and I was starting to worry.

Beau let out a thoughtful hum. "Not so sure about that, Bubbles."

"What? Why?"

"Well, first, because Colbie's a catch. She's smart and beautiful and funny as hell, and the only person with a bigger heart is you." I *loved* that he saw all the wonderful things that made my best friend so amazing. "But also because that's not the look of a man who isn't interested in a woman. That's the look of a man who sees something he wants and has every intention of getting it."

I swung back around in time to see Cade storming off after Colbie, his features set in hard, determined lines. Giddy excitement swirled in my belly like a soda can that had been shaken up. "You know what, baby? I think you might be right." I knew the look Cade was wearing because I'd seen the very same one on Beau's face when he was pursuing me. "This will definitely be interesting. I can't wait to see how it plays out."

Because the only thing better than having my own fairy-tale ending was if my bestie had hers as well.

I couldn't wait to see what happened next.

The End.

Thank you so much for reading, and stay tuned for Colbie and Cade's story, LOVE OUT LOUD, coming soon!

Bonus Scene

Presley

A quick glance at the clock in the corner of my computer screen showed that if I didn't get moving, I was going to be late.

It had been six months since Beau and I were officially together, and he'd informed me earlier that morning that he had a special evening planned for us to celebrate.

It had been a whirlwind six months, for sure.

Our relationship might have changed—all for the better—over the past several months, but the man still had a gift for pushing my buttons and didn't hesitate to do so every chance he had. As always, I gave as good as I got. Sure, we loved each other like crazy, but we still fought as much as we always had, that was just who we were. Only now, instead of ending with me hating him and him pouting like a giant baby, we ended each spat with a rather acrobatic round of sex that always left us both breathless and smiling.

Despite the silly little arguments, I'd laughed more with Beau over these past several months than I had in longer than I could remember. We might still argue and rile each other up, but the good always outweighed everything else. I couldn't remember a time when I'd been happier, and it was all because of Beau. For all the negative in our past, I couldn't imagine my life without him in it. He was my future, my everything. He made each day better than the last.

And not only for me, but for my parents as well.

Because of Beau, my parents' house was in better shape than it had been in years. The dishwasher from hell was gone, along with all the other dated appliances, all replaced with new, top-of-the-line everything. Not only that, but they were finally enjoying retired life. They were officially living the dream and happier than ever.

Mom had taken up knitting, something she'd always wanted to learn but never had the time. Now I had a closet full of scarves because that was all she'd been able to make so far. Thanks to not having to work himself to the bone day in and day out, the chronic pain my dad had been living with had gotten substantially better. That drawn expression he always wore when he was trying to hide his pain was gone, as was the slope in his shoulders. Seeing him standing tall and proud was nearly enough to send me bursting into tears every time.

My parents had worked for so long, living paycheck to paycheck, that it had taken some time for them to get used to the fact that Beau wanted to do everything he could to take care of them. My mother nurtured those she loved with food. Beau's way was to take care of them with money. He was big on spoiling those he loved, something I'd come to learn personally.

He'd explained that, thanks to his professional football career, he had more money than he would ever be able to spend in one lifetime, so if my folks didn't let him spend it on them, it would just sit in the bank.

Finally, they'd relented and started accepting his gifts and generosity. It was so fun watching them enjoy getting everything they deserved, and seeing how happy it made Beau to take care of them only made me love him that much more.

I saved the spreadsheet I'd been working on and reached out to turn off the computer, grabbing my purse just as Donovan knocked his knuckles against the doorframe of my office. "Hey, got a minute?"

I pushed out of my chair, grinning at my new bar manager. "Hey, Don. Just barely. Beau will kill me if I'm late for whatever he has planned, so you better talk while we walk." I started toward the back exit when he spoke, drawing me up short.

"Yeah, about that. We've got a situation out here. I think it would be best if you were the one to handle it."

Shit. My head whipped around, my brows caving into a frown. "Seriously? It's not something you can handle?"

Donovan pulled his face into a wince, lifting a shoulder in a silent shrug. "Sorry, boss."

My head fell back on a groan. Beau was never going to let me hear the end of this. "Fine," I relented on a pout, turning on my heel and following him toward the front of the bar. "But so help me, if this takes longer than five minutes, I'm throwing you right under the bus." I shoved my finger in his face. "You'll have to deal with Beau."

Ready to rip into whoever was causing the scene in my bar that was going to make me late for my special night with Beau, I stomped down the hall behind Donovan as I thought over what I was going to say, how exactly I was going to rip into the person. Only, instead of getting the chance to do that, I jerked to a stop right after rounding the corner, my lips parting on a shocked exhale.

The bar was totally empty. Half the can lights overhead had been shut off, and strings of twinkle lights had been twisted around the pillars and across some of the overhead beams. Candles lined the bar and some of the empty tables, the tiny flames casting shadows around the dimly lit bar and creating a romantic atmosphere.

And there in the middle of everything stood Beau.

I hadn't understood why he requested I wear the red dress I'd worn to our high school reunion all those months ago until I noticed he was dressed in the same suit he'd worn that night, and *man*, he still looked amazing in it.

My belly fluttered at the sight of him. Warmth bloomed in my chest and spread throughout my insides until it took up every bit of available space. A beaming smile split my face in half as my man grinned at me, his hands tucked casually in the pockets of his slacks.

"Hi," I said as I moved toward him.

His eyes did a full sweep of my body, that crystal clear blue darkening as a slight blush rose on the apples of his cheeks. "God, you look so beautiful."

I wasn't sure I was ever going to stop swooning over my man, and I was really okay with that. "Thank you. You look pretty amazing yourself."

He chuckled, running his hand down the front of his button-down. "Oh, this old thing?"

I laughed just as his arm shot out, wrapping around my waist as soon as I was within reach. He pulled me flush against him and lowered his mouth to mine. In the months we'd been together, he'd kissed me a million different ways: passionately, hungrily, softly, tenderly, like he couldn't possibly get close enough. But there was something different about this one. Something . . . *more*.

My heart flip-flopped in my chest as I blinked my eyes open once he finally pulled away. "Wow. That was some kiss." I rested my palms against his chest. "What's going on? Where is everybody?"

Beau's hands came down to my hips, his fingertips pressing in deeply as he pulled me even tighter against him, like he couldn't get close enough. "What's going on is that this is our anniversary celebration. And I kindly asked everyone to clear out so I could do something special for you."

I let out a bubble of laughter. "And they just agreed?"

He arched a brow, one corner of his mouth curling up into an arrogant smirk that only increased his hotness. Not that I'd ever tell him that. His ego was big enough, after all. "What can I say? *Most* people find me charming."

A giggle passed my lips. "Hey, I find you charming. It just took about twenty years for me to get there."

His chest rose on an inhale as he lowered his forehead to mine. "Worth the wait," he whispered, those three words jam-packed with so much meaning it made my skin prickle with goosebumps.

"Bubbles, I have loved you since I was twelve years old. Getting to see you day after day for all those years but not getting to have you was torture." The breath stalled in my lungs as the backs of my eyes began to burn. "These past six months have been the best months of my life, and that's all because of you. You are my happiness, baby. My sunshine. So I have to ask you—"

I sucked in a sharp gasp when he pulled back and lowered to one knee in front of me, right there in the middle of my bar. "Beau," I said on a breath as my eyes flooded, a single tear breaking free and spilling down my cheek.

"Will you keep that happiness going and marry me? Because now that I know what it feels like to have you I can't go back. It's you, Presley. Only you."

I dropped down to my knees on a stuttered sob, a smile stretching across my face so big my cheeks ached. But I didn't care. "*Yes!*" I cried, taking his face in my hands and peppering it with kisses. "Yes. I want to marry you. I love you, Beau."

He let out a whoop of excitement, his long, strong arm banding around my waist as he shot to his feet, taking me with him. I laughed loudly as he held me off the ground and spun in a circle.

"She said yes," he practically yelled, then to my delight and surprise, the doors in the front and the back burst open and people came rushing into the bar. My parents, Beau's mom, all our friends, my staff, practically the whole damn town poured into the bar, cheering and clapping.

My gaze darted around wildly. "What's happening?"

Those blue eyes were shining so brightly as he smiled at me, pure, unfiltered happiness radiating from every pore. He shrugged, placing me on my feet and planting a kiss on my lips that made me swoon. "I told our family and friends so they could be here to celebrate with us. Sorry about all the rest. I guess that small town grapevine was put to work."

"I don't care." I shook my head, unable to wipe the smile off my face. "It's perfect. I love that they're all here. And I love you." A rush of excited giggles burst from deep in my chest. "We're getting married!"

There was a small part of me that still couldn't believe it. This man in front of me had spent years tormenting me, pushing my buttons on purpose just to get a rise out of me. For most of my life, I'd been convinced that I hated him. Now he was going to be my husband.

And I couldn't imagine wanting to spend the rest of my life with anyone else.

More From Whitecap

Crossing the Line

Some lines are meant to be crossed.

Trent Montgomery knew all about loyalty and responsibility. Tracking down his friend's long-lost sister and making sure she was safe was just another job, a favor from someone he cared about. He wasn't supposed to get attached. But when he started to fall for the woman who had been hiding from the world, things got a lot more complicated than he ever expected.

Cheyanne Knightly knew all about living in fear. The life she'd made for her and her daughter was as stable as a house of cards. One stiff breeze could send her whole world crumbling. But when a new guy blew into her small town, stirring up Whitecap's rumor mill, she found herself drawn to him in a way she never expected.

Lies were told. Secrets were uncovered. Lines were crossed. When the truth finally came out, Trent had to find a way to protect the woman who stole his heart while he tried to earn her trust back.

My Perfect Enemy

Rule number 1: Never fall for the enemy.
Rule number 2: Never get involved with a local.

Luna Copeland lives by those rules, which complicates things tremendously when her new boss turns out to be a former one-night stand. As if that isn't bad enough, he's also a world-class jerk. But she just can't make herself stop thinking about their one night together.

When Nate Warren left Whitecap years ago, he was certain he wouldn't come back. But when his daughter starts acting up and getting into trouble, the small coastal town proves to be the best place for her. With an unruly teen on his hands, the last thing he has time for is romance.

Unfortunately, he can't get his sassy assistant out of his head.

When ignoring their attraction fails, Nate decides he wants all in. He just has to convince Luna she wants the same.

Discover Other Books by Jessica

WHITECAP SERIES
Crossing the Line
My Perfect Enemy
Turn of the Tides

WHISKEY DOLLS SERIES
Bombshell
Knockout
Stunner
Seductress
Temptress
Vamp

HOPE VALLEY SERIES:
Out of My League

Come Back Home Again
The Best of Me
Wrong Side of the Tracks
Stay With Me
Out of the Darkness
The Second Time Around
Waiting for Forever
Love to Hate You
Playing for Keeps
When You Least Expect It
Never for Him

REDEMPTION SERIES
Bad Alibi
Crazy Beautiful
Bittersweet
Guilty Pleasure
Wallflower
Blurred Line
Slow Burn
Favorite Mistake
Sweet Spot

THE CLOVERLEAF SERIES:
Picking up the Pieces
Rising from the Ashes

Pushing the Boundaries
Worth the Wait

THE COLORS NOVELS:
Scattered Colors
Shrinking Violet
Love Hate Relationship
Wildflower

THE LOCKLAINE BOYS (a LOVE HATE RELATIONSHIP spinoff):
Fire & Ice
Opposites Attract
Almost Perfect

THE PEMBROOKE SERIES (a WILDFLOWER spinoff):
Sweet Sunshine
Coming Full Circle
A Broken Soul

CIVIL CORRUPTION SERIES
Corrupt
Defile
Consume
Ravage

GIRL TALK SERIES:
Seducing Lola
Tempting Sophia
Enticing Daphne
Charming Fiona

STANDALONE TITLES:
One Knight Stand
Chance Encounters
Nightmares from Within

DEADLY LOVE SERIES:
Destructive
Addictive

Acknowledgments

To Josh, for keeping my dreams alive for me when I'm struggling to believe in myself.

To Jacob, for being so excited that his mom's an author and likes to spread that news far and wide.

To my mom and the rest of my family, thank you all for being the most supportive crew I could ever ask for.

To my writing buddies, Adriana Locke, Dylan Allen, Laura Pavlov, and Kandi Steiner. You guys are a balm to this procrastinator's heart. I'm pretty sure I'd never get a single book written if it wasn't for you guys.

To Karen and Jan, for taking my words and making them into something understandable, and for not firing me when I blow through EVERY SINGLE deadline.

To my ARC team and all my readers, I wouldn't be here if it wasn't for you. Thank you so much for loving my words as much as I do and sticking with me all this time. Here's to more to come!

About Jessica

Born and raised around Houston, Jessica is a self proclaimed caffeine addict, connoisseur of inexpensive wine, and the worst driver in the state of Texas. In addition to being all of these things, she's first and foremost a wife and mom.

Growing up, she shared her mom and grandmother's love of reading. But where they leaned toward murder mysteries, Jessica was obsessed with all things romance.

When she's not nose deep in her next manuscript, you can usually find her with her kindle in hand.

Connect with Jessica now
Website: www.authorjessicaprince.com
Jessica's Princesses Reader Group
Newsletter
Instagram
Facebook
Twitter
authorjessicaprince@gmail.com